Mistletoe Misses

ALEXANDRA GRACE

Cover design by Covers by Jules
Edited by Cayla Cavalletto, Hey Bookworms Editing

Follow me on Instagram and Facebook: @authoralexandragrace

Website: https://authoralexandragrace.carrd.co

*For those who believe in second chances,
and to the hearts that find their way back home—
may love, in all its imperfect glory, be worth the wait.*

Prologue

Maddox

Mistletoe has been good to me, and tonight, I expect it will get even better.

My girlfriend Carmen loves the tradition and uses it to steal kisses from me every December. Since our first kiss under the mistletoe at my Nana's bookshop freshman year, I've developed a profound appreciation for the fancy little plant. While Carmen doesn't need an excuse to kiss me—my lips are available to her, any time anywhere—I'd never deny her the thrill of surprising me. After all, the twinkle that alights her face when she traps me is prettier than a clear night sky, the sun reflecting off fresh mountain snow, or a Christmas light show.

I once thought baseball, snowball fights, or decorating the

Christmas tree were my favorite things, but that was before I discovered the love of the most perfect girl in the world. Nothing beats a kiss from Carmen Delilah Bennett during the holidays or otherwise.

To show her how much she means to me, I've designed the perfect gift for her eighteenth birthday. What better way to celebrate, just five days from Christmas, than with a mistletoe scavenger hunt? After solving the thirteen picture puzzles to discover where to find the locations, she can trap me under each mistletoe for as long as she wants. The night is hers and so am I.

My brother, Cooper, thinks I am stupid for choosing an unlucky number for our big date. But we've had significant moments at twelve places over the years, and I couldn't ignore the gazebo. Everything important in Ember Falls happens at Loving's Gazebo, named after the town's most influential mayor. It's the perfect spot for a night we'll remember for the rest of our lives. Anyway, when it comes to me and Carmen, luck is a moot point. We're soulmates, meant to be together forever, and no unproven superstition will ever change that.

I also expect our relationship to advance in more ways than one tonight. The other surprise I have in store for her will change our lives forever, and I suspect she'll want to celebrate with another monumental moment. I've wanted her desperately, but since waiting until we were both eighteen is important to her, it became important to me. My friends and teammates tease me about being a virgin, but they're just jealous. Carmen Bennett, the prettiest, sweetest, and most talented girl in Ember Falls, is mine, and that's all I care about.

I've been planning for this day since my eighteenth birthday two months ago, but I've known since middle school that I would marry Carmen one day. We'd been best friends and neighbors since birth, but I didn't think of her as more until I saw her playing ball with her brothers when we were nine. She wasn't fragile and whiny about sports like the other girls in my class, and I respected her for it.

I fell for her hard after my Little League team lost the game that would have taken us to the twelve-year-old World Series. I'd been the closing pitcher, expected to shut down the other team for the win, but I gave up a walk-off home run instead. She'd been at that game and knew I'd be sulking in the backyard afterward. She brought over my favorite cookies—peanut butter with chocolate chips—and held my hand, coating my pain with soothing conversation about our beloved Red Sox. In a matter of minutes, I'd forgotten about the game from hell and saw nothing but her—and the Red Sox, of course. That's when I set my mind to breaking out of the friend zone.

It took me three years to earn the boyfriend title. Now, three years after our first kiss, I plan to give her a birthday to remember and a little sparkle for her finger.

In my mind, she's always been mine. Since I'll be forever hers, the modest ring that means so much to me and my family simply makes it official.

"One more to go." I urge as we make our way toward the finale.

She's been lagging and growing more emotional with each riddle solved and kiss given. I'd like to think it's because she's touched by the effort I put into this date, but something about her is off, and I can't take credit. She's less talkative than usual and that alone puts me on alert. I'm the reserved one. Carmen usually fills every lull in conversation with her melodic voice, singing or passing along random gossip or interesting tidbits she's learned about the world. Yet, two hours into this magical night and twelve kisses down, the only noise between us is our boots hitting the icy ground.

Maybe the weather is getting to her. It's frigid in Vermont this late in December, and she's not the only one ready to cozy up somewhere warm. We'll get there as soon as she says yes to the last riddle, and I get my last kiss.

"It's the gazebo, isn't it?" she asks, little puffs of air materializing outside her glossy, pink lips. "A heart, symbolizing love, and a ring. Put that together for Loving's Gazebo."

"Right."

"I should have been able to figure that one out without the drawing. Mayor Loving was your great-grandfather, and I know how much family means to you." Her hand tightens in mine. "It's one of the many things I love about you."

"I'm sentimental. What can I say? Come on." I jog ahead and stand under the mistletoe I hung in the center earlier that day, but she doesn't follow. She stops just outside, the festive string lights decorating the gazebo's edges, casting her features in a somber glow.

"Maddox …"

I hurry down the steps to take her hand to pull her inside. It feels warmer under the lights until I see she's crying. Icicles seem to jam in my veins, and I shiver with dread.

"What's wrong? Tell me, and I'll fix it."

"You can't," she says between sniffs, and more sobs clog her throat.

Without more context about what's upsetting her, I'm helpless and beyond confused as to why regret suddenly clouds her eyes.

"Please let me try." I take her in my arms, hoping to comfort her, but she soon steps back.

"Maddox, I love you."

"I know. I love you, too. That's why …" My fingers slip inside my coat, and I fumble my Nana's engagement ring in the tiny pocket, freezing in place when the words I never thought I'd hear escape her lips.

"We can't be together anymore."

"What?"

"I'm leaving next weekend."

My hand falls to the nearby railing. "Leaving to go where? For how long?"

"Los Angeles … indefinitely."

"You're moving away from Ember Falls and me? Why?"

She hiccups and swallows down the emotion she'd let loose in my arms earlier, and her eyes harden with finality. "You love this town. It's in your blood, but I need more than Vermont or even Boston can provide. And you want a big family. I'm not even sure I want to have kids."

"You don't want a family? Since when?"

"As long as I can remember."

"How come you never mentioned it?"

Her head tilts like I'm stupid, and that's exactly how I feel. "Because you would've tried to convince me otherwise, and I would have let you. Maddox, I have dreams and goals, and I'm not ready to set them aside."

"You're dumping a lifetime of us for a career that's not guaranteed? Do you think a family would hold you back? That *I'd* hold you back? I've been nothing but supportive of you becoming an actress. I go to every singing gig. I'm your biggest fan."

"It's not that."

"What is it, then?" I lean against the rail, needing support to keep from dropping to my knees.

"Maddox, you have my heart. It's just—"

"Not enough."

"I'm sorry."

Sadness wavers in her voice, and I go to her, hoping I can change her mind. Every time I picture my future, she's there. We've been together in one way or another our entire lives. I don't know how to be me without her.

"Don't do this, Carmen."

"I have to. I need to try, or I'll regret it for the rest of my life."

"What about giving up on us? Will you regret that?"

The lights reflect off the unshed tears in the deep blue pools of her eyes, and I'm drowning in them. I have no idea how she'll answer. I suddenly doubt her feelings for me, the depth of our relationship, and my worth to her. For the first time, I doubt us, and it rips me in two.

"I already do."

"Then don't destroy what we've built." I take her hands, and her forehead drops to my chest. A sliver of hope takes flight, and I spout off every idea that comes to mind, praying something will resonate. "I'll wait for you. I'll come visit often. We'll be together as often as we can. Or I'll move to California."

Her head shoots up, and she separates from me again. "No."

"No?"

"We won't have the money to fly back and forth, and there's too much of this place in who you are. I can't be the reason you lose that or put your life on hold."

A chuckle squirts out of me at the absurdity of that statement. "Carmen, either way, my life comes to a screeching halt if you leave. This town means nothing if you're not in it."

"You don't mean that."

"I do." My trembling hands scrub over my face with a sigh. I can't believe this is happening. "I only love it here because it made us."

"Maddox …"

"I want you to chase your dreams, Carmen. You deserve that. If you must leave town to do it, don't leave me, too. We'll figure out a way to make it work."

Emotion chokes her as she shakes her head, mirroring me when I step closer. We do this ridiculous dance, cold, empty space growing between us until she turns and dashes into the darkness. The sound of my frantic voice echoes after her as all I've ever known and loved disappears.

Chapter 1

Nine Years Later

Maddox

"Admin leave? For how long?" The words shoot out of me like arrows, the sharp points aimed directly at my judge and jury.

Captain Emory sits across the desk from me, his arms folded over his uniformed chest. His Boston Police Department badge nearly disappear in the creases of his soft physique. The hard stance tells me he won't be receptive to whining. "At least thirty days."

"Thirty days?"

"You know the protocol."

"I saved lives."

"And ended another. Don't forget that, Maddox."

"Fine." He only calls me by my first name when he has no

patience for my bullshit. "What project do you have me working on until this nightmare is over?"

"Time off," he accentuates. "Not light duty. I expect you to clean out your locker and take a break until the investigation is complete."

"I can't just … hang out in Boston."

Captain is more than my superior, he's a friend. He understands this so-called *break* will hit me hard. Yet, he stares me down, absolute in his decision.

"What am I supposed to do?" I ask, sounding more like a defiant teenager than a veteran cop.

"It's a big city. Find a new adventure or club or go visit your family."

The casual mention of stepping foot in Ember Falls again makes every cell recoil and nosedive into a dark hole somewhere inside me, probably the space where my heart used to be. My hometown is the last place I will go. There must be a thousand ideas better than that one.

"How about taking up a hobby or making some new friends outside of work?" He sighs, realizing I'm barely listening. "Take a hint from Adrian. He's going on a cruise this summer."

"Absolutely not. All I need is this job."

"That's the problem." He lets out a long breath again, propping his elbows on the desk. He's about to give me a good old-fashioned talking to, and I'm expected not to zone out again. If he didn't have two ranks and a decade of service over me, I'd tell him where to stick his advice. "You've already forgotten who you were before you put on a uniform. Your service to our country and this city isn't everything."

"It is to me."

"For goodness' sake, Maddox. You're only twenty-seven years old. You can't keep grinding away here non-stop, wasting your life. You're worn out. It's time to step back and think about what you want out of life before the job's the only thing you've got."

His massive hand slams down on the desk to stop the rebuttal my open mouth tells him I'm gathering. This is bullshit.

"I can pile on more conditions before I let you come back." His hard features soften, cooling the fire blazing in my core. "Maddox, you're like a brother to me, I care about you. When was the last time you did something for yourself?"

My silence provides the answer he already knows. I don't take off. That's not who I am and keeping busy helps me ignore memories I rather not relive. Rushing from one emergency to the next during a twelve-hour shift provides little downtime to think about my past. No rogue thoughts to poke holes in my sanity, pick at old wounds, and make me long for something I can never have.

"December is a few days away," Captain continues, capturing my fickle focus again. "I don't want to see your surly ass until after New Year's. Or, better yet, after you've figured this shit out. Hit the road, take some time away, but steer clear of the station. Don't come back the same Maddox. If you do, I predict we'll all be going to *your* funeral soon."

"Damn, Captain."

"Got your attention now?" He sits back in his chair and waves a hand toward the door. "Go on. Get out of here."

With a dutiful nod, I head out without grumbling. It's not like I have another option, and arguing will only make him more eager to kick me out, maybe for good.

I reach for my badge—the only thing, other than my Army dog tags, that defines the man I've become—flip open the pin and stuff it in my pocket. If I lose this job, my purpose and drive to get up each day will vanish with it.

On my way to the locker rooms, a helpless, ambiguous feeling burrows under my skin. Why am I being punished? It's not like I've done something wrong. Sure, I took someone's life, but it was either him or a kid. The shooter had a rap sheet a mile long, and he shot at me before aiming the barrel at an innocent child. I had less than three seconds to decide, and I responded like I've been trained to do my entire adult life. There had been only one move. Why can't he see that?

Pushing through the scarred metal doors, I'm like a ticking bomb. My uniform comes off with more force than necessary, and I'm nearly bare, just as raw emotionally, when my buddy Adrian enters to suit up for his shift.

"How long?" he asks, knowing the verdict and how much I loathe Captain's decision with one look at me. We've been friends since the academy and spent three years as partners. You get to know a person after spending years of grueling, late-night shifts together and having each other's backs in countless life-saving incidents.

I slip into the sweats I had on when I arrived, reach for my shirt, and yank it on. "At least a month."

"Shit, man." His fingers comb through his hair as he empathizes. "What will you do?"

"I have no idea."

He steps closer and places a hand on my shoulder. "Let's get a beer tonight. Maybe I can help figure something out."

"Thanks, but—"

"Rusty's Bar. 8:00. If you don't show up, I'll come to your apartment and drag you there myself. And based on our last sparring match, you know I can."

"Jackass."

It took two depressing days of sitting in my dark apartment, with only dispatch on my police radio and a case of beer for company, to decide I couldn't continue that pattern for twenty-eight more. On a whim, I pack a duffel bag of essentials, climb into my truck, and head toward Ember Falls.

Home—the one place I swore I'd never go again unless I had a dire, unavoidable reason. Outside of my Nana's third husband's funeral four years ago, I haven't stepped foot in Vermont since high school graduation.

My mom calls often, begging me to visit. Her latest attempts have included some story about Nana's bookshop in near shutdown status. It would destroy Nana to close that shop. There's no way she's let it go so far as to jeopardize its future. It's just Mom playing to my weakness to get me home.

She can stop trying to bribe me now. Thanks to Captain and my rash decision, her wish will be granted soon enough. It's not like I haven't missed my family. Nana is one of my best friends, and my parents are the world's best. I have five younger siblings I'd die for and a town of people who helped raise me. Even after all these years, it's just not enough. Pieces of my shattered heart are scattered across that town, and I have no faith this or any visit will put it back together. Yet, here I am, navigating the early evening Boston traffic on my way to give it a try anyway.

I choose the long route to avoid Fenway Park since tonight's Red Sox game starts in an hour. As if that isn't enough to shut down roads and back up traffic, playing the New York Yankees certainly is, and I don't have the patience to handle seeing all the pin-striped paraphernalia of our rivals in my bleed red and blue city.

The pregame show plays on the radio, helping me focus on

the road instead of what's waiting for me beyond the horizon. But not thirty minutes later, the green, snowcapped Vermont mountains of my childhood appear ahead. With the setting sun tucked behind, glowing like a beacon, there's no ignoring their beauty or what they represent—a past I can no longer ignore.

My path continues toward the little valley town until the heavy snowfall gives me an excuse to delay the inevitable. About an hour outside of Ember Falls, I stop at the first place I find— a bed and breakfast. The simple, two-story, brick colonial home looks innocent enough, and the best part is I'll be anonymous here in Moyer's Ridge.

Stepping inside, Christmas music, pine and cinnamon scents, and bright, flashy decorations cover every inch of the main living space and bombard my senses. My body revolts without warning, and I stumble backward.

"Oh, honey, did we frighten ya?" A woman, wearing a reindeer antler headband and a festive, oversized sweater, rushes toward me. On the way, she snatches a plate of cookies off the coffee table while a man hangs more lights over the living room fireplace. "Coming down out there?"

"Yeah." I brush at the melting snowflakes covering my shoulders and favorite Red Sox baseball cap.

Ignoring the mess I made in her foyer, she holds up the plate, piled high with Christmas-themed sugar cookies. "Would you like one?"

"No, thanks." Maybe I should backtrack and find a quiet hotel room somewhere else.

"How about a place to rest, then? With the storm brewin', we don't have any reservations on the books, so you can have your pick of the lot. Although, that'll change when Ember Falls' Christmas Spectacular gets goin'. Is that what you're in town for?"

How could I have forgotten about the event of the year? It's been a December tradition since the 1940s. For a two-week span, the town nearly shuts down to experience the long list of Christmas events, organized by the mayor and his special committees.

"Pure coincidence. When does it start this year?"

"On the tenth. Sounds like the mayor's beefed up the events list this time. Gonna be doozy."

"Great." Given my horrific bad luck, I'm unable to match her enthusiasm. "Mind if I get one of those rooms you mentioned?"

"Oh, of course, dearie. Right this way."

I follow her into the kitchen, stopping in the doorway as she fumbles through a stack of papers on the built-in desk. On the third drawer she opens, searching for God knows what, she lets out a squeal.

"Georgie! I found it!"

"What? The missing screwdriver?" he calls from the other room.

"No." She flashes a mischievous smile over her shoulder before proudly displaying her treasure.

Mistletoe.

"What are you doing?" I take a cautious step back, and she taunts me with the plastic rendition, holding it up as high as her arm will allow.

"What's the matter, dear?"

Another step back and my feet can't retreat fast enough. My eyes stay trained on her and that godforsaken fake plant like it's a loaded gun. "I'm not a fan of the tradition." Or Christmas, for that matter, since you can't have mistletoe without the holiday.

"I would think a handsome man like yourself would welcome some spontaneous kisses from the ladies." She traps me against the couch in the living room, puckering her lips.

"Leave him be." Georgie scowls at her from where he's hanging lights above the fireplace. "He doesn't want to ruin his suave look with your lipstick."

I glance down at the jeans, flannel shirt, and scuffed boots I put on before leaving my apartment in Boston. It's simple and comfortable—anything but whatever *suave* means. My unsuspecting eyes find the woman again and the bright red, smacking lips on their way to me. She's at least a good six inches shorter, so the mistletoe doesn't quite reach the top of my head, making the traditional requirement null and void in my humble opinion.

Yet, she leans in anyway, and I side-step her. She falls over the back of the couch, catching herself before her legs follow.

"Don't mind my sister," Georgie says flatly, like he's used to her nonsense. "She gets a little excited around the holidays. Here." He hands me a key. "That room has an exterior entrance if you want to drive around back. Breakfast is at seven."

"Thank you." I snatch the key and rush out the door, the sound of his sister's elf-like giggles following me out into the winter weather. At least it's no longer snowing.

Instead of heading to the room to hide for the night, I head toward the roadside bar I passed on the way here. Based on the overflowing parking lot, it must be a good one. All good bars have ice-cold beer, exactly what I need to erase my first mistletoe encounter since the earth-shattering one nine years ago and any lingering memories of both. Even if I'd been prepared for being chased with the dusty twig, I never could have expected it to rattle me like it did.

Ten minutes is all it took for me to regret my presence in Vermont as I knew I would.

After claiming one of the last barstools, the bartender steps up, drying a glass with a towel as they do in cliché movies. He flips the towel onto his shoulder and stares at me while he puts the glass away. "Madds? Is that you?"

I chuckle at the use of my high school nickname, especially since that's how I feel—downright mad at my current circumstances. "Yeah. I think."

"What are you doing here?"

Studying his face, I wonder how he knows me so well, and if I'm supposed to know him. I barely remember anyone outside of my ex, my best friend Jamie, and my baseball teammates. When he shifts into the dim overhead lights, I notice his eyes— one blue and the other green—and it comes to me. Our team manager and biggest troublemaker. He was the lighter fluid to our antics and a total blast.

"Drew? Holy, shit. I haven't seen you since—"

"Jamie's graduation party at his family farm. Man, that was a wild night." He sets down the glass, selects a beer from the cooler, and slides it toward me. "What brings you into town? The Spectacular?"

"Shit no. If I'd remembered that was happening, I would've stayed home. I'm just … visiting family for the holidays." No need to bring up the real reason since I'm trying not to think about that either.

"Where's home these days? I heard you served in the Army."

"After four years as a soldier, I'd done all I set out to do. I'm Boston P.D. now."

"Doesn't sound much different," he jokes before letting out a roaring laugh, but it fades when something across the bar catches his attention. "Madds, I'd love to catch up with you, but are you sure you want to be here right now?"

"What do you mean?" It is either here or the unhealthy solitude of my room at the B&B. I need company and noise to drown out the unwanted emotions my memories induce.

He points to whatever is behind me that's wilted his lively demeanor, and I twist in my seat. At the first sight of Carmen setting up a microphone stand on the tiny corner stage, my heart falls into my gut like I swallowed a brick. She's striking and all grown up, no longer the teenager I remember or the young woman I saw in social media posts.

I'm not proud of it, but I tortured myself by following her actress accounts after she left. When she started posting photos of her at parties and in what looked like dressing rooms with other men, I lost interest. More like I threw the phone into a lake on a temper tantrum, but no one needs to know that.

She bends down to remove the guitar from its case, and her tight jeans show me and everyone in the place the woman she's become. The dark brown cowboy boots and white, off the shoulder sweater have my mouth watering until I remember—*that* is *Carmen*. The girl who broke me and destroyed the future we'd talked about for hours on end. The girl who chose a chance at fame over me. The girl who—

"I'll ask again," Drew breaks into my wallowing and leans on the counter behind me, surely noticing my discontent with this surprise. "Are you sure you want to be here?"

"No." As much as my sanity needs me to, I can't take my eyes off her. I watch her delicate fingers tune the guitar and reach for the mic. She smiles at the expectant crowd before her angelic voice sounds through the speakers. Iron fists grip my lungs as the lights seems to brighten their focus on her, captivating and enraging me at the same time.

What is she doing in Moyer's Ridge? Shouldn't she be living it up in California? Wasn't that the sole reason she left? Why bother with this small-town gig on the wrong side of the country? She hated it here, even going as far as graduating early to escape it sooner.

17

She sings an upbeat country song to engage the crowd, and I recognize it as one of hers. Once upon a time, I had been her preferred song tester as she worked through lyrics. This one, she wrote when we were sixteen. A familiar ache covers my entire body, and I spin back toward the bar, chugging the beer I'd yet to touch. Drew replaces it with a fresh one before I can slam the empty bottle down on the counter.

Her loyal audience cheers like they know the song—a song I thought hadn't been recorded for the world to hear. How is that possible? After a short pause, she starts another, and the roar grows louder by the first word. I recognized the song within the first three notes. It's our song. Our. Fucking. Song. She's singing it to all these strangers as if she didn't write it for a special reason or person. Like it's just part of the show and meaningless.

Shooting off the stool, I slam a twenty-dollar bill on the counter and stalk out the door. The cool breeze slaps my heated skin along my retreat through the parking lot. I don't stop when I hear Drew calling for me. I can't. I need space to breathe, to remember the relaxing techniques that used to help my raging blood pressure, and to forget the love of my life didn't just break me all over again.

Chapter 2

Maddox

The antique iron bell, original to Nana's bookstore, clangs to life above the century-old, wooden door as I step inside. I brace for impact—an ear-splitting squeal when she sees me and her body slamming against mine in an overdue hug.

Nothing happens, and I can't stop disappointment from taking over.

The cash register, sitting unattended on the counter, has my law enforcement instincts stabbing at the backs of my eyes. Nothing in this place is secure. No cameras, no locks on cabinets, no staff. I walk past a row of bookshelves, my boots pounding on the wooden floors and echoing through the aisles.

Still no Nana.

As I make my way to the back, a cracked door and light

coming from inside catch my attention, and I listen for voices and clues. Anyone could walk in here undetected as I did—an easy opportunity to take advantage of or hurt my sweet Nana.

"No, he didn't," a female voice says. "He sent a text."

"I swear. Young people these days." My muscles relax at the sound of Nana's steady voice. She's not being robbed or held hostage at least.

"I should get going. Thank you, Lily. I always enjoy our teatime."

"Me, too, dear. See you next week."

Next comes rustling noises, like they're rising out of their seats. Excited to surprise her, I push open the door and lean on the doorframe, shoving my hands into my jean pockets.

Nana's gray-blue eyes widen with wonder and glisten as a hand cups her mouth. Her long hair has a smattering of gray, especially at the edges, and it's tied up into her usual soft bun. She's thin under her faded Christmas sweater and matching slacks, but healthy, and I'm overwhelmed by her presence.

"Maddy?"

This nickname hits me differently and square in the gut. She's the only one who calls me that, and it reminds me of some of my favorite childhood memories with her—baking or reading by her side, playing games in the backyard, holiday dinners, sleepovers, and everything in between. I didn't realize I had a gaping hole in my chest from missing her until her hug filled it.

"I can't believe you're here." Her fingers grip my shoulders as if she's making sure I'm real. "Why?"

"That's a story for another time."

"And my cue," the other woman says. Stepping closer, she stops beside me and smiles. Before I can figure out her motive for the pause, she rises to her tiptoes and kisses my cheek. "Welcome home, Maddox."

I couldn't have expected this stranger to kiss me, and my defensive reflexes are slow to react.

She hurries through the shop, and I wait for the bell to ring, indicating Nana and I are alone. "Who was that and why did she—" I'm too taken aback to finish the question.

Nana smirks as she points up.

The F-word forms on my tongue at yet another mistletoe sighting, but I think better of it given my current company. I can't possibly detest the plant any more than I do right now. Reaching up, I snatch it and the makeshift hook along with it. Good. Maybe Nana won't try to rehang it.

"That was Harper, the mayor's granddaughter." She waves me toward the two stools behind the counter, and winks over her shoulder. "She's single."

"And this concerns me in what way?" I know exactly what she's getting at, and I'm the furthest from interested as I can get.

"Just sayin'."

"Don't ruin it. I'm still happy to see you."

"Such a sweet boy, you are." She pats me on the thigh as we both sit, her eyes taking in every inch of me in her normal grandmotherly observation. "Catch me up."

Knowing I can't avoid it, I recount what caused my visit and how much I hate it. The unsettling first sight of Carmen in nine years and sleepless night that followed will have to wait until I wrap my head around it … or never, preferably. I'm hoping it was a one and done, and I can forget it even happened. Our lives have taken separate and very different paths and mingling the two would be a horrible idea. I can't trust myself not to say things I shouldn't.

"Did your parents know you were coming?" Nana asks, wanting to scold whoever kept her out of the loop.

"No. I wasn't sure how being here would go, so I thought

surprising them was safer in case I changed my mind."

"I'm glad you didn't. We miss you."

"I miss you all, too."

"Tell me about Boston. Are you making friends, getting out, experiencing all that the big city life offers?"

My hesitation gives away the truth. Outside of work, I barely do more than keep myself alive each day.

"Maddox, you've got too much going for you to let your broken heart stay that way."

When Carmen left all those years ago, Nana was the first person I went to for comfort. She lost her high school sweetheart and first husband to war several years after they married. Her second husband helped start this bookshop before he passed from a massive heart attack. The third, she lost over time to cancer. She loved each one as if they'd been her one and only, like her loss hadn't almost killed her, too. She showed me each time how to survive, recover, and love again. I just couldn't apply that knowledge when the grief happened to me. It took too much out of me to convince myself, no matter her trusted advice, that I wouldn't feel broken forever. That Carmen wouldn't be the only girl I'd love my entire life. And I'd been right.

"I'm not like you, Nana. I'm not good at letting people in."

"You used to be. You were once so kind and generous with your love. It's a special gift, Maddy. And you don't have to be like anyone, sweetheart. You just have to try in your own way." Her soft hand cups my cheek. "You know what I think?"

"I'm afraid to ask."

Sitting back, she surveys me, and I'm not sure I want to hear whatever wisdom she's about to deliver. "I think you coming here at this point in your life is happening for a reason."

"Yeah? Why is that?"

"I have my ideas, but mainly because you need to reconnect with your roots—the place and people who made you who you are."

"That guy doesn't exist anymore, Nana."

"Yes, he does. He just hasn't seen the light of day for almost a decade."

I roll my eyes. Sometimes I wish she didn't know me so well.

"You locked away that sweet boy, and all you need to do is let him out and get to know him again."

"And I suppose you're going to help me do that?"

"Yes, sir."

That answer gives me the sudden urge to flee and avoid the rest of this conversation, but my stand and fight training kicks in while I await her plan. No doubt she has one and it makes me gravely nervous. "How?"

"Don't you worry about that. Just know your Nana has everything covered. By the time Christmas arrives, you'll feel like a whole new man."

"I'm not comfortable with this. Maybe I like my current man card."

"You don't, and no one said change is easy. But everything will work out the way it should if you do what I say."

"Don't I always?"

"You *are* a great listener." The bell on the door chimes as a customer enters, and Nana rises. Before greeting them, she kisses my forehead and whispers, "That's why you're my favorite. Don't tell your brothers and sisters."

While Nana talks about flowers and gardens and searches for the best book to assist her customer with both, I stroll through the shop. It takes only two aisles to find a handful of red flags. Mom hadn't exaggerated about the shop's condition, after all. Broken floorboards, mildew piling up in the windowsills, water damage on the ceiling, cracked drywall, leaning bookshelves, the list goes on.

My biggest concern is the water leak. I don't remember what's above the store, but I know Nana owns the entire building. The side walls are connected to the General Store and boutique on either side, but each roof is separate. She's probably neglected the old shingles since losing her husband. He took care of all the maintenance both here and at their home. If she's neglected her pride and joy this way, I doubt I'll handle seeing her house—my second home—look just as bad and not do something about it.

Then again, all these handyman jobs might be exactly what I need to keep busy while I'm here, especially since I have no idea how Nana plans to *fix* my life. I'm not the only one who has let important things fall to the wayside. Mom said she's been stubborn about doing the necessary work at the shop and won't accept help. That shit stops now because she won't be given an option with me.

A door slams inside the room where I first found Nana. I check her reaction, and she doesn't seem concerned about the noise or the quick footsteps pounding on the wooden floors behind me. I spin to catch them in the act but see no one. Following the noise, I creep along the bookshelves, my big frame making it wobble. I'll fix that first thing in the morning after I get some tools. A fallen full bookshelf could injure someone or cause more damage.

Hearing some rustling ahead, I move closer and peek past the shelf's end. It's not a criminal—at least she doesn't appear to be one. You never can tell these days. A little girl in green overalls atop a candy cane-striped shirt sits on the floor with a pile of books in her lap. Her baby doll blue eyes, near transparent in the sunlight, acknowledge my presence by giving me a once-over. Straight, blonde hair flows over her shoulders and onto the book pages she's reading.

"What are you doing?" she asks like *I'm* the intruder.

"I was wondering the same about you."

"I asked you first."

I hold back my appreciation for her quick wit until I've assessed the situation further. "I'm visiting from out of town."

"How do you know Nana?" She bats her eyelashes at me, all possessive and smug in her position here.

Who is she to call *my* Nana that? I gave her the nickname when I was four years old. Only family follows suit. "I rather you answer that question."

"Do you always evade questions like this?"

Evade? That's a big word for such a little girl. "How old are you?"

She sighs, clearly determining I'm beneath her intellectually, and I'm beginning to think she's right. There are some big books decorating the floor, and she's dancing circles around this conversation. She raises a hand, pops up her forefinger with a white painted nail, and begins ticking off answers to my questions. "Reading. Nana's been my friend for as long as I can remember. Eight. Your turn."

The metaphorical hot-potato she tosses over to me catches me off guard. I try to remember the questions she asked, but like Western movie actors pretending to duel, I'm drawing blanks.

"The answer is yes. Apparently, you evade questions because you keep people at a distance. I bet you're a cop. No, military." My face must have registered my astonishment because she corrects herself. "Both, huh? Double trouble in the emotions category. No wonder you're single."

Holy shit. I straighten, both offended and downright blown away by her intuition and say-it-like-it-is attitude. She reminds me of my little sister, Kendall.

"What's your name?"

"Sadie. And who are you?"

"I was getting to it. Damn." I can't stop my flustered hand from shoving over my short hair. "I'm Maddox."

She chuckles. "No, you're not."

"I'm not?"

"You're not Maddox Henderson."

My defenses activate like I'm eight years old again—but more caveman-style compared to her level at the same age. I lean on the bookshelves and cross my arms to keep from stomping my foot in protest of the disgust in her tone. "Why not?"

"Nana said you're sweet."

"I'm sweet."

Her eyes roll back into her head before landing on her books again. "Don't believe you."

What the—

"How long are you staying in town?" she asks without so much as the courtesy of looking at me.

"Possibly a month, if I can stand it that long."

Her eyes meet mine and hold there, considering my answer. "Okay," she says, like she approves but at the same time doesn't care.

"Okay?"

She answers with an apathetic shrug, then gives her full attention to the books. I'm standing there, frozen to the floor wondering what just happened. I got schooled and dismissed by a human the size of my leg—that's what happened.

With my confidence successfully shaken, I head out, kissing Nana on the cheek along the way. If I could, I'd put young Sadie up against any suspect I've ever arrested. Five minutes in an interrogation room, and she'd crack them open and shake the confession out of them like a raw egg—that's something I'm confident in.

I'm chuckling to myself at the vision of her sitting across a scuffed metal table from a hard, tatted up high school dropout, her feet swinging back and forth under the chair, when I run into someone on the sidewalk. Not ten feet from the bookshop and an hour into my visit, and the past is already slapping me in the face.

"So sorry about—Maddox." Carmen's father stares up at me as if he were seeing a ghost or someone reincarnated from the dead. The description isn't far off.

"Hi, Mr. Bennett. I'm surprised you remember me."

"It's been a while, but I could never forget. You were good to my girl."

The wounds Carmen left pulse and threaten to reopen. When she walked away, I didn't only lose her, I lost her entire family. I'd grown up at her place as much as mine and Nana's. Our families were neighbors and best friends. We spent every holiday, summer, and Sunday afternoon together until her absence added a canyon size hole to those activities. I couldn't continue going about my life as if nothing changed. It hurt too much.

"We loved you like a son," he says. "Still do."

How is that possible? I hadn't been kind to them when they reached out after Carmen and I broke up. I ignored the letters and care packages they sent while in the Army. I never asked about them when family called. As I did with Carmen, I erased them from my life to keep the sorrow and heartache from swallowing me whole and convinced myself that they hated me for it

"You look good. Strong."

"Thank you."

An awkward silence takes over, and he rocks back on his

heels, the round leather bag he carries draws my attention.

"Going bowling?"

"I am. Every Thursday and Saturday."

"Is your wife tending the store this afternoon?" I point over his shoulder toward the general store his family has owned for generations, thinking of all the times I spent there growing up.

"No," he says quickly, then chuckles. "She's substituting at the elementary school this week."

"Oh. Please tell her I said hello."

"Will do." He doesn't waver from his stance, almost like he's guarding the entrance. "Where are you off to now?"

"I thought I'd surprise Mom at work."

He checks his watch. "That's perfect. She should be getting off soon."

"She is?" It's not even noon yet. "Why?"

"She's getting ready for the baby."

"Baby? What baby?"

"Sorry, son. I thought you knew." He taps me on the arm, closing down the subject. "I'll let her tell you all about it. Enjoy your visit, and I hope to see you at the Spectacular. It's going to be a good one this year."

I couldn't focus on anything he said after *baby*. On my way to the truck, I review conversations I had with Nana, my parents, and my siblings. I may suck at staying in touch, especially over the phone, but how could I miss someone being pregnant?

It better not be Kendall's. She's only nineteen. Or worse yet, Aaron's. My little brother can barely take care of himself in college with his studies, baseball schedule, and partying every minute he isn't in class or on the field. Cooper, my oldest brother, would never have a kid before he was married, discharged from the Army, and stable as a civilian. Unlike Aaron who goes wherever the wind takes him, Cooper has a plan for everything. Mishaps happen, but between them, Aaron is the one I wouldn't be surprised to hear had been loose in the responsibility department. Stupid, crazy kid.

Parking in front of the Ember Falls government building in central downtown, I jog through the front courtyard and up the tall flight of old stone stairs.

"Hi, Maddox." A woman about my age waves from the reception desk as I walk up.

"Hi …" Using my investigative skills, I check the nameplate on her desk. "Rebecca." Am I supposed to know her? I've been gone too long. "How are you?"

"Great. Barry proposed." Her left arm shoots out to show me the large diamond on her hand, and I fight the urge to withdraw. Engagement rings and proposals rank high on my list of things I detest, right under mistletoe. And who the hell is Barry?

"That's wonderful. Congratulations," I force out before changing the subject. "Is Mom in?"

"Yes, sirree. Want me to call her?"

"No. Thanks. I'll surprise her."

"Oh, what fun." She claps her hands together then checks the appointment schedule on her computer. "Good timing. She's in a staff meeting, right now. Go make your grand entrance."

Relying on my childhood memories and signage, I locate the Human Resources offices and walk right on inside—unlocked door, no one staffing the front desk, no bells, or security. What is it with this town? Crime happens everywhere—even small towns—and these people need to get it together.

Walking down the hall to the conference room and unsuspecting staff as any criminal could do, I slowly creep closer and peek inside. Mom is sitting at the head of the table in a festive white sweater, her auburn hair tied up into a youthful ponytail.

She reminds me of my sister when she was younger. Kendall wanted to dress and be like Mom in every way. After having three rowdy boys, Mom ate that shit up. They'd spend hours together trying new hairstyles or makeup while we boys played sports or got into messes outside. Whatever Mom did, Kendall shadowed her. She learned from the best how to be the unstoppable woman she is today. They're both strong, fearless, and selfless with their love. Kendall just does it with more attitude.

Mom stands to write something on the whiteboard behind her, and I slip into the room. They're planning for her absence, divvying up responsibilities and adjusting schedules, and I'm struck with curiosity again. Why does she need to take so much time off work?

A woman in a black Town of Ember Falls-logoed shirt notices me, and I silently plead with her to keep the secret. She grins, and I figure that means we're accomplices now. Two more women at the table nod, promising to keep the heist and Mom's oblivion intact.

The mission remains uncompromised until she turns back to address the group, catching me before I have a chance to duck behind something. My fellow SWAT team members would have ridden me for weeks on my lack of ingenuity. Good thing they're not here.

"Maddox?" On the way to her mouth, her hand drops the marker.

"Hi, Mom."

We embrace to a chorus of *aww*s, cheers, and applause, and it feels like I've won the lottery. Sunrays, sugar, rainbows, and all things soothing and beautiful pour into the dark cavity of my bland existence.

She backs away to say, "Meeting adjourned," to her staff then brings me close again. "I can't believe you're here. Is it because of the shooting?"

With Mom working in Human Resources, she understands the complex investigative process that follows an officer-involved shooting. She releases me for the answer and to study me for any emotional stress. She worries incessantly about all five of her children, but I hear that's a mom thing.

"I got a month off and couldn't stay in Boston for that long not working."

"And you thought to come home?" She shakes her head in wonder, matching my sentiments. "All I have to say is *finally*. I'll have to send a thank you note to your superior."

"Please don't."

"I'm only kidding, dear."

"No, you're not."

Her guilty smile ruffles the peace I found in her arms only minutes ago. "Well, I won't embarrass you … this time."

Sitting in the pair of chairs in her bright, corner office, I settle in for another unsettling topic. "Mom, what's going on? I ran into Wally, and he said you're preparing for a baby."

"You saw Wally?" She grimaces, assuming that would have been awkward for me, and she's right.

"Yeah, but that's not important."

"Right. You know we continued fostering after you graduated, and we adopted Oliver and Opal soon after." She continues following my confirming nod. "We had our hands full with twin toddlers but couldn't say no when a child needed us."

"Of course." Not being here while the twins grew up is another regret I carry. We barely know each other—something I hope to correct while I'm here. "But why does this one feel different?"

"Because it is." She lets out a long exhale, her hand pressing against her navel. "It's Isabelle's."

"Isabelle Raine? Cooper's Izzie?"

She grins at the title and nods. Although he'll say Isabelle is his best friend, he's secretly been in love with her since he figured out what that meant. Everyone knows it, except Izzie.

"She got mixed up with the wrong guy after college," Mom explains, "and tried to disappear to protect her baby."

My jaw clenches. "Don't tell me some asshole laid a hand on her." I consider Izzie another sister and would protect her with any means necessary, as I would all my family.

"Unfortunately, and he's dangerous. He found her in Michigan where she moved with her parents after they retired. When she started showing, she came here to hide and have the baby."

"Does she have a restraining order?"

"In Michigan, yes. We're hoping that will stop him from searching for her or assume she wouldn't come back to Ember Falls since her parents are in Michigan. She just needs to keep the baby a secret until he moves on."

"Cooper and I can make sure that happens."

"Maddox …"

I wave off her concern. We're soldiers and have dealt with far worse things than an arrogant prick who likes to beat up defenseless women. "How can she hide the baby?"

"We'll pretend to foster it from an out-of-town family and hire her as a nanny."

"Good. With us all working together, we can keep them both safe."

"Our thoughts, exactly. The P.D. and everyone in town who needs to know is in on it." She grins at me. "It's great to have you home where you belong."

"I don't know if that's true anymore."

"Of course, it is. You always have a home here, Maddox. And thank you for wanting to help."

"That's what I've been trained to do."

"No. It's who you are."

I don't know who I am these days, but I stop myself from disagreeing with her. It would only prolong the uncomfortable topic.

"You're staying with us, aren't you?" she asks.

I hadn't thought past throwing clothes in a bag to come here. That took all I had to give at the time. "I'm not sure. Aren't all the bedrooms taken with the twins and Izzie?"

"We'll figure it out. I will not have my son staying somewhere other than his home. I was being polite when I asked."

I stifle a groan. "In that case, I guess I'm moving in today."

She fakes surprise, earning her an eye roll. "Oh, that's wonderful, son."

Chapter 3

Carmen

"We need to talk," Dad says, not two steps inside the store.

"Alright. Take a seat and help fold." I pass him a red Ember Falls Spectacular T-shirt, but he doesn't sit. This must be serious. "What's going on?"

"Maddox is here."

On instinct, my hands pause at his name. I thought I saw him at my gig last night, but the lumberjack-shaped man with Maddox's features and shaggy hair cut short looked too broken and angry to be the same boy I remember from high school. My Maddox had a carefree way about him, reminding me of a firefly—unassuming and gentle with a quiet beauty that rivaled the sun at dawn.

As I always do to keep his memory close, I sang our song in

my set. Even when the man at the bar stormed out a few lyrics in, my brain couldn't convince my heart it had been him. He's avoided Ember Falls since high school graduation, except for when he came back for his grandfather's funeral four years ago. I hadn't been here, but I heard he didn't stay more than a few hours.

"Are you sure?" I finally respond, unsure if I want to hear him confirm it. If Maddox is here to stay a few hours, days, or more, can I face him? Can I handle seeing him if he despises me, or worse yet, brought another woman with him? I focus on the task in front of me to keep that vision and the ache it causes locked away where it belongs.

"I talked with him myself," Dad says and sets the poorly folded T-shirt on the pile. He'd been watching my reaction too closely to pay attention to his chore.

"Oh." My trembling hands lift another shirt out of the box, and I hope I look more put together than I feel. "Did he say how long he'd be staying?"

"I didn't ask."

"How'd he seem?"

My pulse revs as he pauses to consider the question, then again with his answer. "Haunted."

"That's the opposite of what I'd hoped you'd say. Do you think he's with someone?"

"Honey, you're asking the wrong person. Maybe you two can talk while he's here. Get some closure."

"It's been nine years, Dad."

"Exactly."

Tossing the shirt I attempted to fold three times back into the box, I stalk to the door.

"Where are you going?" he calls as I reach for the old iron handle.

"Out."

"But the store opens in half an—"

The door slams shut behind me, and I close my eyes, letting the winter air wash over me. The scent of pine needles mingles with the crispness of a new snowfall while the faint aroma of gingerbread drifts by from a nearby kitchen. A classic Christmas song plays from somewhere down the street, the familiar melody reminding me there's magic in the holidays.

Sadly, there doesn't seem to be enough of it to erase the thoughts I came out here to escape. The confusing concoction of emotions bubbling to the surface simply because Maddox's name came up in conversation can only mean one thing. Everything I've been telling myself for the past decade—*I don't need him, he's better off if I stay away, it's okay that he's built a life for himself far from mine*—has been nothing but lies.

My cool skin prickles on a breeze, and I feel the ripple through to my core. I'm sick with nerves thinking about Maddox—the man, not the idea of him I dream about—being so close our paths might cross at any moment. Simply accepting this fortifies his place as the center of my world. He doesn't know and certainly hasn't asked for that spot, but it's always been his whether he wants it or not.

Treasured memories, unfulfilled wishes, heartache, and my deepest fears swirl together, making the earth feel unsteady beneath my feet. Maybe it's not the ground but my twisting stomach. I pitch forward to breathe through the nausea when the old metal lock on the bookshop door unlatches from inside. I straighten, suddenly afraid it might be Maddox.

I don't want him to see me like this. When our paths cross, I'd prefer to be dressed in my best *beg for forgiveness* outfit and prepared to stand before him with confidence and say my peace. But can I ever fully prepare to face the only man I've ever loved after breaking his heart and walking away as if it had been easy?

What do I say in that situation? *I'm sorry* will never be enough. I've spent countless nights imagining what I would say if I ever got the chance, but now, those rehearsed words elude me. It's easy to dream when the odds of following through seem slim to none. With his history, that may still be the case, and I'm terrified he might leave before I can get to him.

Though I consider myself a strong woman, I have plenty of paralyzing doubt. It's what kept me from chasing after him when I realized I'd made a mistake, and again when I returned nearly four years ago. Like a fool, I prayed he'd moved back after his time in the Army and let Ember Falls support and heal him. A small part of me hoped he'd come back for me. But Maddox is a man of his word, and he warned me he wouldn't.

I should have tried to find him when I learned he'd chosen Boston after discharge, but I couldn't bear to risk seeing the pain I caused reflected in his beautiful hazel eyes. Worst of all, I couldn't chance discovering he'd moved on and forgotten about me. That last one hits me harder than it should, considering I'm the one who ended things, and I reach for the brick wall to steady myself.

I wonder if that's why he's showing up now. What will I do if he's here to introduce his girlfriend or fiancée to his family? The bitter taste of irony rises into my throat. It's what I deserve. After all, I ended our relationship and prayed for him to find happiness, even if it meant loving someone else. I was stupid to think I could live with that.

Needing support for my wobbly legs, I shift to lean against the wall and shake out my hands in a nervous fidget. The cold air has seeped into my bones while I stood out here without a coat, and I shove my hands inside my back jean pockets to warm them. Punishing myself isn't helping me think, but there's no way I'm going back inside to finish the conversation my dad wants to have. Not yet, anyway.

My eyes scan the street, searching for a reason to move or a safe place to warm up. I land on Latte Da Café across the street. Coffee. Yes, getting coffee is a perfectly normal thing to do in the morning. I push off the brick with newfound determination. Maybe a heavy dose of caffeine will help get me through the rest of this day with a semblance of my sanity intact.

"Hi, Willa," I greet the owner with a little too much enthusiasm on my way into the café. I'm overcompensating to hide the insecurities eating me alive on the inside. It's contained chaos in there, like the store the week before Christmas. Why does everyone do all their shopping last minute these days?

"What are you doing here?" she asks. "Isn't the store about to open?"

"Not you, too. Can't a girl take a break to get a dose of lucidity once in a while?" I chuckle, hoping the casual joke hides the new fractures in my world.

"Girl, you came to the right place." She holds up a finger, telling me to wait, then pushes through the swinging kitchen door. A few seconds later, she makes a grand re-entrance, holding a layered tray with one hand as if it were full of feathers instead of at least three dozen massive muffins. "You want the usual?"

"Not today. Caramel macchiato, two extra pumps of caramel. Please."

She nods to the young barista behind her, who gets to work on my brew. I'm considering adding more carbs to my foolishness antidote in the form of a steaming chocolate muffin when Willa leans a hip against the counter and smiles at me. This can't be good.

"We've known each other a long time," she says, like she

plans to say more and wants to ease me into it.

"Yesssss." I draw out my answer, eyeing her with suspicion. We went to school together, and since I moved back, we see each other nearly every day.

"I know you've heard the biggest news this town has had in a while, or you wouldn't be ordering all that sugar and considering adding more with my scrumptious muffins." Her judging eyes travel down my body and back. "I saw you lookin'."

"I don't know what you're talking about." To keep the guilt from heating my cheeks and giving me away, I reach for a straw on the opposite side of the counter.

"Stop," she calls to her staff with her smug eyes holding me hostage. "No caramel for Miss Denial here until she comes clean."

The girl stops squeezing caramel into the cup to stare over her shoulder at us, her brow pinched in confusion. No one can ever have secrets in Ember Falls. Sometimes, I miss the anonymity of living in Los Angeles.

"Fine." I let out my frustration with a loud sigh. "Yes, I know Maddox is here."

She snaps her fingers in the air, letting the girl know she can finish making my drink. I can't help being embarrassed for us both.

"Are you going to talk to him?" Willa asks.

"I—"

"Lordy, you two were something else in high school. I was so jealous. All I could attract were the playboys and class clowns. You had Best In Show."

"He's not a horse."

"From what I saw, he's built like a—"

"Here's your coffee, Miss Denial," the lifesaver with my caffeine prescription says with a smile and slides the drink across the counter.

"I don't know why I come here," I complain, reaching for my wallet.

"Because you know I have the best coffee, sweets, and advice in town. Although I know you'll deny it because that's the theme of today, you know you need all three."

Willa reaches for the chocolate muffin I fantasized about and adds it to a white paper bag. "This is on the house along with this great advice: Talk to him."

"I appreciate you caring about me, but I need to get back to work." After placing a ten-dollar bill on the register, I make my getaway before more ghosts of Christmas past can be dredged up. I'll face those when I've scraped together the courage and mindset to absorb the consequences.

"Did you see Maddox Henderson this morning?" Chrissy whispers to her best friend Sandra behind the postcard stand. The biggest gossips in town since we were in high school, nothing gets by these two.

Usually, I tune them out while they use our store to pass along town news for hours on end. This morning, however, the topic of conversation has me wishing they weren't being so discreet. Their breathy voices barely travel past the display racks, and my neck aches from craning it to listen.

Everyone in town knows my history with Maddox, and it's bold to talk about him in front of me. Must be a slow news day.

"He was such a gorgeous boy, but all grown up …" They giggle like middle school girls after the popular boy winks at them in class.

I shake my head, wondering where this gossip trail is heading.

"I saw him carrying a toolbox into the bookshop early this

morning." Sandra fans her face with a postcard. "Lily must finally be fixing up the place."

"If he's going to be working there, I might need a few new books for my library."

"I could use a book myself. I also have some things that need fixin' at my place. Maybe Lily will loan him out for a bit."

That's enough. Hopping off my stool behind the counter, I stalk toward them. "Ladies, can I help you with anything today?" I ask, bringing gossip time to a screeching halt.

"Hi, Carmen. We're just looking for a Christmas gift for my brother. He's coming into town for the Spectacular." Sandra glances at Chrissy before turning her narrowed, not-so-innocent eyes on me. "He's single. Are you dating anyone?"

Subtle. "Nope, and I'm not interested in being set up."

"Why not? It's not like handsome bachelors stroll into our little town very often."

Are they talking about her brother or Maddox? Is she insinuating that Maddox is single? Do they know something I don't, or am I projecting my hopes into this strange conversation? "You're right, but I have a lot on my plate right now and dating isn't one of them."

"That's a shame. I guess that means I can set him up with someone else. Someone like Chrissy, perhaps."

Chrissy's eyes sparkle at the idea, and I'm still not sure who we're talking about. I just know I don't like it.

"Anyone but you." Sandra barges on. "Is that what you're saying?"

"I guess so."

"Alrighty. I'm glad that's settled. Ready Chrissy? We have more shopping to do."

"What about the gift?" I call lamely after them as the door closes. My efforts to quell gossip time where Maddox is concerned, may have accomplished something much worse. With the way Sandra and Chrissy work, the Ember Falls collective of unattached women will be informed within the hour that I'm not a concern. They have free and clear access to pursue and flirt and—

"Poor guy," Dad says, shaking me out of my sickening thoughts. He sets down a box of pens and clucks his tongue. "You know they weren't talking about her brother, right?"

My eyes roll at the same time as my stomach.

He ignores my pre-teen-like reaction and barrels on. "If you don't lay claim soon, every unattached female in this town will be trying to do just that, and you'll be further behind than you are now."

Well, that stung. I fight against a wince by glaring at him, ensuring he understands that I don't care for the hidden message behind his comment. I know I have a lot of groveling to do before earning a conversation with Maddox. I don't need a reminder. "Dad, I can have no claim on him. I gave that up long ago, and surely, he hates me for it."

"Maybe." He shrugs. "Maybe not."

"Dad."

"All I'm saying is you'll never know if you avoid him while he's here."

"I'm not avoiding Maddox. He just got here. I'm giving him space to get settled …" *And me time to determine if he's single.* "Before forcing him to do something he doesn't want to do."

"What do you think he doesn't want to do?"

"See me. Talk to me. Think about me," I blurt out, my arms flying up and banging against my sides in helpless exasperation, like we're acting in an over-dramatic 90s comedy. Only there's nothing funny about this situation.

"What about what you want?"

Picking up the box of General Store logoed pens, I stalk to the main counter. "The last time I thought about that, it ruined everything."

"But wouldn't it be nice to know if he does want to see you, talk to you, and think about you in the present and in a new way. Don't you want him not to be angry with you anymore."

"You're not helping."

"Yes, I am. You just don't know it yet."

I lean against the cabinet for support, exhausted from trying to hold together my shredded patience. "Anyway, we don't know he's angry. Maybe he hasn't given me a second thought." That wasn't easy to say out loud.

"You two had something special, honey." He steps up to the counter to prevent me from dodging this conversation again. "He hasn't stopped thinking about you any more than you've stopped thinking about him."

Of course, I think about Maddox. For my entire childhood, he was the center of my world, my best friend, and my safe space. I've missed him more than I can put into words, but allowing myself to hope he hasn't moved on could be more detrimental to my tender heart than living with half of one without him.

Chapter 4

Maddox

Last night, I made a list of repair tasks to accomplish at the bookshop according to complexity and time needed and snuck in a toolbox after closing. First on the list will be checking the second floor to find the cause of the leak … but *after* I soften the opposition.

Expecting Nana to protest and try to hinder my plans for some unknown reason, I stop by Latte Da Café on my way in to get us coffee and breakfast. She won't show it, but she'll be touched by the thoughtful gesture. I only hope it's enough to make her stay out of my way. Then again, no matter how she reacts, I still win. The repairs will eventually get done—just with annoying chatter from said opposition—and I get some one-on-one time with my favorite person. Now that I think about it, this buttering her up idea is for *my* benefit and sanity, not hers.

Stepping inside the café, I'm too busy admiring my cleverness to prepare my introverted self for the young barista greeting me by name. It's a small town. Of course, she knows me and my family, but it's been a while since I've experienced that kind of intimate familiarity, and I'm out of practice.

"Happy Saturday, Maddox," the barista says the second door closes. "I heard you were back in town."

Already? News travels—Wait. Is she ... "Addie Harding? Is that you?"

She smiles in response, reminding me of the little girl I remember from Aaron's birthday parties and games. She seemed to be a good friend to him and balanced his ever-present energy. They liked a lot of the same things, including baseball, and played on the same Little League team until she switched to softball in middle school.

"I haven't seen you since you were eight or nine years old. You're all grown up."

She tightens the loose ponytail on top of her head, her rich chocolate eye showing her amusement before her lips. "That's what happens when you skip town for a while," she teases. "How long are you here for?"

"Not sure."

"You're living in Boston, aren't you?"

"I am."

"Cool. The girls and I are thinking about taking a trip there for my twenty-first birthday in a few months. I hope you'll stay for the Spectacular," she says, switching topics too fast and almost giving me whiplash.

Stay. The vein in my neck throbs like my system is gearing up to do the opposite. That motor hasn't taken a break since I arrived in Ember Falls.

"I haven't thought that far ahead," I say to keep my feet from taking me away without warning.

"Maybe I can convince you to stay longer with some yummy coffee and treats. I guarantee it will be better than anything you've had in Boston," she challenges.

"I live on coffee most shifts, so I—"

"What do you do?"

"I'm a cop."

She leans on the top of the register, eager to re-energize our conversation. "Is that what you've been doing since you left?"

"No. I also served in the Army."

"That's amazing. The Spectacular holds an appreciation dinner for active military and veterans on Christmas Eve. You should go."

I doubt I'll be here then. "I'm not that big on socializing."

"You're socializing with me. See? It's not so bad." She giggles before resuming barista mode. "What can I get ya?"

"Just two black coffees and two blueberry muffins."

She doesn't move to enter my order and stares at me like I spoke an unknown language. "That's so ... generic," she accuses, her brow scrunching in the middle in disapproval. "How can I convince you to stay if you don't try one of our specialties? How about a peppermint latte and a slice of wild berry pie instead?"

"Taking my Nana, Ember Falls' reigning pie-baking champion, a slice from the competitor will get my head chopped off and baked into a pie. Maybe next time when she's not looking," I promise, and her smile returns.

"Okay. So long as there's a next time. Don't go running off again without saying goodbye."

I don't know how to respond to that, nor can I promise I won't, and I'm grateful for the save my vibrating phone provides. After handing her my debit card, I step away to check the text.

Aaron: Dude! I can't believe you're in town. You're going to stay until I get there, right?

Me: Of course. When do your classes end?

Aaron: Next week. I'll be back in time for the Spectacular.

Me: Kendall riding with you?

Aaron: Yeah. If she can pull herself out of the library. She's crushin on some guy working there. [Eye roll emoji] Dude's not even in the ballpark good enough for her, and he's old.

I chuckle. For all the arguing those two do, they're over-the-top protective of each other.

Me: How old?

"Your order's ready, Maddox," Addie announces. "Thanks. I'll be right there."

Aaron: 25

Me: She's only 19!

Aaron: Yeah. Gross, right?

Kendall: You two talking about me?

Aaron: Guess who just barged into my apartment.

Kendall: OUR apartment. Don't forget who keeps this place looking less like a locker room.

Kendall: Hi, big bro. I miss you.

Me: Hi Ken. I miss you, too.

Aaron: How come you didn't say you missed me?

Me: Goes without saying.

Kendall: Have you heard from Cooper? Is he coming home, too?

Me: I haven't, and no one's mentioned anything yet.

Aaron: I bet he shows up with the whole Izzie situation.

Me: Military leave isn't easy to come by.

Kendall: Neither is a connection like theirs.

My stomach knots at the reminder of the connection I once had.

Aaron: Way to go.

Kendall: Sorry, Maddox. That was insensitive of me.

Me: No, it wasn't. Ancient history.

Me: I better go. I've got coffee and Nana waiting on me.

Aaron: Good luck! You're gonna need it.

Kendall: Shut up. Love you, Maddox.

Aaron: Where's my I love you?

"Anything important?" Addie asks with excitement. "Does a criminal case need your attention?"

"Nothing like that. Just my crazy siblings."

"Oh. Which ones?" Nerves shake in her voice, erasing all playfulness.

"Kendall and Aaron."

"Are they coming home, too?"

"Next week."

"That's wonderful." With both hands, she pushes my card and order forward, her friendly smile vanishing. "Have a great day, Maddox."

She pushes through the swinging kitchen doors, leaving me alone in the empty café. Strange exit for someone who seemed content to keep me here talking all day only moments ago. With a shrug, I put away my debit card, collect the bag of muffins and cardboard cup carrier, and cross the street.

Nana must have seen me coming with her special treats.

"Good job," I say as she holds open the door and helps me inside. "That's the kind of welcome customers expect."

"Stop your griping and give me that muffin. I can tell that's what you got in the bag." She snatches the bag from my hand and reaches inside. Without bothering with the paper wrapping, she sinks her teeth into the top of the muffin and groans. "Willa sure knows how to bake bread and pastries, but she's got a thing or two to learn about pies. I'm keeping my crown this year."

"I hope so. For everyone's sake," I add in a mumble to myself.

"I heard that." She takes another bite before giving her attention to me. "By the way, I saw the tools you brought in here. You're not as sneaky as you think."

"Whatever complaining you're conjuring up, I don't want to hear it. This place needs work, and if you won't do it, I will."

"It's not your shop. I'll fix what I want when I want."

"Nope. You gave up that right yesterday when you told me to shut up and listen. Now, I'm saying the same to you. You can try to fix whatever you think is broken in my life, and I'll do the same with the one thing you love as much as family. Got it?"

I expect her to argue, nag, or throw something at me. I never thought I'd hear her to say, "Okay."

"Okay?"

"Yeah, okay. Want me to write it down for you?"

"Damn, Nana. I got it."

"Good."

I remove my muffin from the bag and take a bite, fully understanding Nana's reaction to hers. The symphony of flavors melts on my tongue as I chew.

"Why haven't you fixed the issues around here," I ask, and resign to playing twenty questions when she ignores me. "Do you not have the money? Don't trust Dad with tools?" That got a chuckle out of her. He really is a danger to himself with power tools. Everything I know, I learned from Carmen's father and the Army.

"Revenue isn't exactly flowing steady these days, thanks to online stores, but I'm not dry yet."

"Do you have any ideas for changing that? You need to

adequately support yourself. You can't operate the way you did when you first opened. You have to evolve, Nana."

"You're one to talk."

After that little nugget, we eat in silence until Nana steers the conversation back to my life and ruins the bliss.

"Chrissy asked about you yesterday."

"Who?"

"Bachelorette number two."

"Good Lord, Nana." Snatching up my coffee, I stalk to hall closet where I not so slyly (apparently) hid the toolbox. "How do I get upstairs?" My escape route.

"Stairway in the lounge."

"I'm going up to find the leak. Let me know if you need anything."

Just short of jogging to get away from any mention of my bachelorhood, I rush to the back of the bookshop and locate the stairs, taking them two at a time. At the top, a long hallway connects the bookshop to the building beside it. Two doors break up the long, white wall ahead. The one above the Bennett's General Store has a number on it as if they use it for something. I start with the one closest to the stairwell since it's above the bookshop. The old metal knob grinds through a turn, and I step into an open room.

"You've got to be kidding me."

It's not empty attic space, but a finished apartment with hardwood floors, plumbing, and established rooms.

I cross the room into the outdated kitchen, then down the narrow hallway, passing the bathroom and two small bedrooms. The apartment looks as if it hadn't welcomed a tenant for decades, but with a good cleaning, some paint, new appliances, and plenty of elbow grease, it could be that revenue source Nana needs.

Setting down the toolbox, I check the bathroom for leaks first. Finding none, I move to the kitchen where watermarks decorate the cabinet floor under the sink. The pipe isn't dripping but who knows how long ago the damage was done below.

I grab a wrench and dip under the sink.

"What are you doing?" a little voice asks behind me, and I jump, hitting my head on the old metal pipe.

Crawling out, I sit on my heels to face Sadie. We're eye level with each other, but I'm confident she doesn't see me as an equal with the *you're stupid* look she's giving me.

"Water is dripping into the bookshop, and as you know, water is not good for books."

"No. It would be awful to ruin Nana's collection."

"Agreed. She doesn't seem to be worried, but I am."

"Me, too."

"Glad we agree." I flash her a grin, happy she isn't schooling me again. "What are *you* doing up here?"

"I live next door." At least the Bennett's are smart enough to put their second-floor space to good use.

"Are your parents home?"

"It's just mom and me. She's at work."

She rocks back on her heels and that's when I notice she's holding something behind her back.

"Whatcha got there? Another book?"

She shows me a stack of crumbled papers with deep frown. "It's my lines."

"Are you in a play?"

"Yes. Ellie got the lead role because she has brown hair, but she can't remember all the lines like I can."

"I bet not. What's the play?"

"Snow White. I have to be the evil queen." She huffs and leans on the counter opposite me, her arms folded over the papers across her little body.

"But the queen is a more difficult part to play. I'm sure the director thought you would handle it best."

"How so?" Mirroring me, she lowers to the floor, her pretty, blue eyes holding my gaze with curiosity.

"Have you seen the movie?"

"Yeah. I studied it for the part."

I sigh at her grown up answer, hoping she's spent some time as a carefree child in her eight years on this planet. Those were the best years of my life, and I wish that for her. "No doubt, but did you watch it?'

Her head tilts in confusion, and I settle into a more comfortable position, anticipating a long conversation. "The queen is also the old witch, right?"

She gives me a nod.

"What emotions do you feel when the queen or the witch are on scene."

"Mad, scared, frustrated," she answers after thinking on it.

"Exactly. It takes a very talented actor to play two characters and make the audience feel all those emotions."

"So, the director gave me the hardest part?"

"Yes. A part he would only give to the best actors. Snow White is all fluff." I smile with her as everything unfolds in her mind.

"Thank you." She flings herself into my arms, surprising and releasing me before I can react. "I take back what I said. You are sweet."

Something twists inside me. That fatherly, protector instinct I haven't felt in years bubbles back to the surface and carves Sadie's name into my heart, right beside my siblings'.

"I appreciate that, especially coming from you."

"When you're done here, want to run some lines with me?

Mom and grandpa are always busy, and grandma is terrible at it. Plus, you seem to understand the business."

Amused with her grown up language, I stifle a grin to match her seriousness. "I've had some exposure. I knew someone a long time ago who was an actress and singer."

"Really?"

"Yeah. I used to run lines with her and help her write songs all the time."

"That's cool. So, you'll do it?"

"Let me check a few more things here, then we'll practice."

She jumps to her feet and sets the script on the counter. "Since you're going to help me, I'll help you with your chores."

"Great. I could use an assistant as smart as you."

After crawling under cabinets and in dark, dusty crevices for a while, she sits me on the floor in the living room and hands me the script.

"Does this mean you have all your lines memorized?" I ask, and her chin tilts up. "I love your confidence. Alright, let's see what you've got."

Digging deep into my long-lost childhood, I bring out the amateur actor I'd tucked away. Sadie laughs at my exaggerated accents for each dwarf and especially Snow White.

"You sound like a munchkin from the Wizard of Oz. We don't talk like that," she says between giggles, the adorable sound lifting the clouds that seem to hover over my life these days.

"What do you mean *we*?"

"Girls, silly."

"Oh, right." My palm slaps against my forehead, sending her into another fit of giggles. "I have two little sisters. How did I mess that up?"

"Because you're a boy."

"No, I'm not."

"Since when?"

"Since puberty." A snicker slips out, but Sadie staring at me as if I'm as dumb as the joke has it evolving into a cough. I tap a fist against my chest to clear the non-existent tickle and continue with her prompts.

On the last run through hours later, she recites every word without a hitch, her joy over the accomplishment bouncing off the walls in the empty apartment.

"Way to go, kid." I celebrate with her, my arms flailing in the air as she dances about.

On the last twirl, she falls into my lap. Her arms cover me in both acceptance and adoration, catching me off guard. We barely know each other, but it doesn't take me long to give her the same and realize that this little girl has forever changed me.

"That was so fun. Can we do it again tomorrow?" she asks as she stands, her body fidgety with too much energy to contain.

"If there's nothing else stealing my free time …" And even then, I'd choose her. "I'd love to."

She flashes me a smile to rival the stars, and I wonder if she knows it's a superpower. That twinkle of hers could convince me to do just about anything.

"I better get back to work now and make some progress on the task list." I push off the hard floor to my feet and stretch my sore back. "I've got some more bookshelves to secure."

"And I need to fix lunch."

"You're joking."

"Why would I do that?" she asks, her serious side snapping back into place. "Momma doesn't have time, and cooking our meals is part of my weekend chores."

Shaking my head, I collect the toolbox I set by the door

before our playtime started. "You're incredible, Queenie."

"Queenie?"

"Yeah. With the royal way you delivered that script, you are now Queen Sadie, or Queenie."

"My name and queen mixed together. I like it."

Her satisfaction with the nickname shouldn't have made me as proud as it did, but here we are.

On my way downstairs, I'm marveling at my new friend and don't realize I've walked into a meeting of some sort until it's too late. The lounge is full of women of all ages, sitting in a circle of chairs or beanbags. I recognize Harper, the Mayor's daughter, but that's it. Yet, they all watch me as if they know me and all my darkest secrets.

"Maddox, darling," Nana says, her arm circling mine as I exit the stairwell. "Come say hi to the Book Nook Book Club."

"I don't want to interrupt."

"You're not. I'll introduce you to everyone." Spite glitters her every word. She's not happy with me messing with her shop, but she'll eventually realize I'm doing it for her own good. Until then, I guess she'll be punishing me for it every chance she gets.

With an arm hooked tight on mine, she guides me through the room, forcing me into conversations with each woman. They ask questions I don't care to answer, get too close, and touch me incessantly. After the final awkward introduction, I bolt, bumping into Harper on her way to the eggnog pitcher on a small table by the door. She grips my elbows to steady and trap me.

"Here we are again," she says, batting her lashes.

"Again? Where?"

Her eyes browse the doorframe above us and mine follow. Nana reinstalled the godforsaken mistletoe while I was upstairs.

"You seem like a nice person," I say lamely. "But I'm gonna

go."

Backing away, I catch a glimpse of Sadie snickering at me from the stairs. I already know my fumbling escape tactics make me look like a cowardly fool. I don't need an eight-year-old making me feel like one, too.

Mentally, I add a mistletoe hunt to my to-do list as the number one task. I'm searching this store (and the whole town if necessary) to prevent this unbearable kind of encounter from ever happening again.

Chapter 5

Maddox

Honey, can I speak with you for a moment?" Mom asks from the top of the stairs soon after my shower. Since all the upstairs bedrooms are taken, I set up in the basement. It's mostly unfinished but more comfortable and quieter than most of the places I slept in the Army.

"Sure. Want me to come up?"

"Yeah. Let's talk in the sunroom. I have a fire and beer ready for you."

This is great. She's buttering me up for something. "Be right there."

Like the dutiful son I am, I finish dressing and trot upstairs, rustling Oliver's thick, blond curls as I pass the couch. He's deep into a basketball video game and barely acknowledges me.

Stepping into the sunroom, Mom pats the empty swing

cushion beside her. She tosses the blanket she's using over my legs as I sit and hands me the beer. Mentally preparing myself for whatever she needs to get off her chest, I take a long swig.

"You know we're having our regular Sunday get together today."

"I do."

"It's grown over the years. It's not just our immediate family and closest friends anymore."

I shrug. "That's fine. Are you worried I won't be a good host in my Scrooge mood?"

"No. I raised you right." She nudges me with her shoulder. "I want to give you a heads up about the usual guest list." Her fingers aid in ticking off the invitees. "Nana, of course, and your aunts and uncles. They're excited to see you, so I suspect they'll all come."

"I'm excited, too."

She gives me a smile. "All our neighbors are invited. About half come each week and it varies who. That's the twins' favorite part because it brings all their friends together—the same experience you had growing up."

"It was the highlight of my week." Despite knowing better, I glance across the yard to Carmen's childhood home. Their backyard connects to ours, giving our get togethers the perfect field for killer wiffle ball games. From playing sports, to lying in the shade of a tree, to making out in every private space we could find, we made plenty of memories on every blade of grass. The constant ache in my chest sharpens, and I drown it with half what's left of my beer.

"The Bennetts are expected to come."

Squeezing the bottle to give my rage somewhere to go, I brace for what I know she's about to say. "Including Carmen."

I shoot off the swing, sending it into motion, and stalk to the wood stove in the opposite corner. This news, even though I expected it, smacks me harder than I want it to. How will I handle being in the same room with her? Given my reaction to her presence in a dark bar with a sea of tables and people between us, I guarantee, it won't be good.

Searching for the peace I had before this conversation started, I scan the yard for something to carry my thoughts away. Remnants of snowmen and snow forts created after the last storm dot the yard, reminding me of simpler days. When watching the clouds and wishing for another snow day off from school was my only concern.

"How long is she in town?" I ask, tossing another log into the stove and letting my eyes blur over the new flames.

"She should be the one to answer that."

"I'm asking you."

"And I'm telling you this pain you hold, centering around her, will never lessen unless you two talk it out. You've avoided it for far too long."

Irritation rockets through my system, courtesy of my rising blood pressure. "What if I don't want to talk to her?"

"Your anger isn't doing you any favors," she says, shaking her head, and my skin ripples with annoyance. "Talk to her, Maddox. Hear her story and figure out a way to forgive her or get the closure you need to move forward. I will not let you waste this opportunity and continue sulking alone in Boston. I want my son back."

Her voice wavers, shutting down construction of the wall I'm frantically repairing. First Captain Emory, then Nana, and now Mom. Why can't I live my life the way I want? Being a cop and brooding alone is where I'm most comfortable. I'm not good at communicating or dealing with my heartache. Because of that, I've become a live wire with a short fuse. I'm not proud of it, but it would be in everyone's best interest, especially Carmen's, if we don't have that talk everyone's so hell-bent on.

Yet, the wobble in her voice makes me say, "Okay."

But I can't look at her. I'm already hovering over dangerous territory, and if I see one tear in her eyes, I'll fall right in. With everyone arriving soon, I guarantee neither of us want to deal with another of my broody outbursts.

Proof of that sentiment comes in the form of comforting arms curling me into a hug, and it's all I can do to not crumble inside them.

Leaning against the brick wall in the sunroom where Mom left me to contemplate her unbearable request, I haven't found a way to force myself to move. Every piece of me wants to lash out at this unfair pivot in my situation. To throw a fist through something satisfyingly breakable, like drywall or glass, and take off, never to return again.

But what would that usual Maddox response get me this time? A disappointed mother (again) and no closer to accomplishing the reason I came here in the first place— to find a way past my anger so I can keep my job. Simply being in Ember Falls is a gigantic leap for me. When I'm ready to jump into the next one, I'll face the woman whose memory has kept me in a chokehold for years on end, but I'll do it on my own terms. Mom will just have to accept that.

Away from the evolving activity of arriving guests inside, I decide to stay put until I have a grip on my temper. After my extended absence, everyone is sure to have plenty of questions I can't answer and impossible expectations to meet in my sour mood. I'm not evading. I'm doing us all a favor.

My vibrating phone has me pushing off the wall, grateful for the distraction. At the first sight of my little brother's name and his ridiculous texting style, a rainbow of joy peeks through the clouds, filling me with a rare dose of contentment.

Aaron: Dude, you hangin?

Kendall: You sound like a neanderthal. Translation: Are you attending the Sunday dinner, and if so, are you okay?

Me: I'm fine.

Aaron: Don't believe you.

Kendall: Can I give you some advice?

Aaron: Good Lord.

Me: If you say talk to Carmen, I'm turning off my phone.

Kendall: Definitely not. I was thinking you should let her come to you if she has the balls to do it. If not, you know you dodged a bullet and she's not worth the head space you give her. If she does, you can decide if you're ready. If you're not, tell her you need more time. If she cares for you at all, she'll give it happily, and you'll have another answer without having to ask.

Aaron: Damn, that's a lot of ifs.

Kendall: Zip it, A.

Cooper: Great advice.

Aaron: Coop! Bout time you showed up.

Cooper: Been a little busy defending the country and shit.

Kendall: You're the best!

Cooper: Thanks, Ken.

Cooper: Do what you want, Madds. You don't owe her anything.

Me: Part of me is curious what she'll say. The other wants to keep running in the opposite direction.

Cooper: You can't do both. Want my advice?

Me: I thought you said do what I want.

Cooper: Gut reaction. Got better advice.

Me: What is it?

Cooper: There's nothing she can say to change what she did, but only you can change how you live with it. You haven't been doing a very good job of that, and we all know you're miserable.

Aaron: Damn, that was way better than whatever Ken said. I'm still processing it …

Kendall: Shut up. You can do this, Maddox. We love you.

I've never seen this many people in the house before. The living room, kitchen, dining room, and sunroom are full of blood and found family. Long-time neighbors I'm just now meeting, aunts and uncles I haven't seen since the funeral, and kids of all ages, running in and out to get food or to play.

Carmen hasn't arrived yet, and I'm not sure how to feel about that. Maybe she decided against attending, knowing I'd be here, or maybe she's simply running late.

A couple from down the street, turn from me to their fussy toddler, and that's when I see Sadie enter the living room. Curious, since Mom hadn't mentioned her coming, I cross to her.

"Hi, Queenie," I greet, making her giggle.

"Sweetie!"

I laugh at the sarcastic, rhyming nickname and revel at her cleverness. "What are you doing here?"

"I come every week," she says, her little arms circling my neck before I realize how much I needed the generous gift.

"You do? With your mom?"

"Yeah."

"Where is she? I'd love to meet her."

"Be right back," she yells already halfway across the room, her mission clear.

I feel Mom watching me from the couch with concern, and I have no idea why. This is the best I've felt since our conversation, and I have one little girl to thank for—

Sadie re-enters the room, pulling Carmen by the hand toward me, and I swear my heart stops. The room noise blurs as my body refuses to pump blood and oxygen to vital organs.

Carmen is Sadie's mother? The same Carmen who didn't want children. The one who left me for the single life in L.A. Who's Sadie's father? A vision of Carmen in another man's arms sends a shockwave through my tattered soul, and I can't decide which hurts more—knowing Carmen started a family with someone else or that she didn't want one with me.

Someone calling my name nearby echoes in my head like a baseball bat hitting a metal pipe. Each syllable bangs and ricochets off my skull until the pain it creates is all I feel. My body revolts, sending both chills and fire down my spine.

Self-preservation instincts take over my body because I can't think. The only thing populating is that staying here isn't an option. I can't stand before her and everyone and pretend her presence isn't a knife in the back, another scar on my heart, or acid on my soul.

The living room recliner, kitchen counter, and last doorframe before my escape, support my weight until I stumble outside. The cold air slaps against my face, feeling closer to a spa facial in comparison to what the news I learned inside did to me.

"Maddox."

"Not now, Mom." With my hands on my thighs, propping me up, I gulp for something to fill me—air for my empty lungs, sanity, the bravery I once possessed.

"Maddox, I'm sorry. I wanted to tell you." Her hand falls onto my back, and I shake it off like a sullen teenager.

"Why didn't you? Why didn't *anyone* in our family give me the slightest heads up?" This is not inconsequential news, yet I received no warning text or call and not one *hey Maddox, that girl who ruined your life has some shocking news...* conversation. In their defense, I had adamantly refused to listen anytime her name came up. I'd cut off and shut out anyone who brought her up, and after a while, they stopped. Still, they knew hearing about Sadie would kill me and should have tried harder.

That has my system rebooting into status quo mode— downright pissed—and I put some distance between us. It's safer for her that way. Fury is the only emotion I can process in the storm Carmen's surprise created.

"I never expected you would meet Sadie before Carmen could tell you herself. Nana didn't know you two had met either. Either way, it's not our place to tell you."

"I disagree." Glancing over the yard, now covered in a fresh layer of snow, my breath materializes between large, floating flakes, but I don't feel the cold. As if my body is shutting down from shock, I don't feel anything at all. "I guess this means she moved back."

"She did."

"When?"

Ice crunches under her shoes as she steps closer. "Maddox ..."

"When, Mom?"

"About four years ago."

"I need to go." I stalk off in the direction I'm facing with no plan, no coat, and no patience left.

"Where are you going?"

Ignoring her, I continue through the neighbor's yard to the

adjacent street with only my rage to keep me warm. When the road dead-ends, I collapse to the curb and grip my pounding head with both hands. There's not enough hair to take my frustrations out on, so I snatch up a piece of gravel and sail it down the street.

Scar tissue from a season-ending pitching injury my senior year rips in my elbow, providing something else to focus on. The physical pain feels better than the misery and disappointment I had walking here like a zombie. Snatching up a handful of pellets, I shoot to my feet. One after another, I pitch to no target, each rock representing something I can't control, until I'm sweating and breathless.

When the last rock disappears into the snowflakes, I collapse onto the curb, my forearms perched on top of my knees while I initiate the calming techniques I learned in yoga class. The Patrol Unit liked to grumble about Captain Emory requiring us take up yoga, forcing us to attend class regularly, but the breathing techniques came in handy during emergent situations. But this is nothing like a car chase, barricaded suspect, or robbery in progress. It's my worst nightmare coming true, and neither my beloved baseball nor yoga can stop the—

"Maddox?"

My gaze cuts to Carmen standing a safe distance away, her arms folded across her body against the cold. How long had she been watching?

"Please come inside." The nervous shake in her voice does not go unnoticed, and I find a little comfort in knowing this ambush isn't easy for her. "It's freezing out here."

"I'm fine."

"Please?"

"I said I'm fine."

"Okay." Instead of walking away as my harsh tone advises,

she stomps forward with determination and sits on the curb beside me.

"What are you doing?" I ask, letting out my frustration for the unwelcome intrusion with a sigh.

She wiggles her hands into leather gloves before answering. "Since you won't come in, I'm preparing to shiver my way through this conversation."

We'll see how long that lasts. I can be very stubborn. Not ready to reconcile the girl I once knew with the woman she became in my absence, I turn away. "Did Mom put you up to this?"

"No. I'm as ready for this as you are, but—"

My disdain materializes into a puff of white air. "I doubt it."

"Fair enough." Her hands fly up, then fall into her lap. "But I'm hoping the boy I once knew is inside you and willing to give me a few minutes to explain."

I glance out over the snow-covered street, begging for a distraction. Her familiar scent, the feel of her warmth leaking through my thin layers, the melodic sound of her voice—it's more than my sputtering system can absorb and comprehend. Being this close to her once filled me with contentment. I lived and breathed for her before she stripped my life of meaning without warning.

Thinking about the days and weeks that followed without her still haunts me as if it happened yesterday. I forced myself through those final five months of school, barely earning passing grades, before graduating and giving my body to my country. I didn't care if I survived each mission, and the brothers I gained in the Army are the only reason I did.

"I know what you're thinking."

A broken chuckle leaks out of me without permission. "No, you really don't."

"You're wondering about Sadie after what I said to you that

night."

I turn on her "I can't believe you have a kid." *And she's not mine.* "You gave up your career for her." *But not for me.*

"That's the thousand-foot view."

"Who's her father?"

"I don't know."

"Excuse me?" Struck speechless, I glare at her, and she holds her ground with that unfathomable strength I once admired. But I don't want a reason to admire her. I'd much prefer to stay burning with fury, so I can stop wishing she'd chosen me for that life-changing moment instead of some absentee stranger.

"Sadie isn't mine, Maddox. Well, she is in every way that matters, but I didn't give birth to her."

Relief courses through my veins, but it doesn't erase all the images of her with another man my imagination sent through my brain like a highlight reel.

"Soon after I arrived in L.A., I met Charlotte," she continues through my silence. "We were the same age with similar hair, skin tone, and eye color. At every audition opportunity that needed an actor who looked like us, we showed up and helped each other through the grueling process. We grew close and eventually became roommates." She takes a deep breath. "But we didn't always run in the same circles, and trouble seemed to find her. She wanted to keep Sadie safe and stayed away from the source as much as she could. It didn't last, and she didn't have family to help her. She asked me to be Sadie's guardian if anything happened, and on Sadie's first birthday, she wrote up the necessary paperwork. She died in a car crash three years later."

"That's when you came back to Ember Falls?"

She nods. "I didn't know how to raise a child. I needed help."

"What about your dreams?"

"With Sadie counting on me, I guess I made new ones."

"Like what?" I ask, despite my efforts not to.

"Giving her an incredible childhood like I had and endless opportunities to chase her own dreams."

"She's an amazing kid. You've done a great job raising her."

She grins, pride in her daughter shining through the awkwardness between us. "It was a team effort. My parents, this crazy town, Nana. Everyone here played a part and deserves credit." Her tentative gaze lifts to mine. "She adores you."

"Didn't start out that way."

"Sometimes she's too smart for her own good. It's why she struggles to make friends with kids her age."

A breeze tosses a tuft of snow in our direction, and I notice her shivering. I'd prefer not to care, but I can't help myself.

"You should go back. It's only going to get colder out here with the sun going down," I urge, wondering if she'll take advantage of the escape route or stay.

"After all this time, Maddox, we're finally talking. I'm not going anywhere until you make me."

Her eyes hold my gaze with determination, and I let myself get lost in them. Every adult version of her I tried desperately not to create in my mind through the years, pales in comparison to the real one.

The thick, golden waves of her hair I used to thread my fingers through seem more inviting covered fresh snowflakes. She'd gained a few new freckles over the years, and a subtle line bracketing her mouth. I used to spend hours staring at those lips, and they're the same gentle shade of pink. While she sang or told me about her day, my teenage hormones would draw my attention there and conjure up all kinds of ways I could kiss her. A problem resurfacing now despite all the negativity and despair swirling inside me.

A snowflake lands on her lashes, but she doesn't break eye contact. My fingers itch for the chance to brush it away. To cup her face and see if her skin feels as velvety soft as I remember, but I don't dare move. It's too risky. I don't trust either of us with my heart.

"We should go in," I say to keep from doing something I'll regret. Standing, I wait for her to do the same.

Unmoving, she stares up at me. "I know I have no right to ask this, but can we do this again? Will you allow another opportunity for us to talk?"

"Carmen …" The eyes that used to have the power to make me do anything she commanded are boring straight through to my tattered soul.

"You don't have to make any promises. I'm just asking for more time to do this again while you're here."

"We'll see." It isn't what she wants to hear, but it's all I can give. "Come on. I need a drink."

Chapter 6

Carmen

Kaitlyn, my best friend and go-to for all things Maddox, sits across from me in a window booth at our favorite restaurant. She scheduled this lunch date while we talked yesterday. Sadie had gone ahead with my parents to the Henderson's while I closed the store, giving me private time for a desperate call to her before seeing Maddox again.

"How'd it go?" she asks, leaning over her menu with wide eyes.

"Worse and better than I expected."

The menu flops to the table, a physical representation of how disappointing she found my answer. "That makes zero sense."

"I know, but it's the truth. When he first saw me, it broke him all over again."

I'll never forget seeing him like that—consuming heartbreak

in his eyes and weakening his body. All because of me. How can he hold on to so much destructive emotion? I never wanted that for him, and it seems the universe turned a blind eye to my pleas. For too long, I let my conscience and regret believe my wish for him to find happiness had been granted. That delusion and the flimsy foundation it had been built on shattered the second I saw him.

It took everything in me to go after him when he walked out at the party, knowing I was the last person he wanted to see. But no matter how much time has passed or what happened while we were apart, I don't want to hurt him. He's too tenderhearted, too special, too Maddox.

I summarize the result of our conversation for Kaitlyn, omitting the details—those are meant only for Maddox and me—and brace for the questions I can't answer.

"Once he learned Sadie wasn't mine in the way he thought, he could look at me again. He hasn't gotten past what I did, and I'm not sure he ever will."

"Really? After all this time?"

I nod, unable to form words through the guilt battering me.

"What about you? Were there any lingering butterflies?"

"Kait." My elbow plops onto the table, and I swoon worse than Chrissy and Sandra had the other day at the store. I'm not proud of it, but there's no mistaking my attraction to the broody, hunk of a man who has already fallen in love with my daughter. "I never could have imagined the sweet boy I loved to turn into that. Butterflies weren't the only thing he set into motion with those muscles and beautiful, sad eyes."

"You still love him."

"More than I realized."

With a snap of her fingers, she points a purple fingernail at me. "This explains why you haven't been able to connect with the guys you've dated."

Defeated by reality setting back in and halting my melting, I let a sigh take over. "I've always known. I just didn't want to admit it since I thought I'd never see him again."

"Him showing up like this is happening for a reason, I just know it. It's a second chance." Her hands fold under her chin as excitement sparkles in her moss-colored eyes.

"I don't deserve one. I never should have walked away, but since I did, I wish I would have crawled back to him long before now. We're in this agonizing situation because of my selfishness and fear." Thinking of all I gave up by choice—not because of anything he did—has turned my throat into a depressing desert. I snatch my glass of water off the table and drain half of it. "Anyway, I didn't ask how long he planned to stay."

"Does it matter? If you want a chance to get whatever you're longing for—forgiveness, another shot with him, closure—you need to do whatever it takes to get it, or you'll be alone for the rest of your life."

"Geez. Don't hold back, Kait," I joke to counterbalance the impact that declaration had on my faltering system. "I don't—"

Something outside catches my attention. "Is that…"

Kaitlyn's eyes follow where I'm pointing. "A goat?"

The white goat with light brown spots and two tiny horns doesn't appear fully grown—a teenager if there's such a thing for goats—which is probably why it's causing so much mischief. In between eating live Christmas greenery outside stores and restaurants, it's jumping onto and off decorations and planter boxes like it owns the place.

"Wonder who he belongs to," Kaitlyn says.

"There's a tag on his ear. If they ever catch it …" Amusement takes over my brain as several older men emerge from buildings and fail at catching the spry little creature. "Someone can take him home."

"I'd name him Spot," Kaitlyn decides. "What do you think?"

"It suits."

Ember Falls' most lovable drunk hooks an arm under the goat's neck. He lowers to the ground for a better grip, but Spot's head squirts out with the motion, and he takes off across the street … right at Maddox.

"Holy flannel. Is that …"

"Yep." The word oozes out with a satisfied exhale. No one fills out the humble fabric quite like Maddox.

Confident in save-the-day mode, he swings a coat over his broad shoulders, a few defined abs peeking out from under his red and blue, plaid shirt as his arms slip into the sleeves. Each step he takes toward the naughty animal is fluid, sturdy, and unmistakably male. The years he spent in the Army and on the force clearly prepared his body for action of any kind.

He's the picture of strength and grace, and I wonder if that's because the shadows of our past have been lifted off him in my absence. At the idea, grief courses through me with riptide force. I desperately want to repair our connection, whatever that might be now, but I won't do it at his expense.

"Maybe Spot is a girl," Kaitlyn muses, saving me from my spiraling thoughts without realizing it. Her attention never moves the scene unfolding across the street.

Spot squares off with Maddox, holding his stance, but not in preparation for a battle of speed and agility as he did with the others. It's almost like he's admiring the view, too.

I want to laugh at the spectacle, but I'm too captivated by the lanky boy I used to know showing off his man skills. My mouth waters at those muscular thighs dipping to scoop an arm under the goat's belly. He straightens with ease, carrying Spot on his hip to his navy truck parked nearby.

I recognize the Red Sox sticker on the back and yearn for what I gave up once more. I haven't been able to watch a game since we broke up. That was one of our things. We watched every broadcast we could together at his house or mine, even before we started dating. I miss how simple those days had been. How loved and safe I felt by his side.

A groan hums in Kaitlyn's throat as Maddox leans over the open tailgate to secure Spot to the bed with a rope. "I'd let him tie me up any—" Guilty eyes coast to me, a half-smile telling me she's only half sorry for her comment. "Oops. Got carried away there for a bit."

"Go ahead. He's not mine."

She waves away the declaration. "Whatever your status may be in his life, he's always going to be yours and vice versa. That's the magic of soulmates. Anyone who tries to get between that is just wasting their time."

I turn back to Maddox and watch him climb into the driver's seat. He takes off slowly to not jostle Spot in the back. That's Maddox for you. No matter how crispy his outer layer gets through life's challenges, his heart will always be tender and sweet, like the most perfect, hot cinnamon roll.

Maddox

"Well, look what the cat dragged in." Jamie heaves me into a hug, his palm slapping hard on my back. Outside of Carmen, Jameson Blackwell has been my closest friend for as long as I can remember. We were classmates, baseball teammates, and brothers in arms all four years. "What are you doing here?"

"Why does everyone keep asking me that?"

"Because you've been MIA here since high school."

"Whatever." From the front porch of the small ranch house, I take in the rolling sea of white surrounding us for something else to talk about. "I've always loved this side of the farm."

He steps out and closes the door to take in the view with me. "That right there." He points toward the sunset over the horizon, reflecting off the snow below. "That's why I built here."

"It's perfect." I suck in the cool, clean air, so different from what I'm used to in Boston. No burning scents of exhaust, rotting trash, or day-old hotdogs. Although, that last one isn't so bad, given that I grew up in baseball stadiums. It takes me back to the good ole days every time I pass a stand.

"It's great to see you, man," Jamie says, unzipping his coat. "Come in and let's catch up."

In his small living room, I sink into the brown leather couch. Just like Jamie, his house has plenty of personality with its masculine decorations, wood accents, rustic fireplace, and mementos of the things he holds dear—family, tradition, the farm, and his service.

"I'm surprised I caught you at the house." I remember how much effort the farm requires from the summers I worked here, and with or without chores, Jamie hates to be idle.

"I was on my way out when I saw your truck in the driveway."

"Anything I can help you with?"

He smiles. "It's dinner time on the farm. You know what that means."

"Great. I need to stop by the barn anyway."

"My barn?"

I nod. "Found one of your goats in town."

"No shit?" With a laugh, he leans back and props an arm on the back of the couch. "That little fucker gets out at least once a week, but he doesn't usually go that far."

"Might be time to upgrade your fencing."

"Or breed him. He may be my new spirit animal."

"New?" I ask, shaking my head. Only Jamie.

"It used to be the stallion that took over a year to break."

"That's more fitting. It took us two years to tame you."

The surprise of Jamie's unbridled laughter tips my amusement enough to join in. It's been far too long since I've let that part of me off the leash.

"So, who do I owe a beer?" he asks when his amusement fades.

"What do you mean?"

"I want to know who's responsible for getting you to grace us with your presence. That's no small feat and they deserve a reward. My money's on your sister."

"If it were, she's underage."

He waves a hand as if I'd said something ridiculous. "And I bet you think she hasn't sipped a single bit of alcohol at that big, fancy school of hers. She lives with your brother, remember."

"I try not to think about it."

When he asks again what drew me here, I tell him about Captain's orders and my impulsive decision to return to the place that built me. Like a sad country song, I came back, hoping to reconnect with the person I'd been before disappointment, ache, and loneliness beat me down to a point I no longer recognized myself.

"You came to the right place, my man."

"The jury's still out on that."

"Maybe, but we can make the most of it while you're here and see what happens. Ready to get to work?" He slaps his thighs and rises off the couch with a laugh. "You can fill me in on what's been going on since you disappeared after discharge."

Sighing, I follow him out. "I didn't disappear." Even if I did, isn't it old news? "Don't make me regret bringing your ornery goat back."

We make our way to my truck, and I navigate the twists and turns of the farm's snow-packed roads like I'm a teenage farmhand again. Good to know I can remember something other than pain from that life-altering time.

"Tell me about Boston," Jamie asks between shoveling a pile of manure from the horse stall next to mine and dumping it into the wheelbarrow. "What's the scene like there?"

I straighten to see him fully over the middle wall separating us. "The scene? How old are you?"

"Not as old as you, big guy."

"We're only six months apart, and I wouldn't know about *the scene*."

Ignoring his chore, he props his elbows on top of the wall and glares at me. "Are you telling me that you live in one of the most exciting cities in the country, and you haven't been taking full advantage?"

"That's exactly what I'm saying." There's no relishing a place where the criminals know you by name, and you've turned into a workaholic, trying to forget how miserable you are.

"It's the model all over again."

Bumper, the black colt in my stall, stomps his hooves on the wooden floor, frustrated with us disrupting his peace. I give him a rub to make up for it. "The what?"

"The sexy surfer whose car broke down outside the base our last year. She wanted you something fierce, and what did you do?" He waits for me to answer.

"Nothing."

"Exactly. Teddy was so pissed when you turned her down. He did all the work in the muggy California heat to get her car running again, and she couldn't ignore you for one second to notice."

With a shrug, I push my pitchfork through the soiled hay, wondering if I will be mucking the rest of the stalls by myself. "Wait." I lean on the fork handle to face him, and his smug smile widens, knowing what I'm about to say. "Was he also pissed at *you* for sleeping with her days later?"

"More than my stallion when his supper's late." The massive animal neighs outside the barn as if in agreement.

"Good."

Jamie moves into the next stall and digs in, cleaning the area in half the time it takes me. Guess I'm out of practice.

"So, why the solitary confinement in Boston?" he asks. "When we served together you were always ready for anything and everything—the crazier the better."

"As you know, life's a little different in the real world."

He chuckles and grabs hold of the wheelbarrow handles to push it out, securing the door behind him. "Our time in the Army was real life."

"Yes, but we were rarely alone there."

"Ah. You wouldn't be alone in Boston if you'd get out more."

"You sound like Nana. Are you done?"

"With this barn? Yes. With forcing you out of your comfortable grumpy zone. No." He beams and struts past me and Bumper.

Rubbing the colt's neck when his snout snuggles against my hip, I lean down to kiss his head. "If it weren't for you, I might regret coming here."

Following Jamie out of the barn with my own full cart, I meet him by the wide-plank fence. His heavy hand drops onto my shoulder like he's about to say something profound, and I brace for what might seep out of his gutter brain next.

"How about we saddle up and go for a ride? Like the old days."

I pause, expecting a punchline that never emerges. Weird. "Is our sledding hill clear?" I ask, appreciating his restraint.

"Meticulously maintained." A crooked grin glides into place. "Like the sexy snow bunnies I *entertain* up there."

And there it is. "I'm sorry I asked."

He winks before skimming his hand down my shoulder and slapping it one last time against my arm, the punctuation mark to his prank. Just like the old days.

"Disgusting." My face revolts in response to the irregular proximity of smeared manure to my eyes and nose. Somehow the stench isn't half as bad when it's mingled in hay. "What was that for?"

"First of all, I can't go riding with manure on my hands. Second, your boring existence needed something to … spice it up a little."

"Horse shit is *not* spice."

He sucks in a long breath through his nose, and it comes out in a white haze through his mouth. "It is for a cowboy."

"Then you won't mind joining me."

"What?"

Before he can jump out of the way, my gloved hand dives into the steaming pile between us and smacks against his right pec.

As he realizes what I'd done to stain his clean, tan coat, annoyance paralyzes him. He glares at me with blank eyes before surveying the brown handprint. How did he not see that coming?

He picks out a piece of hay from the globs hanging on and

flicks it into the breeze. "That's just dirty."

"No. It's the spicy farm cologne you love so much."

"Fine. I deserved that."

"And plenty more for the trouble you started literally everywhere we went together over the last twenty years."

"And look how dull your life has been without me." He flashes that trademark grin again—the playboy identifier that won over the surfer and probably countless others since.

"That doesn't work on me."

Chapter 7

Maddox

I can still smell manure and hay as I rip out rusty appliances in the apartment above the bookshop the next day. The special scent seems to leak out of my pores as I sweat through the work. My body also aches in places I never find with regular workouts. Each task on the farm is physical and demanding, but knowing me like he does, Jamie didn't take it easy on me.

After our horseback ride set the *I'm going to feel this tomorrow* threshold, we hurdled it by completing more of the farm's endless chores. We fed and watered the pigs, chickens, goats, and a random llama. I have no idea why Jamie has a llama. He wouldn't give me a straight answer. Then, we returned the dozen horses we corralled earlier to their stalls and did the same nightly care for them.

We worked side-by-side, talking when the task allowed and letting the farm provide the entertainment when it didn't. Through it all, he understood how immersing myself in something constructive was exactly what I needed. The familiar environment, mindless manual labor, and animal therapy soothed me in a way nothing else could.

While rewarding ourselves with a cold beer afterward, he avoided any topic that might lead back to Carmen. His ridiculous stories rolled from one to the next, making me laugh more than I have in the last decade, and I didn't give her one thought. It may be difficult for others to recognize at times, but his heart is the size of a tanker truck, and I hope I've been the friend to him that he's been to me.

Getting my hands dirty with the apartment demolition, keeps the relaxed mood I found at Jamie's flowing through the morning. Nana has been quiet, which probably helps. After opening the shop, I expected her to follow me up here and make her complaints known, but she's left me alone. She could be plotting against me, organizing my next mistletoe encounter, or calling in reinforcements for her mission to *fix* my life, but I feel too good to think about that. I plan to ride this wave for as long as I can before life's little surprises drag me under again.

Moving on to removing the old electrical, the simpler task is quieter, allowing the light rustling happening downstairs to register. I ignore it until the muted hum grows into the definition of commotion, piquing my Nana paranoia.

Speaking of little surprises and the instigator herself, she calls for me from the base of the stairs, surely poised to deliver another surprise to make my toes curl with annoyance. It's like she knew I was thinking about her.

"Maddox! Can you come here?"

I don't bother hiding my dissatisfaction since she's not here to call me out on it and use the adrenaline it provides to pull the last of the old telephone wire out of the wall.

"It wasn't a request," she yells.

"Isn't that what *can you* implies?" I grumble, giving the wire one last yank. The end coils into a dusty pile at my feet like a sleeping snake—not quite as satisfying as I hoped.

Wiping my dusty hands down my jeans, I lean out over the top of the stairwell. "What's up?"

"I know you heard me say come down *here*. Not stand at the top like you're scared to face the firing squad."

"That's how I feel."

"Shut up and get down here. I need you to try my pie options for this year's contest."

"Oh. Why didn't you say that?"

She grins and that should have tipped me off to something afoot, but I ate breakfast too many hours ago not to allow my empty stomach a say. It takes charge of my brain, and my feet take off.

"I need your honest opinion."

The sweet smell of cinnamon, fruit, and buttery crust grows stronger the closer we get to the shop. I'm salivating just thinking about sinking my teeth into each flavor until human-shaped shadows appear on the floor ahead.

"And the opinion of my most trustworthy pie-loving friends," she adds, proud of herself for tricking me.

I freeze, rallying my limbs to make an escape, but her hand on my back pushes me around the corner. That's when the whole set up unveils before me. Gathered beside a table of pies, waiting to start Nana's game, are Mayor Whitacre, Wally, some people I haven't met yet, and … Carmen.

Muscles in my neck constrict and shoot more than just annoyance down to my toes.

Damn it, Nana.

I haven't recovered from my conversation with Carmen two days ago. Having to face her when I've yet to determine my opinions on the matter makes me want to throw a pie like a disgruntled clown at a party.

"Thank you all for coming," Nana says to the group, ignoring the heat of irritation rising off my skin.

She walks away to slice the pies as if I'm not a flight risk. Funny. She's forgotten how good I am at running away and avoiding situations I find uncomfortable, which is almost everything that doesn't require a uniform. My escape plan is already formulating in my mind when Carmen's eyes find me over Nana's head. Her searching eyes say more than she did the other night, erasing my exit map and relocating the temper I misplaced this morning. I don't know what to do with any of it.

"Mayor, you get the first bite honors."

"Music to my ears." His dark mustache wiggles above a smile as he accepts a plate of samples and takes a bite.

From the others digging into their samples, compliments and moans sound off while my body goes numb with resentment. I beg my legs to take me anywhere else, but they stay put, giving me no choice but to accept the full plate and fork Nana passes me with my usual obedience. But she can't control everything. Scooping bites into my mouth like it's an eating contest, I empty the plate in record time. The flavors smelled so good earlier, it's a shame I didn't taste a single bite.

Utilizing my SWAT techniques, I rid myself of the dish on the counter behind Nana and slink away … almost.

"Where do you think you're going?" Nana's voice sounds like nails on a chalkboard at this point. Guess I'm not as covert as I thought.

"I have work to do."

"That can wait. The mayor needs help."

I survey Mayor Whitacre, and he looks perfectly content and in need of nothing. His belly, the same round shape as Santa's, bounces while he bellows a laugh that rivals the man himself.

"I know you're busy, son, but we could sure use your skills to help hang the lights today," Mayor says, dusting crumbs off his dark sweater, and irritatingly corroborating Nana's story. "The Spectacular Committee is too small for the job this year, and we're getting older."

I nod, understanding I'm about to install string lights over Main Street with a crowd of people who'll want to get into my business, instead of experiencing the bliss I found working in the quiet solitude upstairs.

Thank you, Nana.

"Enjoying award-winning pies and recruiting young volunteers for the Spectacular," Mayor Whitacre continues despite his full mouth, "it's been a productive outing to everyone's favorite bookshop today."

Volunteers? Plural? I didn't hear anyone else get guilt-tripped into helping. Gauging the group, the only youngish people I see, ones capable of climbing ladders anyway, are me and Carmen.

"Can you be there in half an hour?" the mayor asks her first.

She nods, then all eyes cut to me. I'm trapped. "Sure."

The mayor refocuses on Nana and her pies, and I dart upstairs. With her scheming complete, Nana no longer seems to care if I escape my entrapment. Frustration pours out of me with every clash of the sledgehammer against crooked, wooden cabinets in the kitchen. Since they're not in good enough shape to salvage, they get the brunt of my pent-up anger.

Twenty minutes later, I plow through the shop to get to my truck out front with my toolbox and ladder in hand—begrudgingly, of course. In my befuddled state, I'm more than startled to find Carmen leaning against the side. I'm flustered and furious, and alarms are going off inside my brain. Her long hair is now braided into pigtails, and she's added one of those winter, knitted hats with the furry ball on top. It gnaws on my nerves how good she makes that ridiculous hat look.

"Hi," she says sweetly as if we haven't spent a day apart.

With a grunt, I stalk to the tailgate and slide the tools into the bed.

"I thought I could hitch a ride with you if you're okay with that."

"Do what you want." What a shame the lightness I woke up with didn't last. I could use that zen to get me through this unsolicited encounter. I don't like how she keeps popping up and catching me off guard.

"Is it me?" she asks cautiously after we climb inside, and I start the engine.

"What?"

"Your mood. Is my being here upsetting you?"

"No. It's *my* being here that's upsetting." More came out than I intended, and I'm internally cursing myself as I back out of the parking spot.

"Because of me."

My head whips to her without permission, and the friendliness she greeted me with at the shop is now cautious remorse. Good. *That* I can deal with.

"It's complicated."

"If it helps, I'm glad you came."

It doesn't. It feels more like an ice pick to the back of the neck. "Why?"

"You may not be willing to accept this, Maddox, but I think of you fondly. Something inside me still flutters when I see you, and I will never forget what we had or how much we loved. What we had was special, and the worst mistake I ever made was throwing it all away."

"Carmen—"

"I know this is a conversation better suited for another time, but in case you can't give me that, I wanted to tell you while I have you captured."

She attempts a half-smile to soften the sharp edges of her confession, but they feel more like jagged slashes across my tender scars. Wounds both from her ripping out a piece of my heart and too many years spent longing for someone who didn't want me.

And now, the thought of forgiving her or stitching together the pieces of me she severed with the force of a blowtorch seems damn near impossible. I doubt that was the intent behind what she said, but if we were to try being friends or more again, I wouldn't survive losing her a second time. And I *would* lose her eventually. If I wasn't good enough for her then, when my heart was whole and wide open, I'm far from worthy now.

"Maddox."

My arm jerks from the sudden punch of heat her touch sends through me, and the truck swerves.

"I'm sorry. I didn't mean to—"

"It's fine." I say that a lot, and it's still difficult to believe.

"No, it's not. Talk to me."

With a hard push on the brake, I shove the truck into a parking space and shut off the engine. "We're here."

Carmen

Maddox jumps out of the truck before I can get a full read on his state of mind. From what he did allow me to see, it wasn't promising.

Of course, he's not ready to hear about my regrets and feelings. I don't blame him for hating me, but I wish he'd talk to me. I miss the inner light that once fueled his joy and brought the same out in others. Whether or not I had something to do with dimming it, he doesn't deserve to live in that dark world. Even if it means having to love someone else to find himself again, I plan to help him get it all back.

Grabbing the handle, I sling open the door with newfound energy and jog to where a few remaining volunteers had gathered. I must have missed a few things while I lingered in the truck with my thoughts because Maddox is already setting up a ladder at the starting point.

"There you are," Veronica, the mayor's wife, says, waving her black-gloved hands in the air as she sashays toward me. "I was told you'd be there, but I didn't see you during the kickoff." Her Pilates-toned arms circle me for a light squeeze.

"I'm sorry. I needed a minute to gather myself."

"Why, dear? Everything okay?"

"I rode here with Maddox."

"Oh." She leans back to observe *my* mental state.

In the truck, where I could talk myself up without distractions, I felt infallible. Having him in my sights again with all his muscled glory and morning stubble, I'm back to hanging on by a thread and all gooey inside. Whenever he's near, I turn into a lovesick kid again. Not the stupid one who thought she could be a famous actor if she left everything behind and went to L.A., but the girl who was fortunate enough to be loved by Maddox Henderson.

"Is he not willing to talk?" Veronica asks, bringing my

attention back to her.

We both glance over at him securing the end of the first string with big, color bulbs to the top of the light pole.

"No. He's not ready." My voice cracks as I say it, realizing he may never be. "And he has every right."

"Don't give up. If talking it out will help, you have to try. Life's too short."

"You're right." With a sniff, I pick up a box of garland to take to the light pole, but Veronica's hand gently folds over my arm to stop me.

Her eyes narrow in on something behind me. "Do you want him back?" she asks, throwing me completely off kilter. Wasn't she just talking about getting closure? Doesn't closure mean letting go?

"I ... I ..."

"Honey, you better figure it out soon or he might move on without you."

"What?" I follow her gaze and find Maddox off the ladder, talking with Jada—the striking single mom, who moved into town last year.

She's perfect for him, and my entire body twists with jealousy. Her deceased husband was a Boston cop and military man. Maddox may even have known him, giving them more in common. Her silky, caramel-colored hair shines, despite the gray, winter sun, and she's as sweet as they come.

He lowers to speak with her five-year-old son and both beam with adoration for each other. Maddox has always loved children, and he's never met one he couldn't connect with. Or at least he hadn't when I knew him.

Jada inserts herself into the tender exchange, watching Maddox with her own adoring eyes, especially when he offers a friendly grin meant only for her. A fresh surge of envy blazes through me, and I can feel my face scrunch from the effort it takes to cool it with supportive thoughts.

I want him to be happy. He deserves to be happy. He seems happy in her presence. I'm happy for him. Happy. Happy. Happy.

"You better go before—"

"I can't." The response slips off my tongue before I can stop it. Didn't I promise to help him find happiness, even if it came from someone other than me? Would Jada make him happy? The mere thought of him holding her, kissing her, and loving her—or anyone else—burns deeper than I care to admit. I want to be selfless. I want to be the one to fix all that's broken for him and for us, but I fear even my best efforts would fall short. Too much has changed, and the gap between us feels insurmountable when it hurts him to simply be in my vicinity. "He doesn't want to talk to me. And Jada is—"

"Stop getting in your way." She nudges my back to get my skeptical feet moving. "Go."

Before I know it, I'm bounding up to them like I have something to say, but I must have left my brain somewhere along the way. Words and sentences don't populate when Maddox's gaze finds me, confusion and agitation clouding his eyes. Is that aggravation for interrupting their sweet moment or from our earlier one-sided conversation?

Jada stands to greet me, ending his glare. "Hi, Carmen."

"Hi," I manage, despite my brain lagging behind in Maddox's proximity.

He steps back to make his exit, suddenly on edge. No more grins. No more easy conversation. *Way to go, Carmen.* "I should get to work."

"Wait." Jada reaches for her son's hand and holds it between hers. She spares me a glance, her nerves showing for the first time, and I can already tell I won't like what she's about to say.

She turns back to Maddox with a smile. "This is our first Spectacular, and Easton wants to sign up for the rubber ducky sled race. We've never done one before, and I was hoping you could show him how it works. I heard you've won it a few times."

"Six, actually, but who's counting?"

Was that a joke? Jealous over how effortlessly Jada uncovered his playful side, I fight the urge to sulk outwardly. Inside, I'm throwing a bratty toddler tantrum.

Maddox's eyes cut my way before ruffling the boy's matching light brown hair. "There's not much to it, but I'd be happy to pass along what I've learned over the years. Sign him up, and I'll be there to help."

"That's so kind of you. Thank you, Maddox."

We both admire the view as he walks across the street, ignoring our awkward presence together.

"I'm sorry, Carmen," she says, putting on an innocent smile. I can't tell if it's genuine or if she's showing off for securing private time with Maddox in front of me. Either way, jealousy continues to pierce through me with the force of shooting arrows. "Did you need something?"

Maddox. I need Maddox in my life again, any way I can get him. There it is. No more denying it.

"I was …" Thinking fast, I shake the box I carried over. "Hoping for help with this. Hanging decorative garland on a light pole is a two-person job."

"How about two and a half? Easton is a great assistant."

"Deal."

Chapter 8

Maddox

From climbing up and down a ladder countless times over four hours, hanging lights over a street, of all things, my legs and back are still sore two days later.

As I sand the drywall patches at turtle speed, feeling every muscle scream in protest, the front door of Sadie and Carmen's apartment opens and shuts. I check my watch, trying to figure out which one of them it might be when Sadie appears in the doorframe.

Her hair, the color of sunshine, is tied back with a white ribbon to match her snow boots and sweatshirt beneath a pink jacket. A matching blue, pink, and white plaid backpack scrapes the floor as she crosses to me.

"Hi, sweetie." She rests an elbow on my shoulder, her pleasant smile dissolving any residual aches.

"Hi, yourself. On your way to school?"

"Yep. What are you doing?"

"Fixing the holes in the wall so I can paint."

"I wish I could help today." Her bottom lip pokes out in a slight pout. "Painting sounds way more fun than math and science."

"Agreed."

"What about after school?" she asks.

"I'll save a wall for you. Which one do you want?"

Her arm stays connected to me as she decides. She points toward the kitchen. "The one under the bar. I can reach all of that one."

"Smart choice. That's why you're the queen."

A flash of sweetness beams in her cheeks before she skips out. Alone again, I get back to work, grateful to have something to look forward to later.

Her thick boots, pounding on the unfinished steps as she runs back up, echo across the hall. "I'm back."

"Thank goodness. I missed you."

"I was only gone a minute." Her hand finds my shoulder again, and I love that about her. Affection and acceptance flow freely from her, making it easy to reciprocate.

"It felt like all day."

"You're silly."

"Was there a reason you came back?" I ask. "Or did you just miss me too?"

"Both. Nana needs you."

With exaggerated irritation, I fall back on the hardwood floor, bringing her down with me. Her giggles fill the empty room, and just like that, the apartment feels more like a home than a shell of what could be. She does the same to me, filling the void where my heart once beat wildly for life.

"I guess I better see what she wants," I finally say. On my way up, I snatch Sadie around the middle and carry her down the stairs sideways as she squeals and laughs. Best. Sound. Ever.

"Nana! Save me!"

Smiling, Nana watches us carry on from the front counter. "You two are a mess. Sadie, you better get to the bus stop before you're walking to school."

"Can't I stay with you today?" She manages to stick out her bottom lip in a pout despite being held upside down. The interesting angle makes me chuckle.

"Nope. School is important, and Maddox has work to do."

"That's okay. I'm his best helper."

My *only* helper, but still the best. I wouldn't want anyone else.

With her face turning red, I flip her right side up and set her on her feet.

"Does that mean you're finally accepting my ideas for improvements?" I ask Nana. Before starting the demolition upstairs, I laid out my plans for updating both floors. She threw out every roadblock she could think of, and I had a solution for each one, including the cost. With my parents and I chipping in, she won't have to spend a penny, and she'll soon have the revenue stream she needs to do more than get by.

"No." She scowls. "I have another job for you today."

"See you after school," Sadie calls on her way to the door, surely sensing another argument brewing.

"Nana, I'm busy fixing *your* building so it doesn't crumble onto your hard head."

"This will only take a few minutes."

If this is her adding another speed bump to my plans, it won't work. Yet, I surrender, knowing I can never refuse her, and let my dissatisfaction be known with a groan before asking, "What is it?"

"My friend is going away for a week and can't take her sweet little girl. She's needs a—"

"Babysitter?" I screech, preparing for my first ever Nana refusal.

"What? No. She can't take her *dog*. Trixie has been her companion since her husband passed, and usually goes everywhere with her. She can't this time."

Muscles I didn't know I had relax as my shock wears off. "Where do I come in?"

"Feed and let her out several times a day. Just make sure she's okay. If anything ever happens to that dog ..."

"Keep the dog alive. Got it." That doesn't seem too terrible. I like animals, and Trixie's care will be a great excuse to get away when the need arises.

"She's expecting you today so she can go over the details."

"No problem."

I pivot to head upstairs.

"Where are you going?" she asks, giving me déjà vu. It's the pie entrapment all over again.

"Back upstairs."

"But she's expecting you."

"You said today, not now."

"Let me rephrase. She's expecting you now."

"Nana," I protest pointlessly. When she sets her mind to something, there's no changing it.

"Go on and meet Trixie before you get too dirty. I promise to stay out of your way for the rest of the day."

I'll believe that when I see it. "Fine, but I'm going to hold you to that promise. Staying out of my way also means no complaining where I can hear you. That's just as disruptive."

"No promises " She winks and goes back to her ancient way of bookkeeping—on paper in a ratty, old three-ring binder.

I'll tackle that issue later. Rolling my eyes, I forego the coat hanging on the door upstairs and head for the truck.

"Text me the address," I call and step outside.

"Maddox, it's so good to see you again," Nana's best friend greets after opening the door.

Her dark gray hair is full of haphazardly placed curlers and only the left side of her makeup has been done. I usually wouldn't notice something like that, but she applies eyeshadow like it's 1980. Her bright pink tennis skirt and yellow and white-striped T-shirt match the eccentric personality I remember from my childhood. She's hard to miss and even harder to forget.

A tiny white snowball of a dog sits snug in the crook of her bony arm as she pulls me in for a hug. She's stronger than she looks and knocks the air out of my lungs.

"Hi, Ms. Dottie. Nana didn't tell me it was you I'd be meeting." That withheld detail kicks my suspicion meter up a few notices. "How have you been?"

"Seventy is the new forty, and I'm living it up."

"As you should be."

"Come in, come in." She clutches my bicep with her free hand and urges me inside, transporting us to a tropical destination. Sand and ocean wallpaper, beachy decorations, and equally high air temperature assault and confuse my winterized system. No wonder she's dressed for summer instead of Vermont's freezing December weather. But that's Dottie for you—always contradicting the norm. Sweat begins to bead on my back, and I'm glad I didn't wear my coat. It must be ninety degrees in here.

"Can I get you anything?"

A fan, an open window, an ice bucket to dip my face into.

"No thanks."

We walk through the beach into another contradictory room. Colorful flowers and plants cover every surface, cascade over the tops of cabinets, and hang from the ceiling. It would be easy to lose Trixie in here, and I make a mental note of it. I hope she doesn't expect me to keep this rainforest alive too while she's gone. My thumb is as brown as they come.

"You're very handsome." She smiles over her shoulder as she removes a cup from the cabinet and sets it on the counter. "I always knew you would be. Your grandfather was the sexiest man in town back in the day."

I'm not sure how to respond to that. "Uh, thanks?"

"I tried to catch his attention in high school, but he only had eyes for Lily. That also runs in your family."

What the hell? I know everyone knows my history, but does it have to be brought up everywhere I go?

"Anyhoo. I appreciate you helping me with Trixie. I tried everything I could to take her with me, but my granddaughter is highly allergic to dog hair. If I want to see her, we must make this sacrifice." She kisses Trixie's little head, making the dog's tail wiggle with delight. "We haven't been apart since I brought her home."

"I'll take good care of her. When should I stop by to feed her and let her out?"

Dottie's eyes widen as she stares at me. It goes on so long I start to panic. Is she having a stroke?

"Ms. Dottie?"

"Maddox." Her free hand pats against her protruding collarbone like she's counting the beats to a song, tears building and threatening to spill. "Trixie needs constant companionship."

"She does? Nana said this was a check in on her when needed situation."

"Lily knows better, and I gave her four pages of detailed instructions to pass along to you. I thought you were here to pick her up."

Now *my* heart is playing a heavy metal drum solo, banging itself against my sternum. I can't dog-sit 24/7. The last thing I need is something dependent on me for survival. I have things to do and my own flailing life to worry about.

"She's never been alone. What if something happens?" Dottie continues to fret. "What if she injures a paw? Who will brush out the knots in her fur or take her for her daily walks? What if she needs something or gets lonely?"

She's pacing through the forest now, conjuring up all the ways Trixie's routine could be disrupted. Is that really so earth-shattering? It's just a dog. Aren't pets supposed to adapt to their owner's life, not the other way around?

"I should cancel my trip. Thanks for coming, Maddox, but I'm going to call my daughter, and—"

"Don't." What am I doing? She gave me a way out. Take it, stupid. Take it and run. "If you're okay with her hanging out with me at the bookshop and at Mom and Dad's, I'll take her."

"Oh, sweetheart." Her shoulders slump and relief spills down her cheeks. Yep, I'm the biggest pushover there is. "That's just fine. She'll be a good girl for you. Won't you, princess?" She snuggles faces with Trixie and accepts all the doggy kisses she wants to give.

Then, Dottie launches herself into my arms, making Trixie yelp. She's less thrilled about being pressed against my sweaty body than Dottie seems to be. She lingers like she's searching for reassurance that I won't let her down. I hope I don't, but it seems to happen even when I try not to these days.

"You two get to know each other while I go print out your instructions."

She hands over Trixie and leaves me standing there like a fool, wondering what in the heck I do now.

Two hours of doggy details and witnessing Dottie and Trixie's multiple agonizing attempts to say goodbye later, I climb into the truck with the miniature dog in tow, weakened from guiding them both through it. If Dottie's over-the-top fretting and pages of instructions tell me anything, it's that her little companion can't be left alone. *Ever.*

It could be worse, I guess. At least she's cute.

Driving back to the bookshop, the tiny dog sits on a fluffy pink bed in the passenger seat. Her round, black eyes peek through a soft, white mane of fur, giving off sad, tentative vibes—like she's not convinced she'll survive the week.

"Give me some credit, will ya? I'm responsible for lives and other irreplaceable things all the time at work."

But never something as delicate as me, she seems to argue with a slow blink.

"You'll be okay."

Parking in the back, I scoop up Trixie in her bed and grab the large bag of toys, food, and supplies Dottie prepared to help make Princess Trixie comfortable in her new digs. She never vacates her spot in the corner of the room while I paint doors and baseboard trim unless I force her outside to do her business. So far, so good. I've got this.

By the time Sadie comes home from school, I've painted the living room and kitchen, saving her wall under the bar for last. The queen plays with the princess more than she paints, and I end up finishing that wall as well, but I don't mind. Her endless questioning and giggles while the dog chases her through the apartment make the work far less lonesome.

Given my usual temperament, I should prefer the quiet solitude over a kid and dog underfoot. With both here, turns out, I don't. I'm not annoyed or counting the minutes until Sadie finds something else to do. Instead, I find myself searching for reasons to keep her with me longer. We have so much fun, I don't realize the sun has gone down until Carmen finds us in the back after closing the store.

"What's going on here?" she asks, surprising us.

"Momma, I'm painting."

"I see, and you're doing a fantastic job."

"I'm helping with Trixie, too." She pets Trixie, who hasn't left her side since she arrived.

"Why is she here?"

Sadie turns to me for the answer, realizing she'd been too excited to ask earlier.

"Nana volunteered me to dog-sit."

"You know she has separation anxiety, right?" Concern, either for me or the dog—I can't tell—hovers in her tone.

"I heard … after the fact."

"Not good."

"It's fine."

"Sadie, are you ready for dinner? I picked up pizza."

"Yay!" She takes off toward their apartment with Trixie on her heels, but Carmen lingers behind.

In the soft lamp light, my mind jumps to a vision of the girl I once knew and how much I loved her, but I can't go there. I turn back to the wall and my task, wishing for the memories and the woman to leave me alone.

"Would you like to join us?" she asks.

So much for wishes. "I don't—"

"Please," Sadie begs from the other room, and if Carmen hadn't sucked the air out of my lungs with her beauty, I might have laughed.

"We'll stay in the present, Maddox. I promise."

Thanks to her confession the other day, her promise to keep our past out of our conversation is not one I can match. Outside of distractions provided by Sadie and Trixie, it's all I think about.

"Please, sweetie!" Sadie yells, and Trixie yelps in response.

No matter how much I dread what an evening with Carmen might do to me, saying no to Sadie isn't in my vocabulary. "Okay."

"You're welcome to clean up at our place. Do you have water in here yet?"

"I removed the sinks the other day. Let me finish this wall…" What am I doing? "And I'll be over." Shit.

"Thank you, Maddox. I'm looking forward to it."

Wish I could say the same.

I linger with my cleanup tasks longer than necessary to gather the nerve to voluntarily spend time with Carmen. The last two times happened unexpectedly, and my man card was traded in for one belonging to a spoiled child who didn't get their way. I can't lose my shit again, but she affects me in a way I can't suppress. No surprise there. She always has, and I suspect, always will.

A better use of our time together would be finding a way past my resentment, instead of trying to live with it. Something, as Cooper so delicately pointed out, I've sucked at doing so far.

After tucking away the painting supplies, I travel the few steps to Carmen's apartment and find the door open. Sadie greets me immediately, and I kneel to receive her embrace. Trixie follows, her tiny claws scraping my jeans as she tries to climb up. Reaching down, I scoop her up with my free hand, and she burrows between us.

"What took you so long? We had to put the pizza in the oven," Sadie complains, but her usual banter adds too much charm for the scolding to have its intended effect.

"My bad. How can I make it up to you?"

She pauses, her eyes grazing the ceiling while she deliberates. "You can come to the duck race with me."

"Sadie," Carmen says, gliding into the room, her tone a warning.

She's traded her General Store-logoed shirt and jeans for a fitted, cotton dress that hugs her figure like it was made for only her. The deep blue in the pattern seems to make her eyes of the same color glow brighter, and I can't pull mine away. She would be stunning in anything, but for once, shock and the familiar pain of old wounds slicing open aren't blinding me. I'm able to truly appreciate her, making something light, fluffy, and uninvited stir in my chest.

"Maddox already has plans tomorrow," she clarifies, saving me from the usual nosedive my thoughts take when she's nearby.

"You do?" Sadie turns to me, a dramatic pout on her cute face.

"I promised to help Easton. It's his first race."

Her forehead falls to my shoulder, and Trixie whimpers at her dip in energy. I'm in trouble.

"I'm sure I can help you both. There's plenty of me to go around."

Her head pops up, and so does Trixie's. "Really?"

"Jada may not appreciate that." Carmen's smile is light and teasing when my gaze finds her again.

"Why not?" Sadie asks, turning to her mother.

"Let's just say, she seemed excited to have Maddox all to herself."

"But Easton will be there."

"It's a man-woman thing, darling."

"Eww."

"My thoughts exactly," I commiserate.

"Maybe me and Mom being there will make it better."

I don't mean to, but my eyes dart back to Carmen over Sadie's shoulder. Her tender grin transports me back to when she was my everything—my dreams, my reason for breathing, my wish list and favorite present for every special occasion.

To keep myself from stumbling down that road again, I kiss Sadie's cheek. "You make everything better, queenie."

"Queenie?" Carmen asks with a laugh as I release my two favorite girls and stand.

"I call him sweetie," Sadie yells as she takes off down the hall with Trixie scampering after her, leaving me unprepared.

Last time I was left alone with Carmen like this, confessions I never expected to hear rocked my system. My overreactive heart isn't helping my nerves relax, and I'm on the verge of making some confessions of my own. *I've missed this. I can't handle being here. I need to hold you. I can't risk my heart again.*

Every one of those terrifies me, so I switch to a safer topic to hold myself together. "She earned the nickname when we practiced her lines for the play."

"Oh, yeah. I remember now. She was so excited that night. You changed her perspective on the part."

"I just gave her another option to think about. She did the rest."

She shrugs then motions toward my dusty clothes and paint-stained hands. "Would you like to wash up?"

"Probably a good idea before I ruin your furniture."

While I wash up at the kitchen sink, Carmen moves about the room, adding place settings to the little square table nearby. There are three chairs, two matching and one added from another part of the house. The table barely fits two people, much less three, and I'm not ready for the intimacy that creates.

"Would you like a beer?" she asks when I turn off the water.

"Sure."

How can she be so casual? I'm crawling out of my skin, alternating between wanting to stay far away and holding her close. Both sound like exactly what I need to survive this evening.

She calls for Sadie, and I'm grateful for the distraction and the calming light she brings with her.

Chapter 9

Carmen

"Are you excited for your date?" I tease Maddox after dinner to get him talking. Ever since Sadie retreated to her room, he's been in his head and impossible to read. How can we overcome the awkwardness between us if I have no idea what he's thinking or feeling?

"It's not a date," he says with zero emotion, and I appreciate the answer.

"We'll see." Can't blame Jada for trying. He did look exceptionally handsome that day—as he does every time our paths cross. He keeps getting better and better the more he loosens up. And tonight is no exception, especially seeing him with Sadie for the first time. Their connection and the way he talks to her, with complete adoration and respect, takes my breath away.

Sitting alone with him on the couch, the soft glow from the nearby lamp highlights his strong, rugged features, and I can't tear my eyes away. Whenever his gaze meets mine, I feel like I'm his—like he wants to be mine again. At this point, I'd do whatever, surrender almost anything, to make that happen. But first, he needs to trust me.

"I'm glad you came over."

A soft grin tips the corner of his mouth, the same honest amusement Sadie brings out in him, and I'm grateful he's no longer looking at me like I'm a monster.

"Me, too," he says before his gaze darts away in a sudden burst of nervousness. "I'm sorry for shutting you out the other day in the truck."

"You have nothing to apologize for. I ambushed you."

"And surprised me."

"You're surprised I still have feelings for you?"

His eyes, green in this lighting, dart to me and hold, searching for the truth. I hope he finds how much I mean it.

"Well, yeah. We haven't spoken in a very long time." A deep breath showcases how much that day haunts him. "I thought you forgot about us," he confesses, giving me a dangerous sliver of hope that our story isn't over yet.

Without thinking of the repercussions, I reach for him, my hand falling onto his forearm to make my point. He doesn't jump at my touch, like he did in the truck, and it means so much. "Maddox, I could never forget. You were my everything."

He skewers me with a sharp gaze. "If that were true, why not try to make it work long distance?"

Something akin to panic with a dose of desperation settles in my gut. This conversation took a sudden grim turn, and I'm terrified he'll shut it down before I can have my say.

"That's the same question I most often ask myself." Too

many times, I've relived the events leading up to my decision and wondered how I ever said goodbye to him. Those same questions only spiraled out of control since he waltzed back into my life. "And I have no explanation other than being a stupid, selfish kid who didn't know how good she had it until it was gone."

If he was upset before, he's the embodiment of raw, unfiltered fury now. His breathing has quickened, and he can't bring himself to look at me—something he had no problem doing just moments ago. The message is clear. He believes that if my career had flourished, or if Sadie hadn't come to me, I would still be gone with no regret over breaking up with him.

Saddened that I make him wonder about my love for him, I find a way to set the record straight. "Maddox, I've always felt this way, not just after everything fell apart. We'd always been together, and the second we weren't, I missed you desperately. I couldn't share my joys or burdens with you or poke at you with endless questions about your day. Knowing you were hurting and not being there to hold you—it was torture."

His hands wring together, knuckles turning bone-white under the strain of his frustration. "You could have changed that," he says, his jaw clenched tight and pulsing.

"I thought I was doing what was best for you." It's a pitiful excuse, but an honest one. "I didn't want you to waste your life waiting for me to chase my dream. But after getting my first job months later, I realized the dream meant nothing if you weren't there to share it with me."

"Nine years, Carmen. You had nine years to tell me this. Why didn't you reach out?" His body shudders in a fight for calm amid his pain and mine does the same.

I feel his every emotion as if it were happening to me, and I hate doing this to him. Hate how much I've damaged him and continue to do so just by being here.

"You were overseas then, and by the time you returned, I assumed you'd moved on and found happiness with someone else. I didn't want to upset that or you."

"Why not ask someone? My entire family knew the truth."

The truth grinds its way through like a dull knife. The truth that he spent years despising me for what I did, hurting alone.

"I heard pieces here and there, but I didn't want to accept it. It broke me to think of you unhappy, and I had Sadie and my parents counting on me." I sigh out my frustration and slink away, cold emptiness filling me instantly without the feel of him to warm me. "I'm not proud of it, but I was afraid."

"Of what?"

"Seeing you with someone else, even though I prayed for you to find her."

"Why would you do that?"

"I wanted you to be happy."

"Being with you made me happy."

My chin quivers from a dam of emotions pushing against my wavering strength, but I can't stop now. He's finally opening up, allowing our exploratory conversation to venture further. "Have you dated?"

He stares at me, surely questioning if he should answer, and I have to wonder if I'm properly equipped to hear it. "Not really. I was married to the service and then to my job."

Although he doesn't ask, he deserves to know everything. "I tried."

"I know."

"You do? How?"

"I followed you on social media for the first two years."

That means he saw things I'm not proud of and later deleted. "None of my past relationships were serious. I didn't understand why they never went anywhere until you came back." *And showed me where I left my heart.* Taking his hand, I hold it gently between us. "My feelings for you are as strong as they were then. How could I give my heart to another when it's not mine to offer?"

"That's not helping." Pulling free, he rises and stalks across the room.

"Helping what?"

He whips around to face me, the unrestrained anger and pain I saw at his parents' house back with a vengeance. "Me getting over you," he blurts, twisting the jagged weapon lodged in my breastbone until my heartache bleeds out.

"Is that what you want?" I manage through the pain.

"I thought I did."

At the past-tense use, hope forms like a soothing bandage on my wound, allowing me to ask, "And now?"

"I don't know." His hands rub down his face and slump by his sides.

"What if I tell you again? Say it plainly so there's no miscommunication. You can let it sink in before deciding."

Cautiously, I cross to him and take his hands. He doesn't flinch or retreat. His eyes find mine and hold me captive while he wades through his emotions. From disbelief to resentment to hurt and finally curiosity. He feels it all, but at least he isn't running.

"What is it?" he whispers, caution shredding his voice and me in the process.

"I love you, Maddox. I never truly understood how much until I saw you again."

His breath hitches and holds, and I can see it strangling him. A hard swallow ripples in his throat. "You don't know me. I'm not the same person I was back then."

"Maybe not, but I see the man you've become and would like

to get to know him better. A trial run second chance, so to speak."

He steps away to put some space between us and turns his back to me.

"You don't have to answer tonight," I offer, not wanting to rush him. "Think about it, and see how——"

He whips around, eyes laser-focused on me. "I think about nothing else, Carmen. Twenty-four seven, you're all I ever think about, even though I try not to."

"Maddox." I want to be comforted by knowing I've been on his mind, but he makes it sound like a problem—like he wishes he could forget me.

I go to him, and he mirrors me, fueling my suspicions and fears. He's so close, but I can't touch him and that may hurt worse than being apart.

"I need more time," he says.

"Okay," I concede. Whatever he wants, he can have it, but I won't let him walk out of my life without a fight.

He watches me a bit, turmoil over what to do evident in his eyes, before heading to the door. Framed in the opening, he looks back at me, and I'm struck once again by how beautiful he is. Everything from his physical appearance down to his generous heart. Kaitlyn had been right, and there's no sense in denying it any longer. Maddox is my soulmate, and without him, I'll be forever lost.

"See you tomorrow," he says, thankfully proving he hasn't shut me out yet, and snaps his fingers for Trixie to follow.

"Tomorrow it is."

Maddox

It's 3:05 AM, and Carmen's confession and request for a second chance has kept me up half the night. My thoughts keep rocking back and forth between frustration that our past came up in conversation and relief that it did. Wanting to take her offer and wanting to take five giant steps backward. Missing her more than usual and being grateful for the wide berth she's giving me. It's maddening.

While our talk tonight opened a few old scars, it also healed others. I no longer feel like I'm suffocating when she's close, and my instinct to run hasn't elbowed me in the ribs, so that's progress. Maybe my feelings for her weren't buried as deep as I thought … or at all.

I sit up and strip my T-shirt off my sweating body. Can I still be in love with Carmen? That possibility has spiked a few internal defense mechanisms, waking up Trixie. She trots up from the foot of the bed to give me a few lazy blinks.

"Sorry, girl." I rub her fluffy head to make up for the sudden movement. Her big, glossy eyes look at me with concern, melting my anxiety like it never had a thorny grip on my throat in the first place.

She barks, and I lie down with a pat on my chest, giving her personal contact if she needs it. She's surely missing Dottie, and my fumbling self isn't helping her cope in her strange new surroundings. Climbing up, she licks my cheek and settles her sweet face on her paws, giving me several more slow blinks until I give her attention. I haven't figured out if that glare is out of annoyance or adoration. With the way my touch seems to settle her, I choose to believe I'm growing on her.

"I could've used your company in Boston," I tell her like she can understand me. "I was offered a position on the K9 team, but my apartment doesn't allow dogs, and I didn't have the energy to relocate. Plus, German shepherds are way more work than you."

Her head pops up like I said something insulting, and my fingers brush down her side, a doggie message to let her know she's perfect in my eyes.

"Don't get your fur in a bunch, I'm glad you're low maintenance. All the women I've met since discharge have been needy, always expecting me to go out and spend time with them."

Trixie's yawn comes with a moan that mimics annoyance, giving me a chuckle.

"My sentiments exactly. So irritating." Settling in to watch her sleep—happy at least one of us will get some rest tonight—I trail my fingertips down her side again.

Seeing her so peaceful helps me find a similar state of being, and I lay unmoving for the next hour, trying not to disturb her beauty sleep. That's why I let out a few choice words when my phone vibrates on the bedside table. All my efforts gone to waste.

Her head and my blood pressure pops up at the sound. Who in the hell is texting me at four o'clock in the morning?

Cooper: You up?

Me: Unfortunately. Everything okay?

Cooper: Yeah. I'm at the airport. Bored out of my freakin' mind. There's only so long I can watch people try to sleep in odd shapes in the godforsaken pleather chairs.

Me: At least you brought your positive attitude with you.

Cooper: Locked up safe and sound in my carry-on. Doubt it will be coming out anytime soon.

Me: Maybe Mom can get it out of you. You're on your way home, right? Or is there some top-secret mission that requires you to fly incognito with sleepy civilians?

Cooper: No mission this time. Other than bringing Mom's special Christmas present. Don't tell her.

Me: I thought I was her present.

Cooper: You're old news now. Time for a newer model.

Me: I guess you can butt in… for Mom's happiness. I might also be a tad bit excited to see you.

Cooper: Why wouldn't you be? I am the coolest brother you have.

Me: And the most conceited.

Cooper: No one beats Aaron on that meter.

Me: True. I take it back.

Cooper: Good. How are things with you?

I check on Trixie, giving me a second to find an answer for that unreasonable question. She jumps down to snuggle next to me on the mattress, and I shake out my arms. It's weird how holding a phone over a tiny dog aches worse than bench pressing my weight in the gym. Seizing the opportunity to find a more comfortable position for a text conversation, I sit up and lean back against the pull-out couch cushion to rest my sore arms in my lap.

"Whew, that's better. Right, girl?"

Her pale eyelids slide closed a few lazy times before resting her chin on the mattress.

"Still don't know what that means, but I'll figure it out."

Getting back to Cooper, I type the only answer that comes to mind in my crazy, whirlwind existence here in Ember Falls.

Me: Confusing.

Cooper: Care to elaborate?

Cooper: Never mind. I guess that means you took your brother's awesome advice and talked to Carmen.

Me: Easy guess.

Cooper: And?

Me: We're seeing each other again tomorrow.

Cooper: Again? Wow.

Me: It's a long story.

Cooper: You want to go, right?

Me: I think so. She said she has feelings for me and wants another chance.

Cooper: Wow. Didn't see that coming. How do you feel?

Me: Confused.

Cooper: It's all making sense now.

Cooper: You don't have to go through with it if you're not ready.

Me: I think I want to. Need to.

Cooper: OK. Stay in control and get what you need before deciding what you want. Everything else is bonus.

Cooper: Signing off. The guy in the chair next to me is snoring, and if he starts to lean my way, I need to be ready.

Me: To provide a comfy shoulder or punch him?

Cooper: What do you think?

Shaking my head, I set the phone down, and my thoughts go haywire in the silence. I have a thousand worries about seeing Jada and Carmen soon. Like Cooper, I've been trained to anticipate the worst-case scenarios before they happen. It's easier to protect yourself and others if you know what to expect. With so many hearts on the line and no clear idea of what might happen during the upcoming not-a-date gathering, I can't stop my brain from racing through all the possible outcomes. Although running away isn't a viable option this time, it the first one to populate.

Having to mitigate Jada's feelings already has me on edge. Add in Carmen's presence to the mix, along with my own unpredictable emotions, and I might as well toss myself over the cliff now. Until last night, I've barely managed to be in the same room as Carmen, and I have no idea how I will react to spending all day with her, much less another woman. At. The. Same. Time.

My muscles tighten in anticipation of so many unknowns, drawing Trixie to my lap as if she feels it too and wants to help. Maybe she'll be my therapy dog while I'm here. If her special kind of therapy helps, maybe I should adopt a dog to take back to Boston. It might be what I need to stay on track there and out of Captain Emory's office going forward.

Chapter 10

Maddox

Arriving at the Rubber Ducky Sled Race registration area in Adeline Park on the edge of town, my eyes land on Carmen and Sadie bundled together by the fire pit ahead. All the prep work I did to prepare myself for this outing evaporates, and just like that, I'm knocked back to ground zero.

Where's Trixie when I need her? It was stupid of me to leave her with Mom, but I already had two women to juggle today and thought I couldn't handle one more. I know how that sounds, but I've been here for less than five minutes, and I'm lost already. I need Trixie and her sweet, cuddly distractions to help me think.

Seeing Carmen again as the nurturing, devoted mother I always knew she could be throws me off balance. Is it wrong that I'm wildly attracted to that side of her and eager to know more? The problem is her other side—the one that makes my heart instinctively brace behind an armored shield while it installs flashing caution signs in all directions. My internal back-off defense mechanism.

But I can't keep letting the past dictate my present, can I? I need to tear down these barriers and reclaim the peace and contentment I once had. For too long, I've been trapped in the cold, lifeless shadow of what was, too afraid to hope for what could be.

Determined, I urge myself to move forward, to take the first leap toward Carmen. But before I get off the ground, Jada and Easton join me, their presence a stark reminder of the promise I forgot about during my daydreaming. I freeze, caught between two women as Jada's gaze follows the focus of mine. Her smile dips ever so slightly, and that small crack in her sunny composure means I'm being a jerk already. I hurt her feelings at the very start of our not-a-date—albeit unintentionally—but she quickly recovers with a resilience I wish I could muster.

Going from a view of Carmen to Jada is a blow to the system, and my thoughts stumble over themselves to get to my lips. A one-word response is all I can muster. "Hi."

"Duckies," Easton says, pointing at the entry table full of rubber duckies in every color.

"Yes, sweetheart. We'll get one soon." Coming back to me, she rests a hand on my arm.

Her touch doesn't have the same effect on me as Carmen's. In fact, I have no response at all. She's an attractive, vibrant woman vying for my affection, and I feel nothing.

"Thank you for coming," she continues. "I'm sure you have plenty of places you'd rather be."

Without permission, my gaze shifts to Carmen through the trees. Is that where I'd rather be?

"Maddox?"

"Sorry." For a distraction, I lean forward to see Easton beside her. "What color duck do you want, buddy?"

"Blue."

"Best color ever, especially for cops like your dad and me, right?"

"Right!" He jumps into the air to smack the hand I held out for him. "I want to be a cop."

"That's awesome. Your dad would be so proud. Now, let's go get that blue duck to honor him."

Easton bounces up to me, and I lift him onto my shoulders. While Jada checks him in with the volunteers, we make our way to the fire pit. Sadie sees us first and jumps up to give me a hug.

"Hi, Easton." She waves up at him, and his heels bang against my abs with excitement. "Are you ready for the race?"

"Yeah!" He shows her the duck he chose. "What color is your ducky?"

Sadie reaches into her coat pocket and holds up her red one for him to admire

"Nice to see you again, Carmen," Jada says, peppering in some forced patience. If she stood any closer, I'd be holding her, too.

"I love your scarf." Matching her tone, Carmen holds her position. She made her intentions concerning me known the other night, and her unwavering eyes seem to be giving the same message to Jada.

"Thanks." Jada turns to me, her arm hooking with mine in a show of possession. Guess she has some intentions of her own and isn't pleased with Carmen and Sadie crashing our not-a-date. I'm still clueless in the what-to-do-next category. "Shall we head to the creek and prepare Easton for launch?" Jada asks, pointing me toward an answer.

"Great idea." Carmen takes Sadie's hand. "We'll come, too."

She flashes a grin at us both and heads toward the trail.

The long walk to the top of the hill is a silent one, except for Easton and Sadie's random chatter about the things they see along the way. To traverse the narrow, wooden trail, Jada leaves her post beside me to help Easton over rocks and roots in our path. Sadie and Carmen guide the line, and I'm the caboose on this awkward train with a full view of my two options.

The weight of their pasts has molded the very different personalities of each single mother. Jada's grace and resilience, after enduring unfathomable loss so early in her marriage and raising a young child alone, is something I deeply admire. Her sweet personality and gentle spirit offer a calming change. Around her, I'm as relaxed as I can be in unfamiliar territory but also unaffected.

Carmen, on the other hand, sends me into a tailspin if I simply think of her, much less see or hear her. She sacrificed the career she worked her entire life for to raise her friend's child—a testament to the selflessness I'd been drawn to growing up. She made me want to be a better person. To put others first and go after what I want without hesitation as she did. But that drive of hers destroyed me once, and it could do so again.

When she asked for a second chance, I wanted to believe we could find our way back to each other. But trust, once broken, is not easily mended, especially after all that's happened. If we were to become something other than exes—friends or otherwise—I need to be able to trust her. Without it, we have nothing.

Outside of Jada and Carmen, and whatever it is they want from me, their children have already woven me into their lives with innocent ease. With Sadie and Easton, there's no questioning where I stand or how I feel. I'm a lost cause, hopelessly devoted to them for as long as they'll have me.

"Over there," Carmen calls as we come to a snow-covered

clearing. Next to a coffee and donut stand is a craft area for the kids to make a sled for their duck out of cardboard, popsicle sticks, plastic piping, and more. Once Easton and Sadie start construction with Parks and Recreation volunteers, she says, "I need some coffee. Anyone like to come along?"

"I already had some this morning, and I should stay in case Easton needs help," Jada answers and waits for mine.

It's a test. The direction I choose—go with Carmen or stay with Jada—will speak volumes about where my heart is leaning and change the entire direction of this train for the rest of the day. Nope. Not doing it.

"You go ahead," I tell Carmen, and Jada beams until I say, "Be right back."

Before she can protest or hold me there with questions, I walk in the opposite direction as Carmen with no plan. Hopefully, I'll see something that will save me soon. I didn't think it through when Sadie asked me to come with her today. I could only think about making her happy, and in doing that, I made it infinitely harder on myself.

I pass a few families standing by heaters and more at the trail's exit. Approaching the information table, a woman in a white jacket and fluffy earmuffs waves me over.

"Hi, Maddox. What are you doing here?"

There's that question again, and per the usual, I'm starting to wish I weren't.

"I'm sorry. You probably don't remember me." She steps out from behind the table and holds out a gloved hand. "I'm Veronica, Mayor Whitacre's better half."

"Nice to meet you."

"Did my husband force you to volunteer at this event too?"

"No. I'm here with …" I find the craft table across the field, giving me time to somehow figure out how to put a label on my companions. *Friends* doesn't fit. *Girlfriends?* Just the plural of that word is ridiculous and wholly false. *Someone I've known my entire life and someone I just met, both of whom are out to make me theirs*—too complicated and embarrassing. I watch Carmen return to the others before giving my attention back to Veronica. By the knowing smile she's giving me, she saw everything I did.

"I get it," she says, and my core heats with humiliation. How can everyone understand me and my life while I'm in the dark about both?

"You do? Maybe you can enlighten me." Where did that come from?

"You're exploring your options … as you should. Live it up and let them fight over you." She winks. "Who knows what you'll discover about them and yourself along the way? You might even have a little fun."

My mouth drops open, too surprised to respond, before I realize and appreciate the rarity of that advice. "You're the first person who hasn't encouraged me to jump headfirst into my past. Thank you."

"You're welcome but stop worrying so much. No one will think you're a jerk if you enjoy your bachelorhood. You're young. Do young people things for once, Maddox."

"I did miss out on that."

"Yes, you did. Now, get back over there and flirt with both if you want. Spend time with whoever gets your motor going. You're not chained to any decision you've made or will consider making. This time in your life is for figuring out what makes you happy. So, do it."

I've been talking to this woman for less than five minutes, and I already love her. "It's too bad you're taken."

"It *is* a shame." She flashes me a playful smile and pats my arm. "Turn that charm on them and anyone else who steals your attention and see what happens."

"Yes, ma'am."

Heading back to the others, I'm feeling better. Even hopeful for an easy, uneventful afternoon, but I'm not sure I can do as Veronica recommended. I'm not a flirt and haven't exercised that muscle since high school, and even then, it was only with Carmen. It's always been *only Carmen*. I wouldn't even know how to start. And if I did, wouldn't I be leading them on? I have no idea what I want or where my actions may take us. Isn't that rude and inconsiderate when I have no conceivable intentions or thoughts of commitment with either of them beyond this month? My job and life in Boston await my return.

Enjoy it, Veronica had said. Yeah, right.

A whistle blows from the information booth, and the entire crowd zeroes in on me as if I made the noise. I stop mid-stride, frozen in my insecurities, as I watch every kid within listening range take off from where they'd been playing to surround me. They meet me with expectation and excitement, and I'm trapped.

"Maddox." I find Veronica standing outside the swarm of kids. She reaches over their heads to pass me a piece of paper. "Since your charm has the attention of our eager participants, maybe you would be best to deliver this information."

"What?" How do I keep getting myself into these messes?

"Just read it and have fun." With a wink, she slinks back to the other awaiting adults, all of whom are expecting event instructions… from *me*.

Skimming the crowd beyond, all the faces blur in my heightened blood pressure until I locate Sadie. *Do what we do*, her lips say, but my pulse races too loud in my ears to know if any sound accompanies the gesture. It's my cue to act my way through this. If Maddox can't gather enough nerve to read a few words off a piece of paper, I should find a persona inside me who can.

Sergeant Henderson emerges first. I've worked many events in Boston, shuffling and guiding patrons for hours on end. And this is *not* the Boston Marathon. It's children and sledding and rubber duckies for goodness' sake. Putting on my cop hat, I read the instructions, accentuating the most important information in my friendly, no-nonsense tone.

"So, what's rule number one?" I ask, holding up a finger to my enthusiastic audience to recap.

"Stay out behind the ducks," they yell in unison.

"Great. What's rule number two?"

"Be safe."

"And rule number three?"

"Have fun!" The group squeals and bounces, many on me, and I end up with a kid on each hip and another latched to my leg.

"You've got it. Now, let the race begin." They all take off in a blur of colorful winter coats and hats toward the starting line with family and friends close behind.

I do this sort of thing all the time, but never once did I appreciate or enjoy it. It's always been about what the job required, not what it meant to the people I led.

"You were amazing, Maddox," Veronica compliments as she hurries by. "Thanks."

"Not like I had a choice."

She walks backwards to face me. "You always have a choice." The mischievous smile returns to her lips to remind me of her advice before she jogs down the path. Will I get to work and find a way forward or sit back and let myself falter once again?

Pivoting to escape both options, I almost crash into Jada and Carmen. I seem to have forgotten all my tactical training the second I stepped foot in this town. Both women stare up at me as if I'd just saved a litter of kittens from a burning building. Take it from me, ladies, I'm not that special.

"Great job, officer," Carmen teases.

Ignoring her, I toss a thumb over my shoulder and change the subject. "We should go find the kids."

"They're right behind you." Carmen smirks, enjoying my unease a little too much. Especially since she has a lot to do with my mood … whether she means to or not.

Spinning, I gladly take Easton and Sadie's hands and leave the women to walk together. This trio combination is one I can navigate, allowing me to settle into Teacher Henderson mode.

At the edge overlooking the starting line, I give Sadie and Easton tips on setting their duck in the snow, keeping track of it among the group, and racing down the slope to the finish line. We'll be close behind if help is needed, but they'll have the most fun following along with the other kids. Stumbling over friends in the deep snow and laughing when ducks get caught in a pile or tip over in the groves are some of the best memories I have. It's pure chaos in the best possible way.

When Veronica calls for the ducky contestants to set up, Jada and Carmen step up to stand on either side of me. They're both quiet—the tension as thick and cold as a block of ice.

"You were amazing back there," Jada finally says with a touch of my forearm, her night-dark eyes finding mine with a few bats of her lashes.

I couldn't be further outside my element. "Thanks."

"I didn't know you were such a showman."

A chuckle spurts out of me at the absurd idea of me on stage. "That's—"

"I did," Carmen chimes in. "He had lots of practice growing up."

The hours we spent practicing her lines as teenagers resurface, and a flame ignites in my core. Those rehearsals were my favorite because they quickly turned into hot, drive-me-crazy make out sessions. I think about kissing adult Carmen like that, but this time with no restrictions, and instantly regret it. That pesky little flame flares and spreads throughout my body, making me unzip my coat to let out the steam.

"You okay?" Jada asks. "Can I get you anything?"

"No. I'm fine." And a liar. "Thanks."

I catch Carmen's smug grin in my periphery, but I don't dare look at her.

"Oh, there's Easton," Jada says when her son emerges from the crowd and waves her over.

"It was fun seeing you work earlier," Carmen says when we're alone but keeps her eyes forward. "There's nothing sexier than a hot cop who's good with children. I think you earned yourself a few more female admirers with that performance."

"Dad says firefighters are better."

"He's biased, and they've got nothing on you, my friend." She waves a hand in front of her face, mirroring the fire smoldering under my skin being this close to her.

"Friend?"

That inquiry has her shifting toward me, and I can't stop myself from meeting her gaze. "Always," she confirms, then adds, "until you decide to claim a different title."

This is when I should say something flirty back as Veronica suggested, but nothing comes forward. The easy confessions that roll off Carmen's tongue rattle me and shut off my brain. I'm searching for something poignant to say when Jada returns.

"That boy is something else," she swoons, her proud momma smile fading as she notices the new heat radiating off Carmen and me. I wouldn't be surprised if it materialized in the frigid air and covered us in a cloud of smoke.

Carmen smooths the loose strands of her hair, like something—maybe me—had tousled it while Jada was away and pulls her knitted hat into place. "Shall we get closer to the action? They're about to start."

I hang back to give myself time to recover, but Jada waits to walk with me. So much for that.

"You should see how excited Easton is. This may be the first time he's felt at home since we moved here."

"I'm glad he's having fun."

"It's because of you. Would you let me treat you to dinner after this to thank you?" she asks, and I admire her boldness.

Any man with half a brain would jump at an opportunity to say yes to that question. Where I stand on the topic is a mystery. My life feels like an unassembled puzzle with no picture or guide. All the pieces of something great are there; I just have no idea how to put it all together. Because of that, I don't deserve the effort she's giving me.

Grabbing my arm, she stops me and waits until Carmen is out of listening range. Her eyes raise to mine. "I know you're trying to find your way while you're here, especially where she's concerned." She tilts her head in the direction Carmen went.

My expression must have exposed my shock, making her say, "There are no secrets in this town, Maddox. It's the first thing I learned."

"Jada—"

"I want you to kiss me, Maddox," she demands, her voice trembling as it floats on a heavy sigh. She grabs hold of my coat and pulls herself closer. The scent of her sweet, coconut shampoo contrasts with the pines and saturated ground around us, and I'm just as confused. What happened to her tranquil nature? Where is this desperate plea coming from? "I beg you to put me out of my misery. Kiss me and tell me you don't feel the same attraction I do."

"Jada, that's not a good idea."

"Is it because she's here or is it me?"

"Whether Carmen's here or not, this is not the time or place for that kind of exploration."

Her eyes flicker between mine, trying to read me. I reach for her hand. "Let's talk privately afterward. Okay?"

"I'd like that." With an unsteady smile, she lets go of my hand and slips both of hers into her coat pockets. "And you're right. Thank you for not treating me like a crazy person. I have no idea where that came from."

"It's okay. Women ask me to kiss them all the time. It's kind of a curse." I force my lips into a broad smile, a sign that I still see her as the amazing woman she is.

"You're the best. I hope you know that."

"I'm working on it. Come on. We don't want to miss the excitement."

The annual Spectacular Rubber Ducky Sled Race went off without a hitch. Neither Easton nor Sadie won, but that didn't matter. They had a blast watching their ducks get lost in the madness and being kids. Often, during the race, I envisioned myself doing this with them again next year, then forced myself not to. Nothing in life is guaranteed, and I haven't a clue where I'll be in a month, much less next year.

Soon after collecting his duck from the finish line, Jada took Easton home to rest, the excitement of the race wearing him out early. She didn't bring up dinner or my promise to talk, and I wonder if there's a reason.

I attempted to keep my focus on the kids and not any one

woman in our weird not-a-date triangle. Maybe my effort to avoid upsetting them by staying neutral did exactly that. Maybe Jada noticed I'm not neutral at all—only pretending for her sake—and that's just as painful. But given my surroundings, I resign to worrying about Jada's feelings later. No way will my wayward thoughts and the events of today let me sleep tonight, giving me plenty of time to figure something out.

"I think this is the most fun Sadie's had at this event so far," Carmen says after the three of us travel to the hot cocoa stand downtown.

I watch her rub her hands together and bounce through the cold evening breeze. Whenever she would do that years ago, I'd hold her inside my coat until she stopped shivering. I wonder if she's testing me to see if the old habit lingers within. Just because I remember doesn't mean I'll take the bait.

"I'm glad," I finally say. "She deserves to be a kid every now and then."

"I tell her that all the time."

While we wait for our orders, she leans on the counter to face me, her eyes gently challenging me to stop resisting the magnetic force trying to bring us together. At least the Maddox temptation competition has ended, and there's only one woman trying to win my attention. Much more manageable… if it weren't Carmen.

Collecting our steaming cups, we find a picnic table under the heated tent nearby. Sadie sits across from us and says something to Carmen, but I can't comprehend it. My brain blocks every other sensory input except where Carmen's body connects to mine—shoulder, hip, thigh, foot. She's so close I can smell her shampoo, starting a competition of my own. Desire and caution course through my veins, and I have no idea which will win out if I'm presented with a choice.

Especially when I can't stop wondering how it would feel to hold her again. To experience her surrender as if I'm the only man she's ever craved. To follow the curve of her body with my hands, claiming her as mine. That's the desire talking.

My cautious side waves another flag. Giving in to that fantasy solves none of our issues. Our connection is far more complicated than sexual desire and gravely wounded. With those scars on my mind, avoid and escape instincts have my leg twitching under the table.

If it weren't for Sadie's energy and the line of curious Ember Falls residents stopping by, I might have found an excuse to remove myself. But alas, the town seems to have sent out a Maddox and Carmen flare, calling everyone to this location to ask all their not-so-subtle questions and keep us here longer than intended.

The news of our being out together will be the talk of the town tomorrow. Carmen seems content with the entrapment and rumors that will spread like a pandemic after this. I, on the other hand, am still floundering to work through the twists and turns of my evolving emotional maze where she's concerned.

The gossip line eventually ends, and I'm exhausted. After walking the girls home, Sadie rushes inside their apartment, leaving me and my awkwardness alone with Carmen in the hallway.

"Thank you for today," she says, holding my gaze with expectation. For what, I don't know, but I think I want to find out.

On the quiet hike here, I talked myself into exploring a little more in hopes that it would help me figure out where I stand on her requested second chance.

"What are you doing tomorrow?" she asks.

"Same as I do every day—working on the bookshop."

"Sadie and I are going to the holiday bazaar and the Christmas Parade and Tree Lighting Ceremony afterward. Would you like to join us?" Then, the hook she thinks I can't refuse. "Sadie is caroling before the parade. I know she'd love for you to be there."

"What about you? Are you singing, too?" My freakout at the bar on my way into town aside—the shock of seeing her for the first time too much to handle in my fragile mindset—I'd like to hear her sing again. So long as it isn't our song. That might take more groundwork, more time, more forgiveness.

Her smile blooms and fills another empty space inside me. "Yes. I'm singing."

"Why didn't you mention that?"

She shrugs. "After my gig in Moyer's Ridge, I wasn't sure how you'd react."

"You saw me?"

"You're hard to miss, Maddox." She blushes, and I love the subtle color on her cheeks and what it represents. "Plus, I was exploiting your soft spot for Sadie." She smiles again, bringing one out in me.

"I'm starting to soften to other things as well," I venture, surprised by how paper-thin my walls feel.

"Oh, yeah?" Something light and sensual flashes in her eyes. It's fast enough someone who didn't know her might have missed it. But I've studied her every expression for most of my life and recognize the one she's giving me now. Biting down on her bottom lip, she leans back against the wall—her invitation and permission to touch and taste whenever I'm ready.

"What are you softening to, Maddox?" she asks in a sultry tone I hadn't heard from her yet.

I'd love to hear more.

I step closer, testing my body's reaction to her proximity.

Every muscle springs into action, like getting a fastball down the middle with the bases loaded. With her in my sights, nothing aches. Nothing longs for what used to be. I'm living in the moment, appreciating the woman more than her memory, even though it terrifies me.

The teasing smile fades from her face as I lean in, primed for the next test. Her rapid breaths brush across my lips. I can almost taste her. I want to taste—

"Momma," Sadie calls, skipping into the hallway in time to see me jump back. Her eyes dart between me and Carmen while contemplating our drastic mood change.

"What is it, darling?" Carmen says gently, and I'd love to know where she found the words. My brain had been wiped clean on my way to our almost kiss.

What had I been thinking? I wasn't, and that's half the problem. I wasn't being careful and cautious, as Cooper rightfully suggested, and now I'm paying the price.

"The knob on the bathroom sink is stuck again," Sadie complains.

"Did you twist it like I showed you?"

"I did. Nothing happens."

"I'll be right there," Carmen says, gently nudging her back inside.

"Kids have the worst timing," she says with a nervous giggle, and I'm thinking the opposite. Sadie may have saved me from jumping off the cliff when I should be taking the stairs.

"I need to get going, anyway."

"Baby steps. Got it." She smiles, and I wish the sight would quiet the storm brewing in my gut as it had before.

"That's probably best."

"No problem. If those steps are bringing you to me, I can wait however long it takes." She reaches for my free hand, sending shockwaves up my arm. "Just keep moving, Maddox."

"I'm trying."

"That's baby step number one checked off the list."

Chapter 11

Maddox

"Hey, Mom," I call from the living room. She's in the kitchen with Izzie, preparing an early dinner before the parade. "I need to show you something."

I snuck Cooper in through the front door when he arrived, not bothering with a sneakier operation since she was tucked away and deep in conversation.

"What is it, Mad—" Her hands cover her mouth at the first sight of Cooper beside me, his arm braced over my shoulders. He's in full camo, his light brown hair mussed as if he drove the Humvee straight here from a training exercise.

"Aren't you a sight for sore eyes," he says, forever a momma's boy, but in the best way.

I watch them embrace and, of course, Mom's crying. I wish I'd had this up-close, outside viewpoint of my reunion with her.

The love pouring out of them is a cooling balm on my wounds, and I could have benefited from this euphoria that day.

"Are Kendall and Aaron here yet?" Cooper asks.

"Not until tomorrow. I can't believe you made it."

"Couldn't miss this guy finally crawling out of his hole." He tosses a thumb at me over his shoulder.

"It's a blessing." She frames his cheeks with her hands, pure joy sparkling in her eyes. "All my kids will be under one roof again. I never thought I'd see the day."

Cooper twists to glare at me, implying it's my fault Mom's been denied this happiness. He's mostly right.

"My bad."

They both laugh at my stupid response, then Mom circles an arm around Cooper's back. "Come. Izzie would love to see you, too."

"She's here?" he asks, and the last part of my heart still intact—the corner reserved for my family—squeezes for him.

He holds his position, preventing her from leading him further, and lowers his voice. "How is she? She's incessantly positive in her emails, trying not to worry me."

"She's doing what she can, and we're filling in the gaps."

"Cooper?" Izzie steps into the living room, the sight of him draining her strength, and she folds under the weight of her emotion.

"I'm here," he says, kneeling before her and letting her crumble into his arms.

Mom and I step away to give them space but can't help but watch. The sweet moment rivals any romantic movie I've ever seen, and thanks to all the fierce women in my life who don't take no for an answer, I've seen more than my fair share.

"What is it with my boys?" Mom whispers, tipping her head to rest on my shoulder.

"I've got plenty of potential answers to that open-ended question."

"Let me be more specific, then. Why do you withhold your heart from the women you love?"

"Mom…"

"You love so completely but painfully silent."

"It's complicated for us both. You know that."

"Speaking of complicated, how'd it go with Carmen last night?" She turns her back to Cooper and Izzie to see my face and wiggles her brow. "I heard talk of you two getting cozy after the duck race."

My eyes roll without consent. "It went as expected— awkward and confusing. We're giving it another go tonight."

"At the parade?"

"Yeah, but early. Sadie and Carmen are caroling. Are you going?"

"Wouldn't miss it." Her hands rest softly on my elbows in a show of her motherly support. "I'm glad you and Carmen are working through things. No matter where you two end up, I hope you can lessen your grip on that stubborn heart of yours."

"It's a slow process, but I'm getting there."

"I know, sweet boy. I know." She pats my cheek, then huddles with Cooper and Izzie, who seem to have wrangled their emotions. "Catch up with Maddox," she tells Cooper. "Izzie and I will finish up in the kitchen so we can all enjoy a meal together again. It's been far too long."

Izzie's gaze lingers on Cooper over her shoulder, and he doesn't acknowledge me until she disappears into the kitchen. "She's glowing."

"Only since you showed up. She's been as pale and down on herself as I've ever seen her."

"Damn. I hate that. She doesn't deserve what that asshole did to her."

"No one does We'll make sure she's safe and keep him out of the picture."

Cooper lowers to the couch, and I sit beside him. He looks like he could use a brotherly talk. "I'm going to submit my discharge papers."

"Really? Because of Izzie?"

"Partly. I've been thinking about it for a while now. How can I stay in Texas while she's in danger? She's more important."

"Than your service?"

"Always. She's my best friend."

"With the way you two acted earlier, it seems like there's more between you."

Cooper pauses, picking at the hem of his pants pocket before answering. "It's been a while since we've seen each other, and she's emotional."

"Or you're in denial."

"You're one to talk," Cooper accuses, flipping the conversation to me. "You say you're fine every time we talk, and you're not. You know that, right?"

"I do." No sense in denying it. Cooper knows me better than anyone and will see through any bullshit. Whenever I need someone to give it to me straight, he's the first one I call, and vice versa.

"Good. What are you doing to fix it?" he asks, getting down to business like he's planning for a mission.

"Starting at ground zero. I'm working on forgiving her."

"How?"

"It gets easier to replace the negative emotions with others the more time we spend together. Although, it doesn't help that I think about us—the way we used to be and the time we lost."

Cooper nods. I must have passed the bullshit test.

"I'm not the only one with issues. What are you going to do about Izzie?" I ask.

"Support her, protect her. Whatever she needs."

"That's not what I meant."

Cooper's eyes roll. "I can't do what you're suggesting until the asshole is out of the picture and she's safe. That's all that matters right now."

Noticing the familiar wavering into unsteady territory in my brother, I change the subject. "What date are you expecting for discharge?"

"As soon as I can get the paperwork submitted and approved."

"That soon?

"She's not Mom and Dad's responsibility."

"Or yours, Cooper. You're not the only person around here who loves her. She's family, and we're happy to help."

"Does that mean you're thinking about staying here permanently?" he asks, and like him, I have very few answers.

"I haven't thought that far ahead. If you'd asked me that when I first got here, my answer would have been an immediate and emphatic *hell no*." I had already started the countdown for the day I could get away before I even stepped foot in Ember Falls.

"No doubt, but I hope that's changing."

"We'll see. I have more to work through and a job I love waiting for me in Boston."

"Are you sure?"

"Of what?"

"That you love being Boston P.D."

"It's all I know."

"You can be a cop anywhere." A smug smile pulls at the corners of his mouth. He thinks he caught me without an argument.

"I have a life there."

"Bullshit."

"Food's ready," Mom announces, saving me from having to lie again and failing another test. Life in Boston means little more than breathing and waking up each morning to do whatever I did the day before like a broken record.

Broken and stuck seems to be the theme of my life and it's time to change that.

After dinner, we head downtown and locate the carolers near the gazebo. Sadie and Carmen hold hands in the front line in matching red coats, plaid scarves, and white knitted hats.

They find us in the crowd during "All I Want for Christmas," but what Carmen seems to want feels different when she looks at me—something I don't recognize in my memories of her.

Desire.

We were kids the last time we were together and had little experience in the sensations that ignite between lovers. As adults, we've given ourselves to others and can recognize the magnet hard at work tempting us. With every encounter, I grow more curious about what it would be like to hold her in that way. To touch every inch of her skin and feel her shiver under my touch. To kiss the lips I remember and explore the different ways our bodies could mold together in new ways. But that's a hazardous road, full of caution tape, cones, and flashing lights, and last night proved I'm not prepared to act on those curiosities yet.

Her eyes stay locked with mine as our private conversation continues through two more songs. Then, Sadie steps forward, breaking my trance, and sings "O Holy Night" solo. She's captivating, and I wonder how I ever lived without her in my life. How can I go back to Boston and not be a part of hers?

The answers are too inconceivable to validate, and I'm surprised the questions even surfaced at this point. After all, I'm a week into my hometown sentence, and there's too much left to uncover, like who I am and what I want out of life. Those two considerations have fallen to the wayside behind my public service, heartache, and everything else.

Captain Emory said I can't return to the force unless I'm a different man, and with the rollercoaster I'm strapped to here, I'm worried I may not find him in time.

"You were incredible," I tell Sadie afterward with a high-five, then turn to Carmen, primed to pay her the same compliment. But her eyes are already on me, picking up where our wordless conversation left off before, and I have no idea what to do.

"Let's go find a good area to watch the parade," Mom suggests, coming to my rescue. She offers her support with a wink as the group begins to move down the sidewalk, and I give her my thanks with a one-arm hug.

We soon find an opening in the crowd that will fit everyone. Sadie, Trixie, and Carmen wrap up in a blanket next to her parents on the curb. I linger behind with my family, contemplating what I should do with my two choices yet again— sit intimately with Carmen or keep my distance. Like at the duck race, each direction sends a different message. If I choose her, it says I'm ready for the next baby step. If I don't, I'm telling her I need more time. I want both.

"Why don't you go sit with Carmen and Sadie?" Mom asks. "Test the waters a bit."

"I don't know if my system can absorb another test. It's been through a lot in the last forty-eight hours."

"There's only one way to find out." She nudges me with her shoulder, making the decision for me. *Baby step number two, here I come.*

"Hi," Carmen says as I lower to the curb. She shifts under the blanket to face me, her elbow on her knee to prop her head up with a soft fist, knocking me speechless with her smile once again.

She's stunning tonight. Golden waves flow freely down her back and over one shoulder under the knitted hat. What little skin I can see glows under the soft lamplight. I imagine the rest of her doing the same in the moonlight while lying bare on my bed…

"Hi," I respond, swallowing down the image before it consumes me. "How was the bazaar?"

"Great. We ate way too many fried treats." She winces and presses a gloved hand to her stomach. "But we chose a Christmas tree. It's getting delivered tomorrow."

"Sounds like a good time."

"Sadie can't wait to decorate it."

"I bet. It was one of my favorite holiday activities."

"Do you have space for a tree at your house in Boston?"

"No," I chuckle. "My studio apartment barely fits a bed and a recliner. I haven't had a tree since I lived here."

At the time, I didn't want reminders of what I missed out on here. But I should have come home just for the holidays to enjoy the family traditions I looked forward to every year as a kid. The boundless love of my family and the magic of Christmas might have brightened some of my darkest days.

I noticed Mom hasn't put up our tree at the house yet. I wonder if she's waiting on Kendall and Aaron so we can decorate it together as a family. Damn, I hope so. I sure could use a dose of reliving some of my most treasured childhood memories.

"It's not the same without the Henderson sibling antics," I add, thinking back to those days with a grin.

Her head tilts to the others behind us, bringing my attention back to her. "Speaking of your siblings, it's good to see Cooper home safe. Your parents must be so excited to have everyone together for the holidays."

"They are. I'm glad we could give them that."

"Can I ask why you picked now to come back?"

With a shrug, I shove my chilly hands into my coat pockets and glance down the street at the gathering crowd. The parade will be starting soon, giving us something to talk about other than my pathetic story.

"I didn't know where else to go," I say. "I had extended time off from work and nothing healthy to fill it with." Just the usual—beer and all-consuming misery.

"What do you mean?"

"I was put on admin leave."

"Why? Did something happen?"

"I took a life."

She pauses her questioning to survey me. There's no pity or alarm in her eyes. "But who did you save?"

"What?"

Holding my gaze, she waits until she's sure I'm listening. "I know you, Maddox. We all change over time, but only so much. I know you wouldn't have done it if you didn't have a good reason."

How could she see that buried side of me? The side I show no one, not even myself. "The suspect turned the gun on a child."

"No."

My nod confirms what she's thinking, and she touches my knee to offer her support. The placement—on my leg, instead of a safer location—and the fact that she hasn't moved it after making the gesture, sends another silent message. And it's not something friends say.

"The time off is just protocol, right?" she asks. "You're not in trouble."

"I don't expect any charges, but the investigation is ongoing."

The first float rolls by, kicking off the annual holiday parade, but she doesn't seem to care. "Why didn't you stay in Boston?"

"My captain suggested I not … in so many words."

She frowns. "How is that their call?"

"He threatened to fire me if I didn't make a change." He didn't say that outright, but that was the underlying intent. He thinks I'm a liability, and knowing what I know now, he isn't far off. "I couldn't do that there."

"What does he want changed?"

"Me."

Fresh tears reflect the festive string lights above us, and I feel the empathy behind them. But more than that, I feel her love. I wish that didn't irrevocably alter things. I shouldn't *want* her to love me at this point in my journey, but there's no putting that puzzle piece back in the box now that it's found its place.

"Maddox …"

"Sorry." For once, I don't say *I'm fine* because it isn't true. Continuing to lie can only be detrimental to figuring my shit out. "Baby steps are happening in more ways than one these days."

"You're doing great." Her hand edges up my thigh as she holds my gaze, watching for a reaction.

It's another test, and surprisingly, I'm okay with this one and what it represents. I like the feel of her hand on me. I like how it erases the world beyond us, allowing space for me to get lost in the moment without distractions. When we're apart, I'm starting to miss the feel of her beside me and the way she looks at me. It's different from how our eyes would meet when we were kids—more meaningful, deeper, powerful. I don't feel like I'm competing for her heart with her other dreams. This time, I feel like it's already mine—all of it.

Everything I thought when I came back to Ember Falls shifted the moment she asked for a second chance. I'd spent too many years convincing myself it wasn't possible. Hope is hard to come by when you're broken. But with every step we take toward each other, it's hope—not love or this new lust growing between us—that puts a section of my heart back together.

It won't be easy to let the rest of my guard down or allow this place to rebuild me, but I'm willing to try. And I want to try most with Carmen.

A contented silence hovers between us, and I don't see any of the parade marching by. There's only her, the anchor to my runaway world.

Chapter 12

Carmen

"Can we go see Santa?" Sadie asks, yanking me back to reality with a tug on my jacket sleeve.

I look around to gain my bearings. The crowd is dispersing across the empty street and there's only a quiet snow flurry and buzz of energy filling the air. Did I really just spend the entire parade losing myself in Maddox? Watching one of his walls crumble as he accepted another piece of me was a wish come true, and only Sadie could draw me away.

Although he kept his hands to himself, he allowed me to connect us. No hesitation or concern for what I might do next registered in his body language or eyes. Those windows into his thoughts gave off mostly positive emotions, and I'll take that all day long. In that one hour, we made more progress than any other since he returned, and I can no longer deny that I'm falling for him all over again.

"I know it's Frank in a Santa costume," Sadie continues, "but we always get a picture with him."

"Sure, sweetheart." I cup her cheek, appreciating my mature girl and wishing for time to slow down in that department at the same time.

She leaps over my outstretched legs to get to Maddox with Trixie following and my hand slips from his thigh. "Want to come, sweetie?"

His attention moves to her and Trixie crawling into his lap. After the leap we made tonight, I'm begging the universe to make him say yes. I need more time. *We* need more time for the idea of us to settle in his mind.

"I'd love to," he says before rising to his feet.

Sadie collects Trixie and reaches for his hand. Surprised, his eyes snap to her before a grin emerges, and she gives him one back, content with his instant acceptance. Unbridled joy sweeps me away like the gentle flow of a river, and my heart might explode if any more beautiful moments happen tonight. But I certainly wouldn't complain if they did.

Listening to them chat on our way to the tree lighting ceremony, it's easy to bask in the warmth of their sweet friendship. I laugh and swoon and chime in a time or two until I remember where we're going. The tree is installed outside the gazebo. The same place where I broke it off with Maddox nine years ago. I'm worried about how he'll react to being there with me again and if it will shatter all we gained tonight as our lives were that regretful night.

Another block later, I can see the top of the tree, and my heart won't stop throwing itself against my ribcage.

When we can go no further, Maddox lifts Sadie so she can watch the ceremony over the crowd. Hoping her sweet face will cool my frazzled nerves, I tilt my head up, but my eyes land on Maddox instead. He holds me captive with that pensive gaze of his, and I have no idea what he's feeling. I'm too frantic to process what I see in him. Given our history, I fear the worst— emotions exploding, a revisit of that dreadful night, unrecoverable setbacks, seeing the cloud of hurt in his kaleidoscope eyes.

I fight against the punch of surprise when his fingers glide down my palm and lace with mine, sending me the opposite message—he's okay and we're even better. After everything that's happened to keep us apart and all we left undone, I have no idea how I got so lucky to have this breathtaking man back in my life. But one thing's for sure, I'll never take him for granted ever again.

We spend the next two hours playing games at the rec center behind Loving's Park. I'm happy to learn Maddox hasn't lost his competitive side, and he brings out the same in Sadie. I laugh until I cry at those two going at it with the bobbing for gifts activity and again at the snowball toss.

Best of all was hearing Sadie giggle every time she tossed the beanbags during Rudolph cornhole. Each bag was decorated as a different reindeer, their thin, dangly legs flailing off their square body as they sailed through the air into boards painted as rooftops. Sadie and I faced off against Maddox—the view of him joking and laughing along with her was all the reward I needed— but I'm happy to report, the girls took the trophy, which consisted of reindeer food for the yard. Sadie tried to soften the blow to Maddox's ego by inviting him to sprinkle the loot at her grandparents' and Nana's houses on Christmas Eve.

"They may be too old to believe in Santa, but everyone deserves a little reindeer magic," she says, too wise for her own good.

He doesn't make any promises, and I try not to let that bother me. We have a long way to go and had too much fun to ruin it with all the lingering what-ifs.

Just before closing, we enter the lobby to get our photo taken with Santa Frank, owner of Frankie's Restaurant and Pub on Main Street. He's been picking up children and smiling through photo after photo all night but doesn't complain when our shoot runs past quitting time. First, Sadie poses with him. Next, she adds Trixie, then me. After the last shot, Sadie invites Maddox into our photoshoot. He jogs over, picks up Sadie and Trixie in one arm, and smiles for the camera, the other arm resting across Santa's shoulders.

That photo of the three of us with Santa, symbolizes more than our reconnecting. Maddox is smiling more, and he seems happier—my number one wish coming true. He held my hand and Sadie's earlier, which means he's letting us in and emerging from behind his cracked shell. Who knew baby steps could feel so good?

"Thank you for tonight," I say awkwardly, standing in the hallway outside our apartment once again after Maddox walks us upstairs. Words aren't forming as quickly as I'd prefer with him looking like he wants another opportunity to follow through on our first kiss.

"Would you ... Um." My hand involuntarily flings itself toward the door in a sudden explosion of nerves. "Like to come in for a bit? I had such a great time I don't want it to end."

"Me too, but I better get home."

"I understand." Disappointment takes over, and my gaze lowers to the floor in a search for a way to stop it. It doesn't seem possible to crave someone this much—to need their touch more than air to breathe—but it's because he withholds so much of himself.

I've never given up the reins before and let the other person call the shots. Any other time and with teenage Maddox, I always went after what I wanted. With this version of him, I have no say in what happens between us, and that's only fair. He didn't get a say when I broke things off, and I refuse to do that to him again. We'll move at the speed he's comfortable with, but it doesn't make it any easier to—

Two scuffed boots step into my view, and his familiar pine scent has nostalgia flooding my thoughts. I've missed this closeness and my body's response to him. Tiny bumps appear in a wave down my arms and legs, and I shiver with eager anticipation. His finger curls under my chin, tugging softly until his handsome face is all I see. Holding my gaze, his eyes darken with a slight sensual haze before lowering to fixate on my mouth.

Yes, please.

His lips part slightly in a decadent tease on his way to me. It feels daring, him tempting me and watching my reaction to this huge step. His hot, rapid breaths kiss my cheek. All I have to do is rise onto my toes, and my lips would be on his.

God, Maddox, I beg. *Please don't stop.* I've been one thousand percent in and waiting for this moment since I heard he was in town. We need to determine if our spark hits as potent as it used to. Based on my body trembling with need for him, I'd bet the store it does that and more.

My hands clench into fists by my sides, knowing I can't touch him without permission.

"Maddox …" His name comes out in an airy plea, and I hope he hears how much I want this. How much I want *him*.

"I have a question." His stripped-down tone sends an electric current through me, and I shudder from the jolt of it.

Holding his gaze, I urge him to stay and fight through any doubt that might be forming. "Ask me anything." *Just don't run.*

"Can I kiss you?"

Relief gushes through me, providing more bliss than a double-size cup of caramel macchiato. "Yes."

In one smooth motion, he drops Trixie and frames my face with both hands. His sensual touch is everything I dreamed it would be—confident, possessive, powerful, yet gentle. From that one motion of surrender, my legs waver, and I clutch his wrists to regain my balance. I don't want to miss one second of this.

His soft lips skim over mine, careful and light at first as if he's letting the good memories of us back in one at a time before giving in to me. I'd love to know where he finds the restraint. My body feels like a new flame—erratic and aching to consume everything it touches. I need more.

An overpowering moan rumbles in my throat, and his muscles tense in response. I didn't mean to give him more signals, but this slow anticipation is torture. Nothing compares to being kissed by Maddox Henderson, and I can't wait any longer.

With my head spinning, I lean into the searing kiss, pouring all I have into it and him until my entire body goes numb. My head takes off like a balloon, floating in a cloud of bliss. I wanted this so badly, and what a relief it is to know the wait had been so damn worth it.

The soft rub of his evening whiskers around his capable lips only adds to his sex appeal. Especially when his hands slip into my hair to angle my head back and deepen the kiss. My own trail up his rigid abs, feeling the strength in them. I can't help but picture all these muscles and what the bulk of him might feel like pressed against me without all these layers. Hungry for more, I go to grip his shoulders just as he releases me, and I stumble a few steps to catch myself.

"You should give me a warning before doing that," I say between gulps of air. The sampling of what he's capable of left me breathless, dizzy with desire, and wishing he hadn't ended it so quickly.

Leaning against the opposite wall, he's as disheveled and dazed as I am. His hand scrubs over his jaw as he studies me. The smooth motion brings my gaze back to his wet, kiss-swollen lips and another round of need dashes through my core.

"I thought I did," he says, the gravelly tone in his voice tipping me off balance again.

"I meant before stopping. I wasn't ready."

"Oh."

"Did you feel it?" I find the nerve to ask. I have to know.

His hands dig inside his pants pockets. "Yeah. Too much."

The good news bubbles through me like a sugar rush, and I can't stop my grin from giving away my satisfaction. "I'm glad." Taking the rare encouragement, I cross to him and reach for his hand. "Are you okay with that?"

"With what?"

"Feeling our chemistry alive and well and then some."

His free hand tucks a lock of hair behind my ear, his eyes following. "I'm getting used to the idea."

I'm grateful for the smile he adds as punctuation to that statement because I couldn't read him. He's stoic again, pensive, and even that is sexy. The man has a thousand different expressions, and each one makes me swoon. "Good. In case you're wondering, I'm already there, waiting for you."

He lowers his head for a safe, tender kiss before saying, "How about we start with a date? Just the two of us?"

Best idea I've heard in years. I'm doing cartwheels inside, but I play it cool to not set off his flight reflex again. I've already gotten far more than I expected and probably deserve. "Seems like the next logical baby step. I'd love to go on a date with you."

"How about dinner sometime next week?"

The ambiguous time frame means he's still hesitant to accept the notion of us. He may be getting better at being near me, but our history hasn't been completely forgotten. If raising Sadie has taught me anything, it's patience, and he's worth waiting for.

"Next week sounds great."

"Will you and Sadie be coming over for the Sunday get together? Aaron and Kendall will be home by then."

"Oh, that's wonderful. We plan to be there. We'll probably head downtown for the Spectacular events afterward. Maybe we can persuade you to come with us."

"We'll see. Sundays are my only drama-free day to work on the bookshop since it's closed."

"Alright." I hold back my disappointment and put on a smile. "If you need a break, there will be a bake sale and plenty of holiday activities to re-energize you." Good grief, I sound like a low-budget commercial.

"I'll keep that in mind." When awkwardness switches off the current bouncing between us, he calls for Trixie and ends the night before I can find another reason to delay the inevitable. "Will you tell Sadie good night for me?"

"Of course."

Collecting Trixie when she trots over, he pecks my cheek on his way by. I watch him escape down the hall and disappear into the stairwell, marveling at him yet again. I'm worse than a cheap commercial. I'm a cliché romantic comedy with dramatic overactors and a predictable plot.

Beautifully broken male character guards his tender

heart from the female character because he's been hurt before and doesn't want to ever feel that again.

Female character pines after him all hours of the day and night, always coming up with ridiculous excuses to spend time with him in hopes of tearing down his walls once and for all.

Whichever absurd scene I'm acting out each time we meet, I know our second chance movie will have a happy ending if my beautifully broken Maddox can release his big, tender heart from its cage.

Maddox

Arriving at the apartment before sunrise, I'd planned to make some progress before the Sunday gathering, but I've accomplished next to nothing with Carmen's kiss on the brain. Doesn't help that the location where it happened and the woman herself are just a few feet down the hall.

Standing outside her door last night, I promised myself I wouldn't get carried away. That I'd stay controlled and use the moment to assess my ever-changing mindset where she's concerned. Want her. Run away. Give an inch. Take two. Let feelings in. Empty them out and start over. I thought I could handle touching her like that. I thought I was strong enough.

At first, I was proud of myself for keeping the kiss somewhat contained, but damn, if she didn't destroy my every expectation and send my dormant desire into overdrive anyway. Fire shot through me everywhere her body pressed against mine. Then, who we once had been flooded my thoughts as if we'd never lost it, and I panicked. Especially when that moan of pleasure fluttered in her throat and sent my resolve to keep things in a safe zone up in flames. I could feel myself crossing every line I drew and had to take a step back before I did something I shouldn't.

That's when regret set in, and it hadn't let up since. I wish I would have shown more of me, but I'd been afraid to scare her, let her down, disappoint her. Would I be enough? Would she feel the same after experiencing that side of me? Would it ruin how far we'd come? I couldn't get out of my head and allow myself to truly enjoy it. And even I know how ridiculous and stupid that is. If I want to try being with Carmen again, it's time I act like it.

The next opportunity she allows, I won't restrain my emotions. Giving myself permission to set them free is the only way to determine if my developing feelings are real. I need to let go, and when I do, I can only hope she'll catch me.

Until I hear activity next door, I keep busy quietly cleaning and measuring for new cabinets in the kitchen and bathroom. I'm writing down the last size I need to order when my phone chimes with a new text message.

Aaron: Dude, you said you'd be here.

Me: You're home already? I thought you weren't arriving until the party.

Kendall: Surprise!

Me: Best one ever. I'll be there as soon as I can.

Cooper: Don't bother.

Me: What does that mean?

Aaron: He's just messin with ya. We couldn't wait.

Me: Wait for what?

Kendall: Surprise!

The thunderous noise of three sets of boots pounding on the back staircase has me tucking my phone away and rushing toward the storm.

Kendall emerges first and launches herself into my arms, wrapping me in unconditional love. A few seconds later, Aaron adds himself to the hug, making Ember Falls finally feel like home again.

"What is this?" Cooper asks, strolling into the apartment.

"A hug. Might do you some good to get one occasionally," Kendall scolds, always on Cooper for following in my grumpy footsteps and embracing it ten-fold. The things soldiers see and do in the Army can do that to a person, and he's served longer than me.

"I get and give plenty of hugs, thank you."

"To someone other than Mom and Izzie," she clarifies with a wink.

"Whatever. Anyway, I was referring to this … Is it an apartment?"

Stepping back from my two siblings, my arms open to the small living room. "Welcome to Nana's nest egg."

"I love the color," Kendall says, guiding a hand over the light gray walls.

"Does she need money or something?" Aaron asks.

"Yeah. She's barely making what's required to keep the lights on—I checked the books—and she hasn't done any building maintenance in years. You'll never hear her admit any of that, though."

Cooper inspects my handiwork in the kitchen. "Not bad. Can we help?"

"I'd love that, but not today. We have a party to go to, and I want to hear about college life." I insert myself between Kendall and Aaron and drape an arm over their shoulders. "Coop can drive while you fill me in."

"Great." Cooper complains. "Now I get to hear it for a third time."

"You'll live. Let's go."

Chapter 13

Maddox

At the Sunday gathering later, Kendall finds me alone on the living room couch and plops down beside me. She takes me in, covering my entire body with her eyes. It's great to see her usual sass hasn't suffered while I've been away.

"I have to say, big brother, I didn't expect to see you so relaxed with *her* here."

"To whom are you referring, little sister?"

"Don't give me that." She smacks my arm with the back of her hand. "You know who."

"Who else, right?"

Her forefinger taps the end of her nose. What does that even mean?

"It's been a crazy few days," I answer, hoping it's the correct one.

She glares at me, her long lashes holding steady above dark eyes. Guess I failed. "And …" she urges.

"And what?"

"You tell me. You can't say something like that and let it dangle."

"Let's just say we've passed a few hurdles and hit our stride, but we're far from the finish line."

There she goes, staring at me again. "That's it?"

"I love you, Ken, but this is not the place for that conversation."

Her eyes graze the room and mine follow. Within listening range, dozens of people are standing nearby. She knows as well as I do how the gossip train works in this town.

"You're right, but you're going to fill me—"

"There you are." Jamie steps over the coffee table in one long stride and sits on it to face us.

"You still come?" I say in awe, reaching a hand out to shake his. Before the Sunday family gathering turned into a block party, Mom would let us kids invite a friend to give us someone to play with. Jamie's been my best friend since kindergarten, which meant he was always here, growing up alongside me and my siblings. He's more like a brother than a friend to us all.

"Every week."

"Except the week I come home," I complain, but he doesn't seem the least bit concerned about my feelings.

"Sorry. You crawling out of hiding doesn't trump an injured thoroughbred, but Ken Doll's homecoming does." He turns to my sister, and I brace for the rousing to begin. Rarely do these two take a break, and their comeback battles are always epic. "Glad to have you back. There's no one to pick on at the farm. The cows have a terrible sense of humor."

"What about that stupid goat of yours? He seems to have

your intellectual prowess."

"He's too busy living the good life with his harem."

"Like I said …"

"You must be thinking about all the boys you're stringing along at that fancy school of yours." He tosses back the beer he brought, obviously proud of himself. But I know my sister, and she's not the least bit embarrassed by whatever he's poking fun at.

Slowly, she crosses her legs and leans forward, threading her fingers around a jean-covered knee. "Jokes on you, Jameson. I don't date boys. I much prefer men who know what they want and have the balls to go after it."

Jamie's jaw gapes open in retort, but nothing comes out. Instead, he stares at her with a dumb expression on his face. Tired of waiting for his equally dumb response, she rises off the couch and struts out of the room.

"What just happened?" I ask. Rarely is Jamie muted by anyone, especially women. He always has something to say to them.

He shakes out of his stupor to drain the rest of his beer. "What do you mean?"

"That weird exchange between you two. Have you—"

"What? She's your little sister."

"Exactly, and seven years younger than you with *teen* in her age."

"Which is precisely why what you're implying isn't a concern."

He's saying the right things, but the words come out a little too shaky to be convincing. Kendall is stunning and doesn't look or act like a typical teenager. The poster child for confident, powerhouse females, she's too fearless for her own good.

I'm not surprised Jamie noticed. After all, he appreciates

women a little too much and isn't afraid to let them know. He's more than earned his playboy reputation, but whatever he's *appreciating* about my sister and her new no-longer-a-little-girl curves, better be kept to himself, including his playboy hands.

Those hands raise in protest, reading my expression. "Come on, man. It's me."

"I know. That's what I'm worried about."

"There you are," Nana says when she finds me, Cooper, and Aaron in the sunroom.

"Which of us are you about to embarrass?" Cooper asks, earning an eye roll from Nana.

"Boy, everything I do is for your own good."

"Okay. What *good* are you doing this time?"

Her grin gives us a warning signal, and we all react instinctively. My abs constrict to prepare for the blow, Cooper slumps back in his chair, already defeated, and Aaron drains his beer.

"I signed you all up to volunteer at an event tonight," she informs us. "It's the biggest fundraiser the Spectacular has each year."

The three of us groan in harmony.

"What is it?" Aaron snatches the beer bottle from my hand and gulps down half.

I snatch it back. "Get your own."

"I'm empty and need the boost to get me through this."

"Shut up, you two." Nana's finger waves back and forth between us. "Just arrive at the gazebo at six."

Together, we check our watches. We have less than two hours to prepare.

"The volunteer coordinator will give you instructions. Do

everything she says," she warns. "The Spectacular is important to our town's prosperity, and we all need to pitch in to make as much money as possible."

"Why can't you have that same attitude with the shop?" I fuss, hoping to gain some leeway in that department.

"I do. You just don't like my old-fashioned ways."

"No. I don't like your—"

"Have fun tonight." She pivots, walking off like she won, and I don't even know what game we were playing.

"I don't like this. She's up to something," Cooper says, as experienced in reading Nana as I am.

"Agreed." I reach inside the nearby cooler and pass around fresh beers. "We better have fun while we can. Someone else can drive us there."

Cooper raises his bottle for a toast. "To us. No matter what gets thrown our way, we always have each other's backs."

"And I have a feeling we'll be needing that support tonight."

"I got you, my brothas," Aaron pipes in, his newly turned twenty-one-year-old at a frat party persona shining through in full color. Damn, I love that kid and hope he never loses his zest for life like his big brothers have.

"You've got to be shitting me," Cooper grumbles when we arrive at the gazebo as instructed. "Where's Nana?"

"You won't find her, and she knows we have no way out now." Trixie squirms in my arms from the sudden burst of tension.

"Hell, yeah," Aaron says after noticing the kissing booth sign hanging above the gazebo's entrance. He's had more to drink and weighs less than Cooper and me, which means he hasn't come down from our prepping activity back at the house.

"Ah, the Henderson boys." A woman inside the gazebo clasps her hands under her chin and makes her way to us, her short, black hair bobbing above her shoulders with each step. "I can't tell you how much we appreciate you signing up. You'll be quite the draw." Her brow wiggles above thick, red-rimmed glasses.

Another groan of complaint escapes Cooper's throat.

"What's the matter, Cooper?" she asks, frowning. "A few hours of kissing doesn't sound like the bachelor's paradise?"

"A few hours?" he screeches.

"Come on. I'll get you set up." Back to her peppy self, she waves a gloved hand and struts back to the gazebo, expecting us to follow. When two of us don't move, she stops on the steps and motions again. Behind her, Aaron mimics her enthusiasm, almost drawing a grin out of me. Almost.

"If we don't do this, we'll have Nana to deal with," I say to Cooper, talking through our sticky predicament aloud.

"You want to kiss strangers and women we've grown up with all our lives?"

"Hell no, but what choice do we have?"

"Plenty. We have skills no one else here has." He gives me a side-eyed smirk, clearly more intoxicated than I thought, and I laugh. It's nice seeing my brother relax for a change. He's always been the serious one of us three boys.

Following his lead, I play along. "True, but we can't use those on all the women who'll want a sliver of us to satisfy their fantasies."

"It *is* nice to be wanted," he gets out before a chuckle. "Come on. Let's get it over with."

We climb the stairs, and Joanna—apparently, that's our kissing booth pimp's name—positions us around three square tables covered in green fabric and shaped like a U inside. She explains the two rules in greater detail than necessary—in summary, no tongue or touching the customers (other than lips and cheeks, of course)—and leaves us with, "Have fun."

I set Trixie on a small blanket at my feet and settle in for an interesting evening. Thirty minutes before the booth opens, a line of customers begins to form outside the gazebo. With each passing minute, the line grows, snaking through Loving's Park until I can no longer see the end.

"Where did all these women come from?" Cooper leans back to ask me.

"Who knows?"

From my vantage point, facing the entrance, many faces in line are unknown to me, but I recognize Jada and the mayor's granddaughter, Harper. Guess she isn't happy with our mistletoe misses.

With a sigh, I zip up my coat as a breeze presses through the gazebo, jostling the string lights lining the ceiling. They flicker and draw my attention, along with a few four-letter words. I shouldn't be surprised a Christmas-themed kissing booth has mistletoe, but I'm caught off guard nonetheless. There's a bunch hanging over each table with another in the center … exactly where I'd installed it on Carmen's eighteenth birthday.

"What's wrong?" Cooper asks, and I answer with a point to the offender. "Ouch."

"Yeah."

"Alright, ladies," Joanna begins, taking her position at the entrance. "The kissing booth is now open. Make your donation with Veronica here."

She motions toward my new friend sitting at a table by the steps, and I'd give anything for her stellar advice on how to get me through yet another uncomfortable situation. I seem to be stumbling into a lot of those lately.

"Enjoy!" Joanna says and steps aside to assume her hostess position at the steps.

Cooper sucks in a quick breath. "Shit."

"Agreed."

"Bring on the chicks," Aaron says, rubbing his bare hands together like he's about to eat his favorite sandwich.

At that, my and Cooper's eyes roll with annoyance.

"Hey, Aaron, did you see Addie's in line?" Cooper teases, and Aaron's head whips around so fast I worry about him getting whiplash. "Who do you think she's here for?"

"You see her? Where?"

"I doubt she came for you, given your history. She must have a crush on one of your handsome older brothers."

"What happened to sticking together through this?" Aaron whines, his happy buzz sufficiently doused.

"You're right. I'm sorry. Anyway, we'll find out soon who she has eyes for."

"Why do you care? I thought your beady eyes only saw Izzie."

I snicker, causing Cooper to turn on me.

"You can't laugh at that," he demands. "Your one-track mind is worse."

"My bad."

"We should've brought the cooler," Cooper grumbles under his breath.

I want to laugh, but my first customer, Harper Whitacre, has stepped up to my table.

"Hi, Maddox. Here we are again." She flashes a timid grin. "Except this time, you can't run away."

"I didn't run," I quip, but we both know better. I most certainly ran away as I always do. For our third mistletoe encounter, she's got me cornered.

She curls her forefinger in a come-hither motion, and I give in, leaning forward on the table to meet her waiting pucker. Her glossy lips barely touch mine, and I'm not complaining. She doesn't either and moves to Cooper's table with a giggle as he braces for impact.

Watching them, I wonder if he's kissed anyone since entering the Army. If I had to guess, my answer would be no. He's too loyal to the woman who holds his heart without knowing it. I'm sure my stellar example isn't encouraging him to take the leap and get out of the friend's zone. Look what happened when I tried it.

Our little brother takes the opposite approach. Aaron gives himself away without considering the consequences, never committing to anyone or anything—other than baseball. He's an everlasting sparkler, burning his chances of ever finding something real with a reckless brilliance that overpowers the world surrounding him. I'm not sure which is worse—his oblivion, Cooper's sacrifice, or my hypersensitivity.

Aaron twists in his seat, excited to see if Harper purchased a kiss from him too. She matches his goofy smile with her own giddy version and makes her way to him. In the full-steam-ahead F-it style he's perfected, he stands for a better angle and lays a long, sweltering kiss on her lips, ignoring rule number one. Cheers erupt outside the gazebo as they slowly part and wipe each other's lips with a thumb. Her arms pump high above her head, encouraging the over-eager crowd on her way to the exit.

Aaron drops into the chair, his usual arrogance taking over his face. "Who's up next?"

"We'll see if you're just as eager when Addie comes to our tables and not yours," Cooper teases, knocking Aaron's excitement down a few notches, and I swat a warning across his shoulder.

"Let him have his fun before he ends up like us."

We get through the next dozen customers without incident or tongues involved, and a quick inspection of the line tells me Jada is about three back from the donation table.

"Great," I let out between customers, and Cooper leans my way.

"What?"

"Do you know Jada Miller?"

"I've heard the name. What's the problem?"

"She's coming up in line. I knew her late husband, and we spent some time together at the duck race. She thinks it was a date."

"Was it?"

"Not to me, but she asked me to kiss her, and I couldn't. Carmen was there too."

"Look at you, proving you're Ember Falls' most eligible bachelor like everyone thinks."

"Shut up." I dismiss the ridiculous comment. "Kissing her seemed wrong then and certainly now."

He shrugs. "You've kissed twenty women tonight."

"I know, but this one is different. We've spent time together."

"Are you and Carmen exclusive?" he lowers his voice to ask.

"No, but—"

"It's just a fundraiser, Madds. Everyone here knows it doesn't mean anything. You're not leading her on or cheating on whatever you got brooding with Carmen."

"I guess you're right."

"Who knows, maybe she has the hots for me and passes you by."

"We can only hope."

To keep the nerves at bay, I don't watch the line but count the women who enter the gazebo. Jada should be next, and when someone stops in front of my table, my eyes reluctantly raise up her coat to her face.

"Carmen?"

"Veronica is rooting for us," she whispers. "And I made an extra donation for her letting me cut the line."

Grateful for Veronica yet again, I make the snap decision to honor her by following the advice I ignored yesterday. A sudden boost of adrenaline has me shooting to my feet to do what young people do and have some fun. Without regard for our audience, I take Carmen's hand and guide us through the tables and down the back exit to a chorus of *boos*. I thought about disappearing with her like this every time I saw her at the house earlier, but I let our nosy company stop me.

She didn't tell me she'd be here tonight, making this surprise feel like the perfect opportunity to follow through on what I promised myself. I won't let an audience or my rollercoaster thoughts hold me back. There's only one way to figure out how I feel about us …

At the first tree we come to, I gently push her back against it and break all the rules. The rules of the kissing booth and the ones I put on myself, preventing my heart from relinking with Carmen's. My hands grip her waist as our lips clash through a kiss I'll never forget. This is how free our first kiss yesterday should have felt. While I enjoyed every millisecond of that kiss, I'm uninhibited and unrestricted by pain with this one, and I never want it to end.

My heart races in my ears, drowning out the world. I can't think of anything except all the ways I've wanted to savor her since she became mine all those years ago. Only this time, she's not telling me to save my passion. Quite the opposite in fact. The verbal and physical cues I'm receiving from her are encouraging me to take more, touch where I want, and explore like we're somewhere private. My blood heats a few degrees as she tugs me closer by the collar of my jacket, and our lips part on a deep, satisfied hum that originates in my toes.

I have no idea why it's taken me so long to do this. The voltage we generate is inescapable, and I'm tired of running from it. Tired of living without this exhilaration, this passion, this woman.

"God, Maddox," she says on an exhale, the hot air grazing my already steaming skin and sending the equivalent of sunrays through my veins. It's twenty degrees out here, but with the way her body melts into mine, the park feels more like a tropical paradise.

"I don't want to kiss anyone else but you."

"Music to my ears," she purrs, her lashes gliding open to find me in sensual slow motion. The undisguised hunger in her cobalt eyes does something to me, and I almost resort to dragging her to her apartment like a caveman.

Reading my mind—or I look as one-track minded as I feel—and says, "Come over tonight."

The thought of holding her through the night flashes a vivid image, and my body shivers with greed. There's no ambiguity in her offer, powering my imagination like an oversized generator, but I can't allow myself to be that selfish. Not this soon. After all, I'd only unlocked the cage around my heart yesterday, and it needs time to acclimate.

"I want to … badly," I confess on a long sigh. The truth is the only answer I can form with her body dumbing down mine. I push a hand over my hair and grip the back of my neck, searching for a way to function like the gentleman my parents and the Army raised me to be instead of a dog in heat.

"Why do I feel a *but* coming?" She continues searching my face for the answer.

"Not yet. Is that okay?"

"I meant what I said, Maddox. You choose the pace. I'm not going anywhere."

"Say it again," I demand, drawing her closer.

"I'm here with you and for only you. However long it takes and whether you're here or in another state, I'm never leaving you a—"

I don't wait for her to finish that sentence. It affects me in a way I can't begin to explain, so I settle on showing her instead. With my body screaming for her, I lower my head for another taste and savor her until Aaron's voice registers.

"Get back here. My lips are getting chapped!" he complains for the entire town to hear.

My forehead presses to hers in protest. Where did my commitment to ignoring our audience and having fun disappear to? "I don't want to go back."

"It's okay. I'll wait for you by the hot cocoa stand. However long it takes."

The reminder hits home again, and I need to hold her again. Except this time, the fog of desire isn't blocking out emotions I've kept tucked away, and I feel things changing. So. Many. Things. All the ways I held her through the many stages of our relationship growing up, pale in comparison to this one, and it's opening something inside me. My heart? Maybe. My willingness to forgive? Sounds like the logical choice. My thoughts on a future I thought I'd never have? No doubt.

With a squeeze of my hand, she disappears into the darkness before I can finish analyzing what she just did to me. It will have to wait until my brain starts working again. My weak, neanderthal legs stumble back to the gazebo only to be received by a round of applause and an irritated little brother.

"Good Lord It's about time," Aaron says while applying lip

balm. "I had to pick up your slack."

"I figured you'd thank me for that."

"I'll thank you for Jada—she is so hot." He shoots me a grin over his shoulder and wiggles his dark brow. "But everyone else has been twice my age or older. More your speed."

All three of our phones chime with a text, saving me from having to respond, and we dig into our pockets in unison.

Kendall: How's it going? [kissy face emoji]

Aaron: Great until Madds dipped.

Me: I'm back so stop your whining.

Kendall: Why'd you leave? Did your lips get tired? [laughing emoji]

Cooper: Carmen cut in line, and he didn't want an audience for that kiss.

Aaron: Which sucked. I wanted to witness their first kiss.

Me: Wasn't the first.

Aaron: WHAT?!

Kendall: No way!

Cooper: Knew it.

Kendall: I need details … again with the

secrets.

Me: I don't kiss and tell. Hence the disappearing act.

Aaron: Damn.

Cooper: Can we get back to work, please?

Kendall: Kissing is work, Coop? You need to get out more.

Chapter 14

Maddox

Over the next two hours, every kiss compounds my need to erase them from my memory with the feel of Carmen's skin. Addie must have changed her mind because after Cooper saw her in the beginning, she never reappeared. To say Aaron is disappointed would be the biggest understatement of the year, but he'll have to drown his sorrows with someone else tonight. I have plans.

When the last woman exits the gazebo, I say goodbye to my brothers, jog across Main Street, and down Braddock Road to the hot cocoa stand. As promised, Carmen is waiting for me, but she's not alone. Addie sits with her at a picnic table, and they're deep in conversation.

She sees me stop inside the tent's entrance, and I have all her attention. Following her gaze, Addie grins at me, then leaves to give us space. She and anyone with a view of us can hear our silent conversation this time. It's loud, palpable, and as compelling as it has always been. So much for keeping our budding reconnection private.

On my way to her, she watches my every step and when I straddle the bench to sit facing her.

"Thank you for waiting."

"I always will, Maddox. Until you say otherwise, and probably even then."

I take her hand under the table to let her feel how much that statement affects me because I don't have the words.

"Where's Sadie?" I finally ask.

"Weekly grandparent's sleepover," she says, letting me know with her eyes that the offer for our own sleepover still stands. "Where's Trixie?"

Jumping up in a panic, I bump my knee on the table and bounce through the radiating pain while searching for her. She's not here. "I must have left her at the gazebo."

"Let's go." She grabs my hand, and we take off toward Loving's Park.

When we arrive, the gazebo has been cleared and no one lingers about to ask if they've seen her. I whip out my phone and send a group text to my siblings.

Me: Anyone have Trixie?

Kendall: You lost that sweet baby?

Me: No time for that.

Cooper: I don't.

Aaron: Nope. So glad you texted. My lips are too sore to talk.

Kendall: You need to find her. Dottie would be devastated.

Me: Not helping.

Kendall: Just making sure you know how dire your situation is.

Me: Got it.

Our park search leaves us empty-handed, and my military, law enforcement, and yoga training do nothing to calm my panic. I've resorted to Dottie's fretting, terrified she's injured or wandering through town cold and alone, wondering why I abandoned her. Give me a reckless criminal over a lost, heartbroken puppy any day. This is torture.

Nearly an hour after working our way through town, we stop at the end of Main Street, and I plop onto the bench outside the pool hall to think. Not only will Dottie be devastated, but Nana will never let me live this down. And if I'm being honest, Dottie isn't the only one who would be upset if anything happened to Trixie. She's kept me company through too many lonely and baffling hours not to form an attachment.

"Maddox ..." Carmen points through the windows of Billy's Billiards and Bar. "Is that ..."

My eyes dart through the busy room and land on Trixie chasing pool balls on top of a table. A bearded guy in a brown leather vest with peppermint candy buttons and a white cowboy hat gently taps them with the cue to give her something to chase.

More men and women in matching attire, tough yet festive, and muscular physiques watch from the surrounding bar tables.

"I've got this."

"Got what?"

With the determination of Santa on Christmas Eve, she shoots inside and stalks toward what I can only classify as a biker gang with holiday spirit. I follow closely behind in case a bar fight breaks out since Carmen looks ready to start one.

"Oh, thank you so much," she says, pressing a palm to her chest in her best Dottie impression.

"Excuse me?" Cowboy Hat asks.

"You found my baby." She reaches for Trixie, but he steps in front of her, blocking her path. Carmen's head tilts as her hand finds her punched-out hip in a *no, you didn't* stance.

"How do I know she's yours?" he challenges. "She doesn't look excited to see you."

"That's because she prefers my boyfriend."

Like Aaron's had earlier when he heard Addie's name, my head snaps to Carmen at her casual use of the *boyfriend* title. The room blurs, combining the conversation and loud, overhead music into the voice of Charlie Brown's teacher—all noise with no discernable words or lyrics. Doesn't matter. I'm too lost, trying to figure out where my opinion falls on the boyfriend matter, to comprehend it anyway.

On the one hand, neither of us is dating anyone else. We're exclusive without labels. On the other hand, we only reconnected a week ago. While I can't deny my attraction or residual feelings for her, there's plenty left for us to figure out.

Shapes and shadows move in my line of sight, but I see nothing until Trixie yelps, yanking me from my trance. Refocusing on my surroundings, I locate her in the biker's massive hands beside me. Her little legs wiggle in the air in a fight to get to me. The evidence must be adequate to convince him of Carmen's earlier statement because he hands her over with disappointment drooping his overly tanned face.

"Thank you so much for keeping her safe," Carmen says over her shoulder while pushing me toward the exit.

The cool air slaps my skin, and thanks to my wayward mind, it's a quiet trek back to the General Store.

She stops outside the building's private back entrance and takes my hand. "You don't have to walk me upstairs. It's late, and I can see you formulating your refusal to extend the night if asked. I'd like to save us both the embarrassment."

"Carmen …"

"It's okay. I understand," she says sweetly, and I believe her.

"Actually, I would like to if you're up for it."

"Of course I am. You never have to ask or wonder."

"I'd like to talk."

Amusement hums in her throat. "Does that mean you're all kissed out?"

"Not where you're concerned."

"Good to know." Slowly, she inserts the key into the deadbolt with a smile, sending a streak of desire straight through my midsection and into regions I shouldn't be thinking about.

We walk up the back staircase, and once inside her apartment, I set Trixie on the living room chair. Exhausted from her adventures, she spins in a few circles and falls into immediate slumber.

"Can I get you a drink?"

"A beer sounds great if you have it."

"I bought a six-pack earlier this week to be prepared for this moment." With an adorable wink, she dives into the refrigerator and joins me on the couch soon after, passing over one of the bottles she carried over.

Following a long pull, I start at ground zero. "When you were talking with the gang, you—"

"The gang?" She giggles, knowing exactly who I'm referring to.

The question was asked just to get a rise out of me, and it worked. I'm back to teetering on an unsteady foundation with the purpose of this conversation coming up next.

"They were obviously a biker gang—threatening or not."

"Got it. Please continue."

I catch her grinning behind the bottle and wish my man card hadn't been ripped to pieces by this whole Trixie conundrum.

"Anyway, I can't stop thinking about you calling me your boyfriend. It's been a long time since I've heard that grace your lips."

"Oh." Sensing my unease, she sets her drink on the coffee table and rests an elbow on the back cushion.

I know she wishes for me to be excited instead of freaked out, but I can only give her honesty. We deserve that much while we're wading through this strange new relationship territory together.

"I was acting," she explains. "And that title was a lot simpler than the complicated truth."

"What truth?"

"That we're exes trying to determine if a second chance is in the cards as we take baby steps toward something neither of us can see from where we're at in this non-committed arrangement."

"That is complicated."

"See? He didn't need to get all up in our business, so I shortened it to something he would understand to get us out of there. I'm sorry if it made you uncomfortable."

I considered my initial physical reaction to the idea and how

I feel now that it's settled in my overworked brain. The before and after perspectives are night and day. "It just stunned me at first."

"And now?"

Wading through my thoughts, I take in my view, and she does the same to me. The soft glow of the lamp on her long waves has me itching to trail my fingers through them again. Her eyes, tinted navy with desire, watch me as I reach for the lock of hair falling over her shoulder.

"I think …" I pause to brush a thumb across her cheek, loving the pink tint my touch puts there. "I'd like to try on the title for a bit."

The confession brings a satisfied smile to her glossy lips before she tucks it away to continue setting up our new arrangement. "That's the best news I've heard in a while, but should we keep it secret while you see how it fits on you? Less pressure that way."

"I'd appreciate that. Nana's already on my case about my life, and I can only imagine the field day she'll have with this. I'm not ready to deal with that just yet."

"No problem. What about kissing? Do you need a break, or can we—"

My hand on the back of her neck lures her lips to mine in the most satisfying response to her question.

"Great answer." Her teeth graze her bottom lip, and I can't decide if she's recovering from the same explosion of need I got or trying to tempt me into doing it again. I'm contemplating it when she says, "Now, I'm wondering about sleepovers. Got a position on those?"

Perfect. How can I focus when I'm thinking about touching her nude body? "Let's play it by ear." *Before my heart implodes.*

"Okay." She scoots closer and drapes both legs over my

thigh. "Will you call me your girlfriend in private?"

"Every chance I can get."

Her arms raise to my shoulders, fingers combing through the hair on the back of my head. It's almost long enough for her to grasp, and I think I'll grow it out for that reason alone. Chief won't care for my hair growing longer—

I've been Carmen's for less than a few minutes and already forgotten about the main reason I came back to Ember Falls. To save my job.

Do I want to save it? I've given five years to that department and built a name for myself as a good, hard-working, ethical cop. But what kind of life did that create for me? Nothing worth nurturing, that's for sure. And after getting Carmen back, do I want to put distance between us again? Starting a new job in a new place sounds overwhelming, and I'd have no idea where to start … if I am even ready for that change.

My brain is flying through all the unknowns at a nauseating speed, and I don't notice Carmen watching me.

"What are you thinking about?" she asks, placing a hand on my chest, concern carved into every feature on her face.

"Boston."

"Oh. What about it?"

"It's two hours away." I link my fingers with hers and rest our hands on my thigh. Her other hand absently combs through my hair. The feel of her fingernails on my skin soothes my racing pulse to a slow jog.

"Do you worry about us surviving a long-distance relationship? Because I don't."

I grin at that. "It's not you I worry about."

"What do you mean?"

I can see her reading into the meaning of my statement, and her conclusions aren't flattering. "I meant my life there isn't healthy—mentally. I love what I do, but it's not enough."

She puts on a grin, her strength building a foundation for us both. "I can schedule my store responsibilities around your shifts for visits, or ..." she guides, hoping I'll finish the thought. I know she doesn't want to be the one to say it since she's been the instigator of almost every step we've taken so far.

"Or ..." I repeat to make her squirm, and it works. The sweet pink color I adore returns to her cheeks.

Lifting my hand, she kisses the inside of my wrist before finding my gaze. "What if you *didn't* go back to Boston?" Letting that sink in, she waits for the answer I don't have. "Whatever you decide, I'll support you, but if you're considering not going even the least little bit ... stay."

She blinks back tears, ripping me in two. We won't be able to keep this obscurity going for much longer. The end of my admin leave is approaching, and Carmen deserves answers. Like she wanted to do for me at eighteen, I refuse to let her push the pause button on her life while I'm learning to juggle the pieces of mine.

While I figure out where my priorities lie and what I can't live without, maybe the answers will come to me if I can relax my overthinking tendencies, clear the fog they create, and break the tether on my heart, as my mother often requests. After all, I haven't had any luck following my usual patterns and habits.

Until clarity arrives, all I can do is hold Carmen and appreciate what we are in each evolving moment of our relationship.

Chapter 15

Carmen

After Maddox leaves, I flop my weakened body across the bed and lie unmoving for hours, marveling at my continued good fortune. How in the world, after all this time, did I get him back? How can a glance, a touch, a kiss from him rock my entire body like we're discovering each other for the first time? How can I prevent him from going back?

The very idea of him choosing Boston keeps me up for the rest of the night. I'm flittering between consciousness and dozing the next morning while brewing the strongest pot of coffee I've ever made and almost don't hear the knock on the door.

"Did you forget your keys?" I call, expecting to see Sadie and one of my parents on the other side. Swinging open the door, my heart slams to a stop. "Maddox."

I force my eyes from his adorable sideways grin to the items he's carrying. A bag from Latte Da Café and two steaming cups.

"Is that what I think it is?"

"Chocolate muffins and a caramel macchiato. I heard it's your favorite morning treat."

"It is, especially when I'm stressed or worried."

"Are you either of those this morning?"

I hold his gaze, choosing to ignore my fretting through the night and focus on the positive. He's here now, and I plan to relish every second I get with him. "I'm happier than I've been in years."

"Good. Me, too."

Closing the distance between us, I frame his face. "That makes me even happier."

His head lowers his head, and like our kiss behind the gazebo, he wastes no time showing me what he's after. He'll get zero complaints from me. Taking hold of his shirt, I pull him inside and kick the door closed. I don't dare dislodge my lips from his as I take the drink carrier and bag and set them on the end table. Nothing will stop me from taking advantage of everything he's offering.

His free hands find their way to my waist inside my open robe and lift me with ease, allowing my legs to lock around him. The decorative cutouts in the door dig into my back as his sculpted body presses against me. Every glorious muscle hardens, holding me in the most satisfying position for a kiss to put our last to shame. It doesn't take long before I forget a world exists outside of our little bubble.

I'm on the verge of requesting something inappropriate for our new slow-burn arrangement when the doorknob wiggles. Sadie's voice carries through the wall, and we freeze.

His eyes widen before gently setting me down. Holding the

door closed with one hand, I shoo him into my bedroom. I'll sneak him out while Sadie gets ready for school.

"Mom! The door won't open."

"I'm coming." I give him a moment to find a hiding spot, then swing open the door. "Hi, baby. I missed you."

She trots in and hugs me, pressing her cheek to my belly. I wonder if she can smell a freshly showered Maddox on my clothes. I certainly can and hope his rustic scent stays with me all day.

"Did you have fun?"

"Yeah."

Before I can close the door, Trixie slips through the opening and stands on her hind legs for Sadie's attention.

"Hi, Trix. What are you doing here?" Kneeling, Sadie gives her excited furry friend all the rubbing she desires. "I stopped by next door to see Maddox, but he wasn't there."

"He … ugh … must have gone somewhere."

Shrugging, she drops her overnight bag beside the couch. "Did you go to the coffee shop?" She waves a finger at me. "In your pajamas?"

Glancing over the ivory silk shorts and tank top combo I'm wearing under my equally silky hot pink robe, I have no lie at the ready. I settle on the truth. "Maddox brought them."

"And he brought my fav." She wiggles the macchiato out of the holder and takes a sip.

"It's my favorite, too. Someone must have filled him in on our secret."

"He's so sweet."

And a lot of other adjectives I can't say right now.

"Shouldn't you be at work?" she asks, digging into the bag.

"Shoot. It's Monday, isn't it?"

"And you're late."

"Thank you, my big girl. Hurry up and eat your breakfast. You've got somewhere to be, too." I peck the top of her head and dash off to my bedroom. I'd forgotten about Maddox hiding here until his head peeks out of my closet. I stifle the scream tickling my throat by slapping a hand over my mouth.

"It's my day to open the store," I whisper, crossing the room to talk without tipping Sadie to our secret. He grabs my robe and tries to pull me into his tiny hiding spot. Despite my willingness to get up close and personal, I somehow find restraint.

Little footsteps pad down the hallway, and my finger presses to his mouth. She enters the bathroom and turns on the sink faucet.

"Come on." Grabbing the front of his shirt, I pull him through the apartment and out the door. "If you need a break later, come see me downstairs," I whisper and go to close the door.

"Wait," he says, stopping the door with a hand.

Before I can ask why, his lips are on mine again, tormenting me in the best possible way. He makes me want to shout his praises to the rest of the town and destroy all the boundaries he's set for our relationship. It would be his fault for melting my resolve with his unforgettable kisses.

"Just needed one more to hold me over."

Pure torture. As he leaves me wanting like it's no trouble at all, I curse him and hold my weakened body up with the doorframe. "Never stop doing that," I whisper-yell.

He pivots to face me, all smug with the status as top man in my life, and the corner of his mouth tips up. "Don't worry. I plan to do that and more next time I see you."

"Is that a promise?"

Walking backward, he holds up two fingers in a pledge, then folds them into a fist over his heart.

And that's just one reason why I will always love him.

"I'm here." Kaitlyn waltzes through the store, her arms held wide to absorb all the praise for gracing us with her presence.

"You're crazy."

"Not exactly the welcome I expected for saving the day, but whatever."

"You haven't saved anything yet. I'll reevaluate your worth once we're finished."

Her hands pop up to her hips. "Tough crowd today."

With a laugh, I hand her a tray of paints. We have exactly one day to decorate the front windows for the annual Spectacular window decorating contest, and we're wasting time. "Let's get to work."

"What's the theme for this year? Snowy mountain views? Dog frolicking in the snow? Snow-covered forest with a tree decorated for Christmas?"

"Why all the snow scenes?"

"White is easy … no color mixing."

"And lazy," I tease.

"I prefer efficient. You only gave me one day, and great artists can't be rushed."

"You'll live." I flash her a playful grin, but it's met with an eye roll. "Anyway, here's what I want. I'd like a young Santa and Mrs. Claus under mistletoe on one window, and a little girl and white dog sitting by the Christmas tree, watching the happy couple on the other."

Kaitlyn's eyes narrow at me. "Is there something you're trying to tell me without telling me?"

"Why would you think that?" I say in my best innocent tone,

putting my acting skills to the test, and she buys it. Damn, I'm good.

"Because you've avoided anything remotely romantic, especially mistletoe, for the last four years," she explains like I haven't been present for my own life. "Wait a minute. Have you been withholding some hot news from me? Did you go to the kissing booth? I heard Maddox was there."

I survey the store over my shoulder to make sure no one snuck in while I was occupied before returning to her, a sly smile peeking through. "Maybe."

"Carmen Delilah Bennett. You kissed Maddox and didn't tell your best friend. What the hell?" Her arms cross in protest.

"Sorry, a lot has happened over the last few days, and I've been busy."

"Too busy to tell your friend the news of the decade?"

"You'll understand why when I fill you in … but later. We have some painting to do."

"Fine," she concedes with a loud sigh.

Climbing onto the base of the wide picture window, I whip the stick-figure drawing out of my pocket and hold it up for her to admire.

"You want me to draw that?" She points at the paper. "On there?" Her finger moves to the window behind me.

"Not exactly like this. You're the artist. Use your imagination."

"Does this Santa happen to have delicious chocolate tones, hazel eyes, and muscles that melt panties, or do we have to stick to regular, boring Santa features?"

"Kait!"

"Just askin' because my imagination is stuck on Santa Maddox."

"Shhh," I get out before a fit of laughter takes over.

Envisioning Maddox in a traditional Santa suit is quite amusing until I start picturing him in something more modern and form-fitting.

My hand jumps into action to fan my flushed face.

Kaitlyn's eyes narrow, studying my physical reaction to my thoughts. "Did you and Maddox …"

"Don't I wish? But no." I lower my voice, dying to tell someone. "We just kissed … a ton."

She squeals, and I panic. We're supposed to be discreet, and here I am word-vomiting our secrets to the first person I see. Granted, she's not just anyone. She's my best friend, and with that title comes the responsibility of keeping all my secrets. Not that I have many of those, making this one, as grand as it is, a light carry.

Setting aside the tray of paints, she grabs my arms so I can't circumvent her questions. "How was it? Super hot? Hotter than hot? Panty melting hot?"

"Goodness, Kait. Stop. I've already said more than I should."

"Why? Is it a secret that you two are *together* together?"

"Yes. Don't tell anyone. We're laying low."

"I bet you are," she purrs, making me heat from within. "Don't worry, I won't say anything, and I'll paint your sexy Santa with hazel eyes. You just won't be able to see them because his eyelids will be closed as he melts Mrs. Claus' panties with a steaming hot kiss."

"You're incorrigible."

"You know this, yet you still invite me over to save your ass."

Picking up the paints, I thrust them into her hands. "Get to work."

"Carmen," Kaitlyn says with concern coating every letter.

"What is it?"

She points out the window. "Is that your man with a … baby carrier?"

I search the sidewalk and street and find Maddox walking toward the hardware store with Trixie snug in a sling tied across his torso. A snicker escapes at the absurdity and adorableness of those two. "Yep, that's Maddox and his second favorite girl. He lost her the other day, so he's probably making sure he—"

"Are you his first favorite?" She wiggles her brow and smirks.

"No. That would be Nana. I'm much lower, after his mother, sisters, and Sadie."

"At least you're back on the list."

"Amen to that."

Once the first window is finished, we break for lunch and settle on ordering delivery.

> **Maddox:** Are you free for a private lunch date?
> I'll bring sandwiches.

"Why are you blushing?" Kaitlyn asks, surprising me, and I jostle my phone. The rest of the store had faded away at the first sight of Maddox's name. "Is that from Hot Santa?"

"Yes. I think I'll change his name in my contacts to that for the holidays."

"Wait until he stuffs your chimney with his big—"

"Kait!"

"What? I was going to say bag of presents."

"No, you weren't."

"We'll never know now, will we?"

With Kaitlyn looking over my shoulder, I roll my eyes and re-read his text.

"Go. I'll order a pizza and keep working."

"I can't let you do all the work."

"Yeah, you can. Santa is too hot to ignore, and you'd just be in my way."

"Gee, thanks."

"I know you remember your so-called scratchy drawing. Compare that to this glorious art." She fans a hand across the window, her face alight with awe over her superior talent before she comes back to me, expecting the same.

I poke out a hip, my hand perching there as I glare at her. "If I didn't know how selfless you're being, I might take offense."

"Hey, I'm just happy one of us is getting some, keeping us afloat. I almost killed myself during the last four years of your excruciating sex ban, trying to hold us above water."

"What does that mean?"

She points a long, red fingernail at me, and I have the feeling I'm about to regret asking that question.

"Remember all those late-night talks about my escapades in the city and all the juicy details I had for you when I got back?"

"Yeah." The word draws out in way too many syllables, and I wait for the bomb to hit.

"That was keeping you wet and ready for this moment."

"Ugh." I stalk off through the store to find a place to respond to Maddox's text in private. "Now, I'm offended."

"No, you're not. You're excited to be finally carrying a load. Or you will be when his big bag of presents arrives."

Trying not to think about making my own late-night juicy details, I type my response five times before getting my fingers to work without typos.

Me: Name the time and place.

My heart feels like it's in a jump rope contest with my stomach as I await his response.

Maddox: Your apartment. 20 minutes.

Feeling bold, I add a little spice to my reply.

Me: Will any promises be fulfilled during this private lunch date? I want to ensure store coverage for an adequate amount of time.

Maddox: Might want to call in reinforcements.

Me: Mmm. I love a man who keeps his word.

I hit send quickly before I chicken out and erase the boundary-crossing comment. Several minutes slip by without a response, and I worry I've said too much.

Maddox: Good. Over the years, I promised myself I'd do a lot of things if I ever got the chance.

Me: Like what?

Maddox: I'd rather show you.

With anticipation clawing its way through me, I dip into the back storage room and let it out with a scream. Then, coolly, I type my response.

Me: Can't wait.

Chapter 16

Maddox

For forty minutes, while our sandwiches grow cold and soggy, we make out on her couch like teenagers left alone in the house. We make great use of every minute and come up for air, surprisingly, with our clothes still on.

She's lying on top of me during a rare break when a thought escapes my mouth. "It's hard to believe we're here."

"Here in my apartment or together?" she asks with a giddy giggle.

"Together. I never thought I'd see the day."

She props her chin on a hand to see me, a pretty smile brightening the room. "It's good, right?"

"Yeah, it is. But, unfortunately, all good things must come to an end."

"Don't say that." All the joy and hope I saw in her seconds

before dissipates into concern as she sits up. "I'm not ready for this—" she waves a hand between us "—to end."

I adjust my position to sit beside her. "Me neither. I was referring to this private lunch, not us." I mimic her hand waving. "It's time we got back to work."

A groan in protest that could be mistaken for another sound sends my head into a tailspin, especially when she climbs into my lap. Long, touchable legs straddle my hips as she squares off with me, her arms resting on my shoulders.

"Thank you for making my day special." She lowers to press a tender kiss on my lips, careful not to ignite anything we can't finish. "When can we do this again? How about you come back tonight and watch some Christmas movies with us?"

I glance over at the small pine tree in the corner by the window she set up earlier today, reminding me.

"I think Mom's planning something for us tonight at our place." The night of the parade, while we shared a piece of Nana's maple cream pie, I mentioned how much I missed our tree decorating tradition. She got so excited she almost choked on a bite and snatched her glass of milk. Streams of milk trickled down her chin as she drank and cleared her throat. Watching her laugh and cough and spew milk was the cutest thing I'd seen since Sadie's victory dance after our Rudolph cornhole match.

"How about tomorrow night, instead?" I suggest. "Aaron said something about a Santa Pub Crawl. Know anything about that?"

"Too well. It's another Spectacular favorite. Not as popular as the Henderson Boys Kissing Booth but high ranking in the fun category."

It's my turn to groan. Since replacing my kissing memories with her lips, I don't need any reminders of what I endured.

"What is a Santa Pub Crawl?"

"You dress up as Santa and visit all the participating bars in town. It's a great revenue boost for local businesses. Each place will have a different holiday-themed bar activity going on."

"Sounds like fun … except for the costume part." An involuntary grimace of disapproval scrunches my face.

"Come on. No one can fulfill my sexy Santa fantasy but you."

Taking hold of her arms, I separate us. "Stop right there. You have a Santa fantasy?"

"Not until you showed up."

"I don't look like Santa."

"No, you do not." Laughing, her hands run down my torso. "Wait until you see the store window painting. With the rumor mill running at full capacity already, I'm definitely winning the contest this year."

"What did you paint?"

"I just designed it. Kaitlyn and all her artistic talent is bringing it to life."

Confused, I hesitate before asking, "And it includes your Santa fantasy for the entire town to see."

"Yep. Winner, winner, chicken dinner." She points at herself and leans in for another taste of me.

Catching her unaware, I pick her up and toss her into the chair. The intrusion disrupts Trixie, and she barks in protest as she usually does when something interrupts her beauty sleep.

"Where are you going?" Carmen yells as I throw open the door and rush out without explanation.

Her rapid footsteps and Trixie's yelping echo behind me, but I've got a good five-second lead down the stairs. I exit through the back door and take the alley on the other side. It barely fits a trash can, but I'm on a mission, and it's the fastest route. My sweatshirt sleeves scrape against the brick until I squirt out onto the sidewalk in front of the store.

Trixie arrives next, and I gently toss her inside the bookshop before returning to Carmen's store. Looking over the painting, I'm face to face with a rendition of myself in a skin-tight red T-shirt with white trim, tool belt, and accentuated biceps and chest—okay, maybe those are true to size—and black work boots over jeans. A startled woman stares at me through the glass, her paintbrush frozen in mid-stroke on the curve of Santa's ass.

Carmen skids to a stop beside me with a huff, and my eyes dart from her to the supposed Mrs. Claus in the scene. It's Carmen in a skimpy red dress and black, knee-high boots. Her curves are also accentuated in all the right places, and we're kissing, quite seductively, under the mistletoe.

"Wow," is all I can say.

"You don't like it?"

"I didn't say that. Kaitlyn is *very* talented."

"Chicken dinner," she brags, then sobers. "Is it too revealing? I know you wanted to keep things quiet. Say the word and I'll erase it all if you're—"

Curling her into me with one arm, I cup the back of her head with the other and dip her back with a kiss that could fog up the windows if we let it go on too long. Passersby stop to ogle and gossip, but with Carmen in my arms, I can't seem to muster a care.

"You as a Claus is so hot." I peck her nose and set her upright before I ignore the dangers of the rumor mill again.

"Right back at ya, big guy."

Standing next to me, with her hand lingering on my pec and my arm around her waist, it feels as cozy as it used to. Right. "Do you have an outfit like that for the pub crawl?"

"No, but if it gets this reaction out of you, I'll find one."

"If you do, I'll suck it up and dress like Santa."

"Sexy fantasy Santa?"

"Who else?"

"What's on your face," Aaron asks, his brow pinches in the middle while he sits in the chair beside me in the living room. Propping an ankle on his thigh, he leans back and studies me.

I unravel an arm from around Opal, who hasn't left my side since I got home, to drag a hand over my jaw. It wouldn't surprise me if tomato sauce lingers there from dinner. Mom's lasagna is my favorite, and I scarfed down two heaping portions like it was my last meal.

"Ahh, it's gone now."

"What was it?" I ask, checking my hand and sweatshirt for evidence.

"A smile." His laughter erupts, making Cooper and Dad turn from their posts by the fireplace to stare.

I catch Opal chewing on her bottom lip to hide her amusement. "Don't encourage him."

"Come on, you have to admit it's weird," Aaron says when he stops laughing at me long enough to speak. "You and Cooper are the only grumpy Hendersons. If you jump ship, I worry Cooper will be lonely." He holds a grin, proud of his joke, until Mom pops him on the back of the head. "What was that for?" he asks, glaring up at her.

"You know. Don't ask stupid questions." She waves a hand for him to join her, and he flinches, instincts to protect him from another potential punishment kicking in. "You can make it up to your brother by helping bring the ornaments from the basement."

"How is that helping Maddox?"

"When you all were little, getting the boxes was his job.

Today, it's yours."

He grumbles on his way out with Oliver on his heels but knows better than to argue with her.

"I'll help," Kendall announces, probably to save the evening by ensuring he doesn't screw anything up. He seems to have tuned out all the lessons on organization and situational awareness we get during our childhoods and lives more haphazardly than the rest of us. And she knows this better than anyone.

"Thanks, dear." Mom clasps her hands together and breathes deep. "Archie, can you grab the new boxes of lights from the kitchen? This year we're going all out."

"On it."

"What can Cooper and I do, Mom?" I ask, not wanting to be idle.

"You can sit back and enjoy yourselves."

"That's not in our DNA."

"How about humoring me just this once? You'll get first honors with the decorations when—"

"Oh, no." Cooper's hands fly up, making Opal snicker. She shared a room with our sister until she went to college and knows what's about to come out of Cooper's mouth. "I refuse to take that from Kendall and have to hear about all next year."

"What do you mean?" Mom asks.

"As the baby .. no disrespect O," he says to Opal sweetly, and she smiles up at him like he's her favorite. Jealousy pinches at my ribs, and I make a note to step up my big brother game. "Kendall always goes first. We accepted that long ago."

"Ditto," I chime in. We're both traumatized from her toddler years and beyond when she had to prove she could do everything her brothers could and do it better. She had to go first and set the standard for everything. It's not entirely her fault. We played into it, wanting to ensure our girl's happiness. "We'll go last."

"Not this year," Mom protests. "You've both missed too much." Tears coat her pretty brown eyes, and we both immediately relent.

"Okay, Mom. Whatever you want."

"Ditto," Cooper echoes with a crooked grin.

"Marilyn," Dad says, gliding into the room with the boxes of lights and a wrapped gift perched on top. Kendall and Aaron flank him with containers of Christmas ornaments. "We want you to open one of your presents now."

"I will do no such thing. It's not Christmas," she complains.

"You'll want to open this one. I promise."

"Do it, Momma," Kendall urges, setting down the plastic container she carries.

"Alright."

Dad hands her the gift, and she carefully removes the red and gold wrapping like it's as precious as the gift inside. She peeks into the open end and bursts into sobs.

We all move in and place a hand on her, giving her our support while she lets her emotions flow.

"What is it?" I mouth to Cooper, wondering what could touch her so profoundly.

He mouths something back, but I can't make it out.

"What?"

Trying again, he frames a box shape with his hands and wiggles an index finger.

Seriously? What the hell is that? I can't remember the last time I played charades.

"It's a photo printer, dummies," Kendall says, rolling her eyes. "She can print pictures she takes with her phone from this monumental evening of having us all together and put them in this." She holds up a matching gift bag.

Mom cries more into her hand before accepting the bag. Reaching in, she pulls out yet another box.

"What is it?" I mouth to Cooper, and he shrugs. We're sorely out of touch with today's technology, gift-giving, and everything that makes Mom happy, it appears. Speaking of gifts, I haven't done a lick of Christmas shopping. Maybe Carmen can help. She owns a retail store, after all.

"It's a set of picture frame ornaments, magnets, and regular A-frames so she can sprinkle current photos of your ugly faces all over the house," Kendall says, bringing us up to speed with her usual flair.

"We all know you'll take up ninety-percent of them," Aaron complains.

"That's because I'm not ugly."

Mom's still sobbing when she ends the teasing with a group hug—the best damn hug I've had in a decade. "Thank you," she manages, and the same sentiment builds on the tip of my tongue.

I feel the urge to thank my family for loving me despite all I lack, all I've missed, and all I have yet to make up for.

"Let's take our first picture," Kendall suggests and gathers us all in front of the fireplace.

All the boys, naturally, are herded to the back, a line of mischief and stature that doesn't belong in the front. Elbows fly left and right and anyone within arm's length gets impromptu rabbit ears. Oliver bounces on the fireplace hearth, trying to match the height of his brothers. Cooper puts Aaron in a headlock at some point—a gentle reminder that it's never smart to mess with a soldier. We don't take shit from anyone, not even little brothers.

Kendall and Opal huddle in front, their smiles poised in contrast to the immaturity happening behind them. While Mom takes in the sight of her boys acting like fools and her daughters showcasing their perfection, Dad clicks away. He knows not to stop taking pictures until he's captured the moment Mom's been wanting for years. Based on her face lit with the biggest, watery smile, we did it, and she couldn't be happier.

We start decorating the tree the way we always do—each of us taking turns hanging our favorite ornaments. Some of these treasures have been part of our tradition since I was a baby, but the calm lasts all of three turns. Some of us—Kendall and Aaron—grow impatient with the casual flow of things. As it always did when we were kids, the peace morphs into a relay race, and then a full-blown free-for-all. We're climbing over each other, elbows out, scrambling for the best ornaments, pushing our way to the tree as if our very lives depend on it. I'm amazed we don't knock the tree and surrounding furniture over in our frenzy.

The chaos is magnificent, transporting me back to when I was twelve. When life was pure joy and the world was a playground. Euphoria washes over me, and for a bit, I'm tempted to let it carry me through the rest of the night. But since Aaron's falling behind his big brothers in this activity, he challenges us to a flashlight snowball fight outside—something he thinks he can win. It's a game we played every winter as kids, and since I haven't experienced it with the twins yet, I'm the first to accept.

Soon, we're running around in the cold darkness, completely absorbed in the game as if our lives depended on it. We build snow forts and form alliances to take out the opposition either by snowballs or brute force. Aaron teams up with Kendall and Oliver, but they don't stand a chance against me, Cooper, and Opal. Cooper and I bring strategy expertise and years of training. I was an accurate baseball pitcher in high school, and my snowballs never miss. Opal, fierce and more ruthless than Kendall, is quick to throw herself into the fray for the sake of the team. I watch her and think, with a swell of pride, that we may have a future soldier on our hands. Oliver tries to make a dent with his speed and athleticism, but with Kendall barking orders more than she plays and Aaron going rogue, the three of them are easy targets.

Our team's victory is one snowball away when Dad calls from the back deck, bringing us out of the war zone. "Who's ready for the gingerbread house decorating contest?"

It's time to enter his territory and start another Henderson tradition. Each year, the firefighters have an internal competition to see who from the station gets to compete in the Spectacular Gingerbread Decorating Contest. Dad always wins and practices his Spectacular-worthy design during our humble competition. One of these days, someone will overtake the hierarchy. My bets are on Opal. She's quite the artist and has the most patience for placing all the tiny candy pieces.

After changing out of our wet clothes and warming up by the fire with hot cocoa, we gather around the dining room table set up with a buffet of every kind of candy and icing imaginable. Aaron starts trash-talking before my ass hits the seat cushion, and I can't wait to shut him up.

"You all will be eating my crumbs when I grab second place," he announces, and no one takes the bait but me. They've all had more practice at ignoring him.

"Only second?" I ask. "You don't think you can beat Dad?"

"No one beats Dad. We're all playing for runner-up."

"I hope that's not how you approach your baseball games." I pause when a snort bursts out of Cooper. "If so, it's gonna be a rough season."

"You know I play to win, but this ain't sports. It's candy and crafts and not exactly my speed."

"Yet, you still run your mouth."

He beams at me. "Are you sure you want to participate? All this sugar might sweeten you up. Wouldn't want to hurt your reputation."

"I could use a new one of those, but it doesn't matter. You won't be here to see my transformation anyway."

"What's that supposed to mean?"

"It means you like to talk a big game but rarely follow through. Let's make proving me right interesting. If you're still sitting there in fifteen minutes, I'll pay you fifty dollars." I take the bill out of my wallet and place it on the table for motivation.

His eyes widen. Fifty dollars will buy a lot of cheap beer for parties when he goes back to school, and I know that's where his mind went.

"I'll raise you twenty," Cooper adds. "I'd love to see him finish something that doesn't involve baseball."

"Amen," Kendall says, laughing.

Aaron scowls at her then comes back to me with his chin lifted. "You're on." Sheer determination paints across his face as he digs a knife into his icing container.

I get started too, and glance up at Dad's a few minutes later. It's not fair how he can manipulate the sloppy building materials and make them look good enough for a magazine photoshoot. My big, fumbling fingers can't get the candy where I want it or make it stick. Not to mention icing is everywhere, especially where it shouldn't be.

As predicted, Aaron loses patience within the first ten minutes and struts to the kitchen for a drink. Oliver follows suit, always in Aaron's shadow, and they roughhouse or play video games to wait out the rest of us. Looking over at Kendall's progress, she's too meticulous and won't be finished by judging time. Cooper's, well, his looks like a kindergartner made it during recess. If the task can't be attacked with military precision, he's lost, but at least he looks to be having fun. He should be, Izzie sits beside him, helping him more than she works on her own.

Since Mom's the judge, she's sitting back chatting, sipping wine, and taking pictures of the fun. She laughs at our stupid comments and lack of skills, giving me another sound I wish I could bottle and keep with me wherever I go.

"No more candy," she announces when the oven timer sounds. "Meet me at the kitchen island and present your designs."

Yes, the competition is that serious. We all get in line by order of age. Dad's last, of course, but he prefers it that way. It's his chance to round out the judging and put us all to shame with added drama.

Opal kicks off the judging, and Mom studies every inch of her house. I'm impressed with her use of green and red gumdrops on the roof. She took the time to slice each one in half before placing them on the icing, making them look more like festive shingles. Looking down at the glittery sugar crystals I used with lazy abandon, I should have thought of gumdrops. They're much cooler. She also created trees by separating and twisting strings of Twizzlers and adding fluffy snow with cotton candy on top of green sprinkles for grass. There's even a walkway made of chocolate bars and smoke from the chimney in the form of blue cotton candy. It's incredible.

"I think we have our first contender, Archie. Hope you brought your best," Mom teases.

"Don't you worry. Opal, honey," Dad says, leaning around me to address her. "I love you, but you're not winning this year."

"That's okay," she says sweetly.

Next, Kendall sets her house on the island. She steps back

and chews a nail while she awaits the evaluation. Kendall didn't add any trees or special features to her house since she hadn't finished, but she did a great job on the basics.

"Very nice, Ken. You were the only one to use mini-Hershey bars for the roof. It's a unique choice, and the red sprinkles on the edges were the perfect accent." She knows Kendall would appreciate the *unique* compliment more than something generic about her effort, like Cooper and I will probably get.

"Thanks, Momma."

Izzie would be up next, but she tired of the excitement long before the judging began and escaped to her room. Cooper didn't want her to be left out, so he set their houses on the counter, side by side, as the two of them always are. I wish she were here to stand beside him now because he looks to be coming apart at the seams. He's fidgety and scowling more than usual.

"Well," she begins, searching for a few kind words. It takes her a full minute to find them. "It's better than last year's at least."

"I tried my best."

"And I'm proud of you." She pats his cheek and motions toward the bedrooms, giving him permission to go where his heart longs to be.

Half of me wants to slap some sense into him before he leaves and demand he man up and tell the girl how he feels. The other half can relate to his hesitation. I know he loves her, but he's too afraid to lose her friendship if she doesn't feel the same.

Dad nudges me from behind to wake me from my thoughts, and I add my house to the little neighborhood.

"Maddox," Mom swoons. "I'm impressed."

"Don't lie."

A hand lays over her heart in mock displeasure. "I would

never."

True. I give her a nod of apology and accept her compliment.

Unlike the others, she doesn't mention my decorating techniques or choices. Instead, she pushes aside the tray holding my house and leans both elbows on the counter. "Tell me what's given you this new glow."

"I don't know. Lots of things." Reliving my childhood, being with the people I love most, seeing them happy and thriving, rebuilding my heart, and letting go of my anger. Why am I feeling so peaceful? All of the above. "I like seeing you smile."

"You're the sweetest, but I know of another reason."

I try again, digging deeper. "I'm glad I'm here?" It comes out like a question, and I hope it's the right answer because it's the truth.

With a slap on the counter, she reaches across to frame my face with her hands. "Best Christmas present you could ever give me."

She continues to take me in, and after a while, Dad pulls out a stool and sits with a dramatic sigh. "I guess no one cares about all my hard work."

Mom's body doesn't move, but her eyes scrunch closed, tears forming at the corners as her lips roll together. The sight of her face turning red while she holds back a laugh, brings one out of me too. Except I turn it loose. *Sorry, Dad.*

Before I know it, Mom joins me and braces herself against the counter, gulping for air between spurts.

"What's so funny?" Kendall asks, jogging back into the kitchen.

"Me, apparently," Dad says, his mustache twitching with a chuckle.

Kendall glances between Mom and me and back again before landing on Dad. "You've never been *that* funny. What happened?"

Chapter 17

Maddox

T hankfully, with the pie baking contest coming up later this week, Nana already had plans for a practice round and sleepover with Sadie and the twins, giving Carmen free rein to experience the pub crawl. I'm picking her up, and we're meeting my family, Jamie, Kaitlyn, and her date downtown. There's no way we won't make a scene at each place we bombard simply by the sheer number of us—not to mention the antics that will ensue given the attendees.

I can't wait.

Cooper: Check in.

Aaron: 10-4

Cooper: Wrong answer.

Aaron: House.

Cooper: Where in the house? I don't see you.

Aaron: Basement.

Me: Why are you in my room?

Aaron: You don't want to know.

Kendall: Present.

Cooper: Wrong. How many times do we have to do this before you all just report correctly?

Aaron: Every time.

Me: At the store picking up Carmen.

Cooper: See. It's not hard.

Aaron: That's what she said.

Kendall: Not happily.

Me: How would you know?!

Kendall: [angel smiley face emoji]

Cooper: Hurry up. Dad's getting impatient.

Kendall: When is he not?

Cooper: Don't forget... Strong smells in confined spaces (like cars) make Izzie nauseous. Forgo cologne and perfume.

Kendall: I remembered.

Aaron: Gotta change.

Cooper: Unbelievable.

Standing outside Carmen's door in my red button-down shirt and jeans—the best I could do on such short notice—I've got the jittery nerves of a hormonal teenager. The image of her in a tight top, flowy skirt with faux fur trim, and shiny boots like in the window painting has disrupted my entire day. I made little progress on my task list, anticipating this very moment.

I raise a fist to knock at the same time the door swings open. Carmen, in the most perfect outfit for her delectable shape, leans on the doorframe and beckons me with her eyes. Her hair flows over the fur lining of the low dip of fabric across her breasts and up her shoulders. The fur on the skirt stops at mid-thigh above a teasing of fishnet hose and black high-heeled boots

"Damn."

Young Carmen made me want to sing with her, curl up by a fire to read, and take long walks along the river. Finally being able to appreciate the woman she's become brings a whole new list of activities to mind—most of which are unspeakable in this stage of our exploratory situationship.

"Does that mean you like what you see?" she asks, stealing the air from my lungs with a new sultry wisp in her tone.

"More than I can say."

"You wouldn't be breaking any rules if you did. We're both adults."

"Maybe later. Right now, all I want to do is kiss you."

She smiles, knowing she has me right where she wants me. "What are you waiting for?"

Taking her face in my hands, I find her waiting lips and walk her backwards until she lies back on the couch to receive me. I catch myself before crushing her and use my position to sustain a slow, savoring pace.

"You're so beautiful." The words tumble out of my mouth without the eloquence she deserves. She's always been the standard, and that will never change.

Her eyes glisten with either gratitude or sorrow, I can't tell, and before I can study her further, she hides her face in the curve of my neck. "I could stay here in your arms all night."

"But we have plans."

"Exactly."

I press my lips to her cheek then stand, lifting her off the couch. "Maybe we can come back here after we finish crawling."

Her head tilts in amusement. "Is that a baby step or drunken date reference?"

"Doesn't matter. Either way, I have a feeling I'll be on my knees for you tonight."

Carmen

How am I supposed to respond to that? I'm silently begging my body to move. To drag him by the collar to my bedroom to see if he'll follow through on that prediction stone-cold sober.

Sadly, my rational side takes charge and makes me say, "Let's go enjoy ourselves and see where we land."

He helps me into my long coat, and we find the others waiting for us outside the store.

"'Bout time." Aaron fusses, adjusting the oversized belly under his traditional Santa costume. He holds up the event flier—our signal to follow him—and leads the way toward the first bar.

At the back of the group, Maddox threads his fingers with mine, and I lean into him to whisper, "I was too busy seducing you to tell you how gorgeous you look in all your sexy Santa-ness."

He grins, and I swear my toes tingle from that one small tip of his lips. "That's okay. I'd much prefer a seduction over a compliment any day."

With a quick kiss on my forehead, he holds the door open for me to enter after the others.

It takes only a few minutes to secure a table to seat the group, and we order dinner and drinks. Some of us even sign up for karaoke, while others claim they'd never touch a microphone.

We learn that Aaron is one of the former since he's the first in our group to be called to the stage. Instead of a Christmas song like everyone before him had chosen, the music to "SexyBack" by Justin Timberlake starts, and the full restaurant erupts. With each added dance move and butchered lyric, energy rumbles through the room again. Most everyone here knows to expect this from him, but he has a handful of tourists on their feet, cheering for more. It's impossible not to cringe at the scene he's making but also appreciate the free-spirited way he puts himself out there. He's Maddox's opposite in every way.

"Are you sure you two are related?" I ask him, earning a chuckle.

"He's an anomaly, for sure."

I smile at a long-time waitress here as she walks by our table, and she bends down to talk to us over the noise. "I'm rooting for you two."

My eyes dart to a dumbfounded Maddox. He watches her scurry off but says nothing. Several minutes later, I'm given the *you're up next* signal from the DJ right before one of our high school classmates tiptoes to the table.

"I knew this day would come. I'm so happy for you," she says.

Although Maddox sits next to me, he's kept me at a distance physically—his attempt to subdue the rumor mill in a public setting. But he doesn't realize he lost control the second we stepped inside together.

As he spins in his seat to face me, giving his back to the others, I survey the surrounding tables. Too many eyes are watching us for his comfort, and it shows in the new lines bracketing his eyes.

"What's happening right now?"

"Everyone knows our secret."

"How?"

"Oh, honey." I don't dare touch him in case he's thinking about retreating. "If the window painting wasn't blaring enough, the kiss you planted on me in front of it certainly said it all."

"That was yesterday."

"You're not in Boston anymore. News travels faster here."

Surveying his thoughtful expression, I ask, "What do you want to do?"

He's silent for a beat, then the best words I've heard in a long while flow from his lips with resolve. "Sing our song to me."

"Maddox … I … Are you sure?"

"Ready for your special treat?" The crowd's deafening applause in response to the DJ prevents Maddox from answering. I watch for any hesitation or concern from him as the DJ continues. "Put your hands together for Ember Falls' country music sweetheart Carmen Delilah." The use of my stage name instead of the one I wrote on the form causes a flash of pain to darken Maddox's eyes, but he quickly recovers.

"Go."

I only half believe that he understands what he's asking for, but at this point, I have no choice but to accept every inch he offers and trust him. He's in for a little surprise, though. He doesn't know I rewrote some of the lyrics.

The night he waltzed back into my life and flipped it upside down, I couldn't sleep. All I could do was the one thing that used to bring me the most peace. I wrote a song. The drive to write left me when I escaped Ember Falls, but that night, nearly ten years later, the words flowed again—all because my muse was back.

The audience quiets as I speak with the DJ to change my song and step to mic stand. With a microphone in hand, I'm rarely nervous, especially with Maddox watching, but the spotlight is shining on more than just me this time. It's on us.

Supercharged butterflies take off in my belly as the guitar strums the first notes, sending the first time I ever played that chord flowing through my mind. I had been sitting on the floor of my childhood bedroom for hours, seeking the right combination of notes and words to tell the boy I loved how much he meant to me.

And here I am again, singing my heart to the man I love.

"This one's for you, babe."

The audience's collective gaze follows mine to Maddox. Despite everyone witnessing our heated exchange, his eyes never leave my face. There's no mistaking how he feels about what's happening between us. It's the moment I've been waiting for since we talked on the street curb that first Sunday. Now that it's finally happening, those electric flutters surge again, and I doubt they'll ever stop.

He's ready for me.

Maddox

My brain struggles to comprehend what my ears are hearing. For one, I can't get past how stunning she looks with the lights on her. Everything about her—her ocean-blue eyes, angelic voice, unwavering conviction—as she pours her love into the lyrics takes my breath away.

> *Now for a thousand miles*
> *And for all of our years*
> *We'll never have to question*
> *We have all we need here*

I hear Mom gasp behind me and feel Kendall's hand on my arm, but I can't look away from my world singing to me like she used to. Except this time, it hits me harder and square in the chest. We may have drifted apart over the years, but true love never diminishes. In our case, the time apart seems to have made it indestructible.

I wish I had seen it sooner
But glad I see it now
From this day 'til forever
We'll make every second count

Every word fills me with a shot of liquid courage, and as she belts out the final note, I rocket to my feet and make my way to the front of the stage. She opens her eyes and finds me standing there, accepting the love she poured into the song, and jumps into my arms.

The applause is louder this time, cheering on an ideal more than us—the romantic belief that love can survive through adversity and destructive life choices. Love is the foundation of hope. Without it, all is lost. If I've learned anything since returning to Ember Falls, it's that *I'm* misplaced without love in my life. The love and support of my family, the people who give me a place to call home, and the woman who makes me whole.

With Carmen using her entire body to hold me, I can see that now. I'd been wasting away, a wandering, and numb fraction of the man I want to be, for far too long. It feels incredible to be me again.

"I guess it's official," she says as she unravels her legs and finds the floor again. "I'm your girlfriend in public and private."

"And I'm your boyfriend."

"Want to seal that with a kiss?"

To answer, I dip her back as I did outside the window painting and kick it up a level, more than lust fueling the gesture this time. I know we have an audience and that they're hanging onto every movement we make, but if they're going to butt into our moment, we might as well give them a show.

"That was quite the scene you made in there," Cooper says on the way to our next destination. Carmen had been intercepted by Kaitlyn as soon as we exited the bar, who is surely phishing for the same information Cooper will be in this conversation.

I size him up, not surprised that he didn't wear a stitch of Christmas-themed clothing. At least I made an effort.

"Gotta give her credit, though," he adds before I can respond. "I thought it would take longer."

For what he's implying, all he'll get from me is a scowl.

He ignores me and shrugs. "Maybe you've embellished your feelings on the matter over the years."

"I don't embellish."

"No. You've always been a straight shooter unless it involves her. Then, you tuck tail and run."

"Not anymore."

"Thank goodness. Now Mom can stop praying for your dumb ass to come out of hiding."

An audible exhale forces its way out of my body. It would be nice if people would stop bringing up my poor choices. I was a dejected recluse. I get it. Can we move on now? "I wasn't hiding."

"The hell you weren't. Welcome back to the real world, dumbass." He slaps my back and jogs forward to catch up with Izzie.

"Hell yeah," Aaron yells, and I stretch to my toes to see what he's so excited about.

The sign outside our pub crawl destination number two advertises their featured activity: beer pong.

"Ever played?" Kendall asks after the hostess guides us to an open table and sets down a stack of red and white-striped plastic cups.

"More times than I can count. I'm scared to ask you."

"I'm not a child anymore, Maddox."

"No, but still underage."

"College parties don't care about your age."

"I don't need to hear that but hope you're talking about drinking."

She shrugs like it's no big deal. It's a mountain of a deal when it comes to her. "That and other things. I'm not a virgin, you know."

"Holy shit, Kendall." I chug the cup of spiced beer that appeared in my hand during this groundbreaking conversation, hoping to rinse that knowledge from my brain. "Does Mom know?"

"Drove me to my birth control appointment with the gynecologist herself."

"When?"

"Senior year. Right before Jamie popped my cherry."

Beer spews out of my mouth and floats to the floor like a rain shower. "Jamie?"

"Shhh. Mom doesn't know it was him, and he's right there." Her eyes widen with a tilt of her head in his direction a few feet away. "Don't get your panties in a bunch. He didn't seduce me or anything, and I was eighteen."

"Not helping."

"I wanted to see what all the fuss was about, and I figured he knew what he was doing."

"Kendall!"

"He didn't want to do it if that makes you feel better. But he'd rather it be him than some irresponsible boy at school who couldn't find his way around a girl's—"

"Stop. For the love of God, please stop." My head is pounding from resisting the urge to kill Jamie and fighting back unwanted mental images of him with my little sister. I'm also reviewing our previous conversations to determine if he lied to me.

"I'll withhold further details if you promise not to go all protective big brother on him. He doesn't deserve that."

"If you didn't want me to do anything with this information, why say it?" This conversation rivals the confusion and irritation I felt talking to Sadie my first day back, only quadrupled.

"I don't know. I guess I wanted you to see me as a woman, not the little girl I was when you left."

"I see you. Proof isn't necessary."

"Isn't it, though? You freak out over everything that doesn't paint me as an innocent child."

I empty my beer and reach for one of the beer pong game's full cups to Aaron's exaggerated complaining. Ignoring him, I drain half of that cup, too, hoping it will help me get through the conversation that just won't end, no matter how much I beg it to.

"Why did you have to pick my best friend?" I finally ask. As much as I don't want to talk about them together, I have to know.

"I trust him."

"So did I."

"Do. He's done nothing to discredit himself."

"You sound like his defense lawyer."

She smirks. "You've already tried and convicted him in your mind. Apparently, he needs one."

"What about all the arguing? I thought you hated each other."

"Hate is a strong word, Maddox. We butt heads a lot and challenge each other, but I don't hate him. He's a good man and a standard my potential dates must live up to, or I don't waste my time." Her hand raises to the arm crossed over my roiling stomach. This conversation is brutal. "You and Dad are top of that list, too. If my man doesn't love me as hard as you loved Carmen and Dad loves Mom, I don't want it."

"I don't know what to say, Ken." My arm moves to her shoulders, and hers lock around my middle.

"I do. Thank you for showing me how a real man treats a woman." Her eyes twinkle in a playful warning signal. "Just so you can stop planning his funeral, Jamie is as real as they come, too."

"I know, and I'm glad you understand what you deserve." I kiss the top of her head. "And you deserve the world, Ken. Don't ever settle for anything less."

"That was intense," Carmen says after I shut down Aaron's boasting in a one-sided beer pong match.

"For him, maybe. He's a six-pack in, and we just started."

She laughs. "I was talking about you and Kendall. For a while there, you looked like you were about to claw through a wall."

"Very observant."

"Not really. You've usually been easy to read."

"Another one of my curses."

Stepping in front of me, she tucks her hands into the back pockets of my jeans. Delight bubbles in all the right places inside me at the sudden turn of events. "I think it's sexy."

"Guess it's a good thing since I can't stop it." Holding her against me, I bend to plant a quick kiss on her lips.

"Anything to worry about with Kendall?"

"No. I think she was trying to tell me she admires me. She just took a long and excruciating route to get there."

"Oh really? What did she—"

Excitement at the table erupts, and we shift in time to see

Mom and Dad position themselves to face off.

Turns out, Mom's terrible at aiming a ping pong ball but has an unnatural beer guzzling talent. When did my perfect mother learn to down room-temperature beer like a frat boy?

"I taught her that," Aaron brags to the stranger-to-me beside him, squashing my curiosity.

"Should have known."

I snuggle up to Carmen and enjoy the crazy that is my family until it's time for our next destination. Aaron's keeping us on a tight schedule. He doesn't want to miss any of the pub activities tonight. Although, I wonder how much longer he'll be in charge. Things are bound to go askew whenever the text on the brochure starts to blur through his drunken eyes.

Chapter 18

Carmen

After an hour of line dancing to Christmas songs sung by popular country artists at the third pub and another of holiday-themed trivia at the fourth, Maddox and I find ourselves in a corner booth at the fifth, passing the time with altered board games. I watch him concentrate on picking the right piece from the customized tower of Jenga, tailored to keep the conversation and festive fun flowing. His brow lowers, and his tongue curls at the corner of his mouth as he removes the little wooden block.

It's an adorable view, but I'm over being separated from him by a table, room, or dance floor. I want to hold him, kiss him, and bring him to his knees. I want to show him my love and feel his surrender without an audience in the way. He has only two weeks before he must return to work, meaning we don't have the luxury of time to play games—board games or other.

"Interested in walking me home?" I ask, leaning on the table to talk over the noise of the lively bar.

"Are you tired?"

"No. Quite the opposite."

He stares at me, hopefully reading my intent correctly.

To spell it out for him, I add, "I'd like to have you all to myself."

"Really?" His voice has a sudden huskiness to it, his sex appeal showing through his emotional window. That will come in handy when I seduce him later.

"How do you feel about that?"

On the way to mine across the table, his hand sideswipes the tower, sending the red and green blocks crashing to the table and sliding in every direction. "Damn. Guess the game is over. You win."

"If that's your way of saying yes, I'm a winner in more ways than one." Rising out of my side of the booth, I join him and bend my legs over his. Dark, mossy eyes watch my every move. That tender way he soaks me in with adoration and bewilderment will never get old. I hope he always looks at me like that.

Running a hand up his shoulder, I cup the back of his neck and bring his forehead to mine. "Stay with me tonight, Maddox."

His answer takes longer to emerge than I like, putting me on alert.

I straighten. "Whatever you can give me, I'll take it happily. Just stay with me."

"Okay."

That one little word activates something inside me, and I can't wait to show this stunning man what I'm willing to do to make him happy. He deserves that tonight and every day for the rest of our lives … if my good luck holds and I'm gifted a lifetime with him.

On our way out, no one tries to talk to us beyond saying goodbye, and we're dashing down the sidewalk toward my apartment with minimal effort. For all the times the people in this town rummage through our business, at least they know when to leave us be. It's their way of cheering us on, and I love them for it.

In a matter of minutes, we're standing outside my apartment, shivering and breathless, but it isn't from the frigid jog to the store or climbing the stairs. I'm happy to report that my seduction plans weren't needed, and we're too consumed in each other to unlock the door. His hands are everywhere I need them to be, and for once, he's not holding back.

I'm on the verge of luring him to the floor in the hallway when he asks, "Where's the key?" His lips trail kisses up my neck, and I can't think. I need this—need him—and I don't care where my keys are.

"I … God … In my …" As his mouth consumes mine, he somehow removes the keychain from my purse. The man has many talents, and I plan to explore and exploit every one of them over the next several hours.

"Don't move," he rasps, like I could if I wanted to. With one hand on my hip, he unlocks and pushes open the door, tossing the keys inside with a clatter.

His eyes come back to me, drinking me in as he does while the pad of his thumb traces my cheekbone. I'm drunk with love and giddy to get everything I've longed for when something changes in his eyes. The past and his fears are creeping back in.

"If we do this," he begins. "We can't go back to the way things were."

"Good. I don't want to live without you again, Maddox.

Ever."

He sounds like he wants to trust me but can't fully yet, even after how far we've come this week. I did that to him. To us.

"Whatever happens after this, we'll figure it out together. Come inside."

"I want to. More than anything."

Tingles of hope radiate under my skin, and I take his hand, gently urging him not to let doubt separate us. "Give me a chance to show you how much you mean to me."

I take a tentative step back toward the open door. Another step, and he follows. Several more take us inside, and I shut the door. Finding his gaze, I see competing emotions holding him captive. He wants me, but he's afraid I'll hurt him again. I get it. This is a monumental step for us so soon after reconnecting. Yet, at the same time, it feels like no time has passed at all. We understand each other, always have, and no amount of time apart will ever take that away.

I don't know what he'll decide to do, but whatever memories he allows us to make, I'll cherish each one. This night marks the start of our forever—a forever I should have claimed long before now and will never stop fighting for.

Maddox

The sun is starting to peek through the evergreens behind our house and cast interesting shadows through the sunroom. I've lost count of how many hours I've been sitting here, overthinking and reanalyzing my decision not to stay with Carmen last night.

Everything in me wanted to let go as she asked. I heard her words of affirmation. I felt the love pouring from her touch. I know she's put down roots for Sadie. Yet, I'm too damaged to accept that she won't give all that away without warning.

And it's not just her I'd lose this time. Her daughter has stolen a piece of my heart I never want returned.

"This is a nice surprise," Mom says, finding me in the sunroom before dawn the next day. She checks the stove on her way to sit beside me on the swing. "But I didn't expect to see you back until later. Did something happen with Carmen last night?"

"Yesterday was a big day."

"Yes, it was. I'm proud of you for letting your heart guide you for once."

Frustration leaks from me with a long exhale, and my body shudders. "It didn't last once we were alone."

"What's holding you back?"

I pick at the hem of my sweatshirt sleeve, wondering the same thing. "Probably a host of things, but most of all, I think I'm scared to lose her again."

"Maddox, you can't live your life in fear based on something that happened when you were kids. You're both different people now."

"I know."

She twists to face me and takes my hand. "I'm glad you didn't give your body to her before you are ready."

My head whips to her, and she smirks. I will NOT talk about sex with my mother. Kendall was bad enough.

"But ..." she barrels on to make her point, noticing my sturdy reluctance to continue. "It was nice seeing you smile again and witnessing your big, mushy heart open up. Can I give you one last piece of advice?"

"You've been gearing up for it. Why stop now?"

"Such a smart boy. Here it is." Her delicate hands, holding one of mine, tightens in a supportive embrace. She thinks I won't like what she's about to say. "You'll never find forgiveness or happiness unless you reconnect with your true self. You were put on this earth to love, Maddox. You're a teddy bear. Own it, and let people love you in return."

With a kiss on the cheek, she disappears inside, leaving me with only my thoughts for company. Normally, that would be a concern, but the last two weeks have changed me. Carmen had been right all those years ago when she said Ember Falls was a part of me. When my self-sabotaging stopped, this place was waiting, ready to save the day and my life. I never thought healing would find me, yet here I am, thriving in the one place I thought would break me. Instead of hurting more, my heart has been pieced back together like a patchwork quilt.

For the first time in a long while, I'm free from the steel grips of pain and anger, allowing me to review all the advice and helpful pushes I've received with more clarity. I'm grateful for my sweet mother and her poignant words, Captain forcing me to take a hard look at myself in the mirror, Ember Falls breathing life into me, my siblings reminding me about the importance of family, and Sadie and Carmen providing a future I'm excited about.

I'll figure out what to do about the life waiting for me in Boston later. Today, I want to watch the sun come up and bask in what it represents—a new day, a new future, a new me.

"There's my girl." I'm greeted by a wiggly and excited Trixie when I step into the bookshop later that morning. She covers my face in tiny dog kisses until I tuck her into my coat.

"Did you have fun last night?" Nana asks, catching my gaze over her readers and ancient notebook sitting open on the counter.

"I did. You ready for the pie contest on Monday?"

"Yep." She keeps staring like there's more she wants to say.

"What?"

"Nothing." She goes back to her notebook as if that *nothing* wasn't laced with a whole lot of *something*.

"Out with it."

Setting down her pen, she straightens and crosses her arms, taking me in over the glasses tipped low on her nose. "You look different this morning."

Playing the game, I peek down at my open coat, flannel, and jeans. "Same old clothes I always wear."

"Nope. That's not it. You look … more rested."

"That can't be it. I spent half the night on Mom's swing then watched the sunrise. Quite the view."

"You didn't do anything else last night? Nothing that would wear you out for a good night's sleep?"

My hand stops petting Trixie in faux shock. "Nana, are you asking what I think you're asking?" Sadie would make fun of me for days if she'd witnessed this horrific acting display.

"Oh, for Pete's sake. Did you spend the night with Carmen or not?"

A satisfied grin takes over my face. Funny how she doesn't like having her usual manipulation used on her.

"I am not talking about that with you."

"Why not?" she complains, moving out from behind the counter to prevent me from escaping this ridiculous ambush. "We tell each other everything."

"You weren't exactly upfront with your scheming to bring us together all this time. I wouldn't be surprised if you recruited

Sadie to help you."

Taking her time, she removes her glasses, setting her eyes on me with finality. "It worked, didn't it? My *scheming* fixed everything to where you're happy, she's happy, and your mother isn't having stomach pains anymore."

"Wait. What?"

"Yeah, you big idiot. You've given your poor mother ulcers with all your moping and throwing yourself into every hazardous situation you could find. Are you done with that now?"

"Shit." My fingers comb through my hair. Just when I thought I'd hit my stride, I'm knocked backward with the force of a bungee cord off a skyscraper. "When was her last attack?"

"Just over two weeks ago. It's another reason she reduced her hours at work." She steps closer, her hands gripping my biceps. "All that's in the past, Maddy." Her voice is gentler now, sympathetic like she's talking to an injured child. Maybe that's how she sees me. Poor pathetic Maddox. "There's nothing you can do about it. All you can do is strive to be better than you were the day before."

I swallow down the emotion clogging my throat, but my voice breaks anyway, showing her I'm as weak as she thinks I am. "I'm trying, Nana."

"I know you are, sweet boy."

Holding me as she did after Carmen left, I let a new round of fear, sorrow, and regret seep out of me in sobs.

"Come." She takes me into the lounge and sits me down, soon handing me a cup of tea like I'm one of her guests. "What's bothering you, Maddy?"

"Everything. I've missed so much—the twins growing up, Izzie's situation, Mom being sick, Sadie …"

"And time with Carmen."

"Of course. I've been so selfish and stupid."

"You were hurting. It's hard to see past that in the moment."

I set the cup on the table, not trusting my unsteady hands. "It was more than a moment, Nana. Nine years."

"Yes, but what did I say?"

"It's in the past and can't be changed." A sigh rattles through me because I can do nothing else with my mounting annoyance. "Every time I think I've turned a corner something slaps me backward. I can't help but wonder if I'll ever be whole again."

"You may never be, and that's okay." She pats my hand, drawing my attention back to her. "The good news is you're not alone in that damaged place. I live there, too. I've lost three husbands, and each one has taken a piece of me with them."

"How does it not get to you?"

"Because in the short time we had together, we loved enough to last a lifetime. You and Carmen did that as kids. Don't you know what you two reconnecting as adults means?"

Soaking in every word, I shake my head.

"You're lucky. You can have a second amazing lifetime of loving her if that's what you want. She's already offered. All you have to do is accept that she's your future."

"What if it doesn't work out? What if she walks away again?"

She gives me that all-knowing grin she keeps at the ready. "There are no guarantees in love, sweetheart. That ambiguity is part of the allure."

This woman never ceases to amaze me. An unexpected chuckle casts out most of my anxious energy. She may drive me crazy most days, but she's my Nana and there's no one else like her. "No wonder everyone comes to you for advice. That was beautiful."

With a proud smile, she points to something behind me. "See all those people?"

I twist to browse the fifty or more photos tacked to a bulletin board.

"I've helped each one find their happily ever after," she says.

"How?"

"They come to me lonely or hurting, and I set them on a path to find what they need to heal. Like I did with you."

I give her a slow eye roll, ensuring she knows exactly how I feel about that comment. It's dangerous to leave anything to interpretation with her. "You're taking credit for me and Carmen?"

"We already discussed this." Her eyes repeat my gesture but with more sarcasm as she rests an arm over the back of the chair all smug and proud of herself. "Who do you think pushed her to talk to you that first Sunday gathering? Who kept forcing you two into close proximity situations? Who found reasons to babysit so you could have uninterrupted love making time?"

"Nana!"

"Which you wasted. Stupid boy."

"Good lord. If I give you some credit, will you shut up?" I beg. She may have meddled unnecessarily, but I would've gotten the same result in my own time … probably. Either way, I'm grateful. She just doesn't need to know that. Her ego is big enough for the two of us.

"That's plenty for today," she concedes.

"Thank you, but for the record, I had to do the work. That counts for something."

"Yes, it does, and speaking of that." She shifts to the edge of the chair and clasps her hands together. Here we go again. "I have another job for you."

"What is it?"

"Wow." She pauses, seemingly waiting on something. "No complaining? No whining or melodramatic sighs?"

"You said I couldn't do that anymore." And her *jobs* aren't as bad as I make them out to be. It's just more fun to give her grief.

"Such a good boy." Her soft palm taps my cheek sarcastically. "I volunteered you to install some Christmas decorations today."

"Where?"

Ignoring me, she removes a folded piece of paper from her pocket and hands it to me. "This is the address."

"You're not going to give me any information?" I shouldn't be surprised at this point.

"Nope. Consider it community service. Do you need me to watch Trixie?" At the mention of her name, her little snowball head pops out of my coat.

"Thanks, but she can stay with me." I've missed her snuggles and cute little quirks. "I'm guessing I need to go now."

"That's usually how this works."

"Fine." Setting Trixie on the couch, I rise and help Nana to her feet to get my fill of her embrace. She may be a lot to handle at times, but her love is felt down to every cell that makes up who I am. "Thank you."

"I love you, Maddy. Don't forget, you're doing the best you can. It's all any of us can do."

With a nod, I collect Trixie and head out, stopping in the doorframe to admire the matriarch of all the amazing women in my life. "Love you, too."

Chapter 19

Maddox

Sweetie! Sweetie!" Sadie runs through the apartment above the bookshop, finding me scrubbing the new tile floor in the bathroom after school. She jumps into my arms, waving a white envelope above her head.

"Oh, my goodness. What's all the excitement about?"

"I got it."

"That's great. What is it?"

"The part."

"Part of what? A puzzle? An apple? A car?" I tickle her belly, making her giggle, but she's too consumed with her announcement to play. Setting her on her feet, I kneel ready to listen.

"No, silly. A part in a TV show in California."

"What?" I crumble to the floor, the day Carmen left swirling through my head like drunken wasps. The memory stinging as sharply as it had back then. "You're going to California? For how long?"

"Not sure. My agent says I could be in movies next."

I stumble through my devastation, picking up the words she wants to hear along the way. "I'm so happy for you. You'll be amazing."

"I need to tell Nana." She pecks my nose and takes off.

I can't believe this is happening … again. I can't believe Carmen and Nana didn't tell me this could happen… again. Everyone acted as if I had nothing to worry about. That my inability to let go of the past was the problem. The way I see it, I have every right to be cautious and guard my permeable teddy bear heart with a fucking titanium cage.

My phone chimes, and I nearly rip my jeans pocket pulling it out with a force to match my fury.

> **Dottie:** I'll be home in an hour. I can't wait to see my sweet baby. I've missed her so. Can you bring her to me?

When the universe has you under its heel, it just keeps on kicking. My trembling fingers type the opposite of what I want to say.

> **Me:** Sure. Meet you there.

I need air. I need to get out of here.

"Maddox," Nana calls from downstairs. "Can you deliver my pies to the fire hall?"

Jumping up, I gather Trixie and her stuff and race downstairs, grabbing the box of pies sitting the counter on my way out. I don't wait for instructions and take a chance on having to answer questions about yet another drastic mood swing. I can't hear more about Sadie's news. I just want to run away.

Arriving at the fire station, the first person I see is my father, standing outside a closed garage bay with his arms crossed, like he's been impatiently waiting for me to show up after curfew. "What the hell?"

I park the truck and let it run—half to keep Trixie warm, half for a quick escape.

"How's it going, son?" he asks as I climb out.

"I've got Nana's pies."

"You can put them in the BINGO Hall, but that doesn't answer my question."

"Dad, I love you, but I'm not in the mood for another lecture. I've already gotten one from Mom and Nana today, and I have somewhere to be." Stalking past him, I head inside and hand off the pies to the baking contest volunteers.

"Hi, Maddox. It's good to have you home," someone I either don't know or don't remember says on my way out.

Home. I was beginning to think I'd found that elusive place until it all was yanked from my grasp in the same way with the same dream. I can't pretend my world isn't falling apart again. The parking lot blurs, but I trudge on until two strong arms catch me mid-stride. My dad is almost my size, and at my pace, contact with him feels like slamming against a brick wall.

"Son, breathe."

"Dad, I just want to—"

"You're not running today, my boy. Sorry."

Shaking my head, I find my balance, but his hand stays on my back for support. "I'm fine."

"You sound like you say that a lot."

"Yeah."

"It's okay not to be, you know?"

"So everyone keeps saying."

"What can I do? Buy you an ice cream cone, take you to the park, throw a football?"

His mustache tips up at the corners in a smirk. It's the goofy expression I remember from my childhood and cools a few charred nerves. "I'm not a child," I say in stubborn protest.

"I'd still do it if it would help."

Somehow, I feel better knowing that. "Thank you."

"Where are you off to?"

"Dottie's on her way back."

"Oh. You better get Trixie there before she arrives."

"I know. I'm just not ready to lose her, too."

"Who else did you lose, son?"

"Doesn't matter anymore."

"Alright." His big hand slaps against my back before vanishing inside his coat pocket while he takes on a no-nonsense fatherly stance beside me. "You'll be home for dinner tonight, right?"

He wants a promise that I won't hit the road in my mood, but he won't get it. "We'll see."

On my way back to the truck, a text arrives.

Carmen: I miss you. Join us for dinner tonight?

"One problem at a time," I say to myself and fling the phone onto the passenger seat.

Carmen

"Hi, baby. How was school?" I ask Sadie after work and plop down on the couch next to her. It's Dad's turn to close the shop, giving me plenty of time to cook dinner for our get-together … if Maddox ever responds.

She closes her book and crosses her arms. "Where have you been?"

"I had to pick up some inventory in Moyer's Ridge and scheduled a few gigs while I was there. Did you need something?"

"Sort of."

"Why didn't you call me?"

"I did. You didn't answer."

"Sorry, babe. Service is spotty there, especially in the warehouses. What's up?" I tuck the strands of hair that had fallen into her face behind an ear. "Why are so sad? Talk to me."

She pouts, and I'm gearing up to comfort her when she points at me with a wide smile. "Gotcha."

"Yes, you did. Been practicing your emotional acting, I see."

"Yep. I need to be ready."

"For what? The play isn't until spring."

"I got the TV show."

"You did? Oh, sweetheart. That's amazing. Although, I'm not surprised. Your audition was a no-brainer." This time, she lets me bring her into a hug and cover her face in kisses while she giggles. "Let's celebrate tonight."

"Can Maddox come?" she asks, and I love how she wants to share her life with him as I do.

"I've already invited him, but he isn't responding to my texts."

"That's weird. He acted a little weird when I told him, too."

Air catches in my lungs, making my next words squeak out shakier than I'd like. "What did you say to him?"

"That I was going to be on TV in California."

Thick and jagged tears blur my view of her. I can only imagine what Maddox is thinking and hope Sadie's surprise hasn't hurt him beyond repair. Fear presses against my lungs. I should have told him. I expected her to get the job and knew how it would affect him, but I'd been too focused on rebuilding our relationship and didn't think ahead.

"What's wrong, Momma? Did I do something wrong?"

"No, of course not. I'm so happy for you. You've worked hard for this and deserve it." I kiss her forehead to piece myself back together. "Let's have dinner backwards and celebrate with dessert while we wait for him."

"Yay!"

"What do you want?"

"I'll see what we have, or maybe Nana has a pie downstairs."

"Good idea." She hops off my lap. "You go check with her, and I'll call Maddox."

She runs downstairs, and my frantic fingers can't call him fast enough. I punch the wrong app and contacts in my haste, finally hitting CALL when I get it right. Waiting for him to answer, I curse myself again for blindsiding him. It didn't help that Sadie's eight-year-old understanding of the world didn't tell the full story, surely giving him an unnecessary and painful bout of déjà vu.

Of course, I get his voicemail. I call again. Nothing.

Me: Please call me.

I try his mother next.

"Hi, Carmen," she says in answering

"Hi, Marilyn. Is Maddox there?"

"No. He went back to Boston."

I take a few seconds to breathe through the shock wanting to paralyze me. "He went— Why?"

"He didn't tell you? I swear." She lets out an audible sigh. "Everything okay?"

"I'm worried." Needing somewhere for my energy to go, I pace the room.

"What happened?"

"Sadie told him we're moving to California."

"She got the part?" Marilyn's excitement would be heartwarming if I wasn't panicking about Maddox's interpretation of that news.

"Yes, but I'm sure it feels like my eighteenth birthday all over again to him."

"Oh no. And with the news about Adrian," she trails off, empathizing. I recognize the concern in her voice, and it only amplifies my own. I could be patient if she'd been cool and confident that everything would be fine. But she knows something, pushing me until I'm one nervous jitter away from jumping in the car and driving to Boston to find him.

"Who's Adrian?"

"His friend and former partner at work. He was shot early this morning and in surgery when his captain called. Maddox wanted to be there when he woke up."

"How terrible. Did he go alone?"

"That's what he's used to doing. So stubborn."

"I hate that." His friend is fighting for his life, and Maddox has no one to turn to for support. He's probably worried and hurting, both for Adrian and because he thinks he's losing Sadie and me. "Do you have his address?"

"You're going to Boston?"

"I have to. I'm not letting him go through this alone, thinking I'm leaving him again."

"Alright. I'll text you the address. Why don't you bring us Sadie? She can play with the twins and ride with them to school in the morning."

"Thank you, Marilyn. Do you know if he has Trixie?" If so, at least he'd have her for company.

"No. Dottie returned today."

"Dang. He was attached to her." Yet another loss for him to absorb. "Sadie and I will be over soon. Thank you."

Before packing a bag for us both, I send a text to Maddox.

Me: See you soon. I love you.

Chapter 20

Maddox

I t's after midnight by the time my exhausted body begins the three-block trek from the parking garage to my apartment building in the snow. One block down and icicles have already formed on the tips of my collar and hood.

As if enduring the unexpected drive to Boston and five grueling hours at Adrian's bedside at the hospital wasn't enough, I've been honked at, screamed at, and flipped off for God knows what. Even the smell of hotdogs didn't soothe the familiar ache that curled around my ribcage the second I left Ember Falls. No one called me by name when I entered a building, and I haven't been forced into a hug or kissed once.

Being another body taking up space here used to be my favorite thing about this city. How depressed had I been to find false solace in that? I've been back for less than a day, and my world has resumed its usual blank and meaningless status—a grayscale version of the man I want to be. The one I found in Ember Falls.

I never thought I'd say this, but I miss home. Not this dreary place and my boring apartment. The home I found over the last few weeks in the town I once loved as much as baseball. I miss my family, the crazy people in town who treat me like one of their own, Trixie, Sadie, and Carmen. I miss short walks to restaurants and long get-togethers with friends. I miss the fresh air, mountain views, and goodness that lives and breathes in every corner there. I didn't realize how much all that changed me until I left it.

Every step I climb to the front door of my apartment building takes the same effort as four. Doesn't help that I've ignored my hollow stomach since lunch yesterday. The stress I've been under for the past twenty-four hours has replaced any hunger pangs I might have had with nausea and drained me of all energy reserves.

My phone vibrates in my pocket, reminding me I've also ignored it all day. In a hurry to get to Adrian's hospital room, I accidentally left it in my truck, the single digit-temperatures emptying the battery in my absence. I had to charge it on my way home just to get it to turn on.

When the phone started working again, several missed calls and text messages appeared, but I'll have to check them after I get inside and thaw out. My frozen fingers couldn't push the tiny buttons right now anyway.

Foregoing more stairs, I use the elevator for the first time since I moved into the fifth-floor apartment. I'm concentrating on my popsicle fingers in their search for the right key on my keychain and don't see the person huddled on the floor in the hallway until I trip over them.

"Maddox," the groggy female voice says before she gets to her feet. She sounds aggravated that I woke her up with my big foot, but in my defense, I never expected someone to be sleeping outside my door.

Wait. How does she know my name?

She removes her hood, and long, golden waves tumble out and settle outside red, swollen eyes.

"Carmen? What's wrong?"

I step closer as she leaps at me, throwing her legs around my waist. After the day I've had, I need this and allow myself to soak in the feel of her warm, unwavering embrace until we've both had our fill.

Securing herself there, she leans back to see my face.

"Are you okay?" I ask, detaching a strand of hair caught on her wet eyelashes.

"I am, but I was worried about you."

"I'm sorry I didn't tell you I was leaving. I could only think about getting here in time." It's probably not the answer she wants to hear, but it's true.

"I understand. Your mom told me what happened. Would a kiss help?" she asks shyly. "I know it would help me."

"Come inside."

She holds onto my coat on our way to the living room couch, then settles on my lap after I sit. Her lips send healing light and energy through my veins, coloring my black-and-gray world with her love.

Drawing back, her eyes glisten in the moonlight while she surveys me. "Tell me about your friend."

"He responded to a domestic dispute. Nothing out of the ordinary until the neighbors got involved, escalating the call to a brawl with multiple weapons. He took a stray bullet while trying to break it up." I pause at her gasp. "The bullet missed a major artery in his leg by an inch, but I didn't know that until he came out of surgery. Because of the fight, it took longer for EMS to get him to the hospital, and Captain said he'd been close to bleeding out. I couldn't take any chances."

She nods, understanding I needed to be here for him without my having to explain. "Now, it's my turn."

"Your turn for what?"

"To explain. Sadie told me what she said about her acting job, and I was scared you wouldn't come back and give me the chance. I didn't want you to think I was leaving you."

The news and fog of hurt it caused flood my memory. I don't realize my tired body reacts, giving away my feelings on the matter until she lifts my gaze to hers with a hand on my cheek.

"Maddox, we're not going anywhere. She got it wrong."

"What?"

"Yes, she was selected for the role, but we're not moving to California."

"How will she …"

"We'll have to fly out there occasionally, and that's where her agent lives, but most of the filming will take place in Boston, ironically. Other than her being the obvious choice for the part, we can easily commute here whenever she's needed on set. It was a no-brainer."

"You're not moving?"

"No." She grins. "Ember Falls is our home."

Reveling in that good news, I take her hand, kiss her palm, then hold it against my chest. "I was thinking that on my way here. It's my home, too, and I miss it already."

"Does that mean you're not staying here?"

She fights back a smile until I shake my head to confirm.

"What about your job?"

I think about all the years I dedicated to the department and wish my decision to resign had been a harder one to make. "I planned to make it official tomorrow … later today," I correct since it's already morning. "But I wanted to wait until Adrian was stable, so I could tell him first. We've been through a lot together on the force."

"Maddox, that's wonderful. I bet our police department would love to have you."

"I've already been offered the job."

"You have? When?"

"Another Nana errand. She must have sensed I was thinking about it and sent me to help the chief's wife, conveniently before he left for work."

"She's good." Her eyes shift to our hands as she contemplates her next words.

"What is it?"

"The last few weeks have been a whirlwind, and I'm so happy you've chosen to stay in Ember Falls," she says easing into her question. "How are you feeling now … about us?"

There even being an *us* again fills me with a pride I haven't experienced since I was a teenager. "I feel like keeping it going—no more holding back, no hesitations, no fears. How does that sound?"

"Like my next love song."

"I could go for a song right about now." Her soft, sensual tones have a way of soothing me no matter the situation, and I love the way her eyes make love with my soul when she delivers the lyrics. "Sing for me, Carmen."

With a kiss, she stands and removes her coat, the moonlight casting a soft glow on her through the curtainless window. She takes my breath away in any situation, but in the intimate darkness with her singing softly to me with no overpowering music or rowdy bar patrons, I'm more than speechless.

I'm in love.

You will be the song I won't stop singing
The future I believe in
The best part of my day
You will be my comfort and my laughter
My happy ever after
My favorite choice I've made
It's nice to know the best is yet to come
It's nice to know our lives have just begun

Through every line of the new lyrics, I hear our story and find myself again. Only I'm better than I was before because this stunning woman makes me better, whole, stronger.

She finishes, blushing under my dumbfounded gaze until the words I should have said the second I saw her again flow from my lips. "I love you."

She sucks in a breath, her lashes blinking faster than I would be comfortable with if I didn't know she's fighting back happy emotions.

"Maddox, I love you, too, and always will." Lowering to her knees before me, she runs her hands up my outer thighs.

Her touch sends my system swirling with a sudden surge of need. "I thought that was my move."

"What?"

"Getting on my knees."

A playful grin rolls across her lips. "The way I remember it, you chickened out."

"I did no such thing. I saved it."

"For what?"

"Later." In rising, I pull her to her feet and into my arms. "First, we have to make up for lost time."

Five hours. That's how long I proved to my girl how much I love her. Taking in the view of her in my bed, I can't believe I'm not continuing what we started earlier. My teenage self would be grossly disappointed, but I have bigger plans that need to get underway. Once everything is set into motion, we can experience more of those lazy, lingering mornings for the rest of our lives.

I leave her a note and the spare key and make my way to the hospital. Stepping outside, the weather matches my mood again. Last night had been unkind and dreary. After a life-changing few hours with Carmen, the sun shines cheerfully down on me from clear skies.

On the way to my truck, I stop by the bagel stand and order my usual. No one asks about my day or when I'll be back just to visit, and that's fine. I'll soon be free of this place, left to endure it only when I attend a Red Sox game or visit during Sadie's rehearsals.

Traffic is hell at this commuter time of day, and I get to Adrian's room twenty minutes after visitation starts.

"You're back." His voice sounds like he swallowed razor blades for his last meal. Despite enduring emergency surgery yesterday, he's sitting up in bed like it's any normal day, white bandages covering the top of his hand, forehead, and thigh. He turns off the TV and flings the remote onto the nearby tray with a *clank*.

"Where else would I be?" I reclaim the stiff chair my ass put a permanent dent in yesterday and roll it up to the bed.

He eyes my coffee. "That smells amazing."

"I would have brought you one, but I didn't know if you were allowed to indulge yet, and I didn't want to end up beside you. Your doc is scarier than Captain."

"She's great, right?" His brow pops up twice before a grin emerges.

"I take it your flirting talent wasn't injured in the shooting."

"Nope. Just my ego. Damn drug dealers should never win."

"Agreed, but they haven't. You know who they are, and they haven't killed you yet."

A nurse stops in to bring breakfast—I'm glad there are no razor blades on the plate—and check his vitals. The task could have taken less than five minutes if they'd stop flirting. Even in his condition, he can't help himself. He reminds me of Jamie but on a humbler scale.

"So," he begins when the nurse reluctantly pulls herself away. "Is my condition really this dire or is there another reason you stopped by today?"

"I thought you were going to die last night, so forgive me for making sure you're alive this morning."

"Thanks, man. I feel the love."

My eyes circle to the ceiling and back before confessing, "And I needed to talk to you."

"I knew it."

Taking a deep breath, I set the coffee cup aside and lean forward with my elbows on my thighs, my legs bouncing with pent-up energy. There's no reason for these nerves. I know he'll offer his support. "I'm resigning today."

"About time."

The response I expected still makes me chuckle. "Was I really that bad?"

"Yes, and then some." A touch of annoyance flows among the sarcasm, and given the way I took off, I deserve it. "I've never seen you like this before."

I smile at that. "Like what?"

"Happy."

Ouch. "That's because I haven't been for a very long time. I thought I was okay with that. Turns out, I didn't realize what I was missing."

"I'm proud of you."

"Thanks."

He takes a bite of egg, grimaces, then pushes the tray away and refocuses on me. "There must have been some dramatic things happening over there to cause so much change in such a short time."

"Buddy, you have no idea."

"I'd like to. Tell me about it."

Until it's time for my meeting with Captain Emory, I fill him in on the magic of Ember Falls and my plans for when I return.

"You're one lucky son-of-a-biscuit."

"I guess I am. Who knew?"

"Not you. That's for damn sure, or you would have done this shit years ago."

It's one of my biggest regrets. Right after letting my broken heart fester and stop me from going after Carmen soon after she left. I ran instead of fighting, and I'll never forgive myself for it.

"Maybe I'll be lucky like you and find the woman of my dreams on my trip," Adrian says, grinning.

"I hope you do, buddy. I highly recommend the lifestyle."

"What lifestyle? Monogamy?" He puffs out a breath of disapproval.

"Exactly. Ever heard of it?" I tease. Like Jamie, he has no problem showing off his bachelorhood pride.

"She'd have to be special to warrant that impulse, and I seriously doubt the perfect woman exists."

I beg to differ but keep it to myself. One day, he'll learn as I did.

"Hi, Captain. Thanks for meeting with me on such short notice," I greet, closing his office door and taking a seat when he motions toward the chair.

"You better have a good reason for coming back here before your time is up."

"You're not happy to see me?" I joke.

His elbow lands on the desk, and he raises a thick finger to start the count. "I've got a wounded officer, four with the flu, two on maternity leave, and one dumbass who needed a longer admin leave than necessary. What do you think?"

That last dig is aimed at the dumbass sitting across from him. "Did the investigation come back yet?"

"A week after you left. It didn't even need investigating."

"You took me off rotation for no reason?"

"Are you complaining?"

I pause to mull it over. If Captain hadn't found a reason to send me away, where would I be now? "No."

"With that settled, let's get to the point of this meeting. I've got a lot of work to do."

"Alright." I drop the letter I wrote at a patrol room desk on top of his.

"What's that?"

"My resignation … effective immediately."

"Maddox, I didn't send you away to make you quit." His big brother voice is back, poking at my conscience. I haven't hated my job. I just hated who I became in it.

"I know. You did it to save me, and it worked. I've found myself along the way, and that version of me doesn't have a purpose in Boston. I'm moving home and starting over."

The side of his mouth tips up with pride. "I'm happy for you."

"You're the second person to tell me that today." It feels good. "I'm happy for me, too and have you to thank for it. It's been a long time."

"I didn't do anything but give you an ass-kicking when you needed it. You did all the hard work."

"I'm indebted to you anyway and always will be. Thanks for having my best interest in mind for the unnecessary punishment."

"Wasn't a punishment. It was a kick in the ass. Totally different."

Laughing, I rise and reach out a hand to my superior, mentor, and friend. "I'm going to miss you."

"I'll miss you, too. Now, get. I have more blasted paperwork to do, thanks to you."

"My bad." I go to leave him to his blasted work, then stop by the door. "Merry Christmas, Captain."

He looks up. "You too, brother."

From there, I make my way through the station, saying goodbye to the friends I've made over the last five years. It's embarrassing how few that number turns out to be, but that just means I have no regrets leaving it all behind.

Exiting the garage, a text from Carmen plays through the truck speakers.

Carmen: Everything okay?

Me: Better than okay. I'll tell you all about it when I see you.

Carmen: Are you on your way?

Me: Be there in thirty.

Carmen: Good. If we hurry, we can beat Sadie home and surprise her with the good news.

Me: Hmm. What news is that?

Carmen: [eye roll emoji] That you're moving to Ember Falls.

Me: Oh that! Think she'll be excited?

Carmen: More than. She's been wanting a little brother or sister.

I slam on the brakes, snatching up the phone to read the message myself as if the robotic text reader is messing with me. The driver behind me honks, then darts past in the other lane.

Me: That's a big leap. We just had sex for the first time today.

Carmen: That's usually how it happens.

Carmen: But I wasn't suggesting right away. When we're both ready.

Me: I'm not hating the idea.

Carmen: We'll talk when you're loving it. We

have all the time in the world.

Me: Thank goodness for that. I love you.

I don't wait for her reply. With our future on my mind, I push on the gas and head toward the apartment for the last time.

Chapter 21

Maddox

Hello?" I call when I don't see Carmen's father in their store. Since Carmen and Sadie went to the final chorus practice before the Spectacular Holiday Sing-along, I know he's here.

"Maddox." His hand pops up over a shelf before he emerges at the end. "It's great to see you. What brings you by today?"

"I was hoping you'd have time for a quick chat."

"I always have time for you. Come have a seat."

We both claim a chair in the sitting area near the front windows.

"I'm sure you know that Carmen and I are dating," I begin.

"Yes. She filled us in after you two got back from Boston last week."

I nod, agreeing that there's no reason for her to keep it quiet.

After all, I've already told everyone I could think of.

"We're going out for her birthday tonight, and I'm hoping you can bring Sadie and meet us for dinner."

"We'd love to, but are you sure you want us to crash your date?"

"I am."

"Alright." He concedes. "What time?"

"Seven o'clock at Frankie's. I have a table reserved." Emotion jams in my throat as I gear up for the second reason I stopped by.

"Is there something else?" he asks after we sit in silence a suspiciously long time.

"Yeah. I've never stopped loving Carmen, and Sadie now means so much to me. I want to be a part of their lives forever."

His lips tip into a slow crooked grin. "Are you asking what I think you're asking?"

"I plan to ask Carmen to marry me."

"Hallelujah." His hands fly into the air as he lets out his spontaneous joy. "I always believed you two would find your way."

"Thank you. Should have happened long before now."

"Maybe, but that's irrelevant. Love each other and never stop fighting. Nothing in this world can compete with what you are together. It's special."

I don't have the words to express how much his support means to me, so I reach out to shake his hand, only to find myself hauled to my feet with it and trapped in a fatherly embrace. Little else beats the love of family, real or found.

"Does this mean I have your blessing?"

"Son, you've had my blessing since you were twelve years old."

Thinking back, I chuckle. "That's when I fell in love with

her."

"I know. You're an open book, Maddox. The whole town knows how you feel with one look at you."

"Not sure how to take that."

"It's a good and beautiful thing. Don't ever hold it back, son."

Carmen

"Wear something comfortable," Maddox yells from the kitchen table where he's coloring with Sadie.

Sighing, I kick off the three-inch heels I'd just slipped on.

It's our first date since we pledged ourselves to each other. Not to mention this day holds a lot of dead weight in our relationship. I hope to shed and replace it tonight with a memory we'll want to cherish.

"It would help me get dressed if I knew what we were doing," I call back.

"Lots of walking. Plan for that."

Ugh. How can I knock him speechless with snow boots and a warm sweater? Winter gear doesn't exactly scream seduction. Oh well. There will be time for that after our date.

"Ready yet?" he asks three outfits later. "You're—"

Maybe I *can* rattle him speechless with no skin showing. "Is this okay?" I'd settled on a pastel pink, fitted sweater, jeans, and ankle boots shortly before he appeared in the doorway.

"You could wear a garbage bag and still be the most stunning woman in the world to me." His hands slide to cup my waist and hold me close. "Happy birthday."

A response gathers in my head, but it's wiped away with the

first touch of his lips. He takes his time, loving me with his whole body, and it's all I can do to keep from throwing him on my bed nearby.

"I want you," I try not to say when his mouth moves to my neck, but my thoughts find a voice anyway.

"Later."

"No. Now, please." His lips find mine again and open instantly, showcasing yet again why I can't keep my hands off him. It's meant to hold me over and shut me up, but it only amplifies every needy fantasy that's been percolating since he returned.

"Later. We have plans." With a peck on my nose, he takes me back to the kitchen—not my first choice, but a night out with the man I love ranks at a close second. "Let's go, queenie."

"I get to go on your date?" Sadie asks, standing on the kitchen chair.

"What do you think you're doing?" I scold. "Get off there before you fall."

She jumps down and crams her crayons into the box.

"You don't want to go with us. Gamma and Pap have planned for your favorite holiday activity."

"Gingerbread houses?"

"Yep."

"Come on." Maddox turns his back to her so she can jump on and the three of us make our way to the door. "We'll walk you downstairs."

"I can't believe you recreated my birthday scavenger hunt. I thought you hated mistletoe." My arm circles his as we stroll toward the gazebo for the last stop. I'm tipsy on too much wine and his resolute love.

"I did until recently." He winks over his shoulder. "We deserved a do-over."

"I love it and you."

We climb the gazebo steps, and he positions us in the center. The entire structure has been lined with holiday lights, and the large Christmas tree nearby provides even more festive lighting in the dark park. Like standing on a stage under spotlights, anyone walking by will have a full, high-definition view of us. I'm grateful Maddox no longer cares who sees us. His boundless love shines through every look, touch, and word, no matter where we are. Let the town watch like we're stars in a romance movie. Our story is better anyway.

I search for the expected mistletoe and find it dangling from the center. I didn't have the mindset to check for it the first time he brought me here, and I'm excited to benefit from it this time.

Taking my hands, he plants his feet in front of mine. "Nine years ago, I had a speech prepared for your thirteenth mistletoe location. Would you like to hear it?"

"More than anything."

He kisses me softly, then straightens to meet my gaze. Overwhelming hope fills me and heals every crack my regrets left on my heart as the sweet love of my life chooses me for a second time.

"You and your happiness have been my only goals for as long as I can remember. I knew you were more than a friend when I saw you play ball in the backyard when we were young. I fell in love with you when you brought me cookies after my team lost a baseball game."

"It wasn't just any game. It was one of those once-in-a-lifetime games."

He lowers to kiss me again, touched that I remember. "And our first kiss freshman year changed my outlook on so many things. I already knew I'd always want you with me, but that kiss made my life depend on it. I've never loved you more than I do today, but somehow, I know it will pale in comparison to how much I'll love you tomorrow and all the days after. I want to be the one you wake up to, the first person you call, and the last man you ever love."

"You are also my first and only."

A grateful smile lifts the lips I adore. "Remember what I said before the Santa crawl?"

"Mmm. Something about being on your knees."

"Your eighteenth birthday was the first time I wanted to do that for you." He reaches into his coat pocket and lowers. "I'd planned to give you this."

His boundless love covers me like a warm blanket, and the world fades into the distance. Glittering in the lights between his forefinger and thumb is a diamond ring. I couldn't have fathomed he would want to do that then, and I'm just as stunned now.

"You were going to ask me to marry you that night?" I manage, amplifying both my love for him and the guilt I carry.

"What's wrong?" He rises and grips my arms—the same way he did all those years ago to keep me from walking away—and all that regret he washed away comes roaring back.

"Nothing and everything. I wish I'd never left you. I wish we could have had the last nine years together. I wish—"

"Carmen, I don't care what we did or didn't do then. It's in the past, and don't forget, I threw us away, too."

My head shakes fast, sending the tears I hoped wouldn't fall zig-zagging down my cheeks. "No, you didn't. You had every right to be angry. I hurt you."

"But despite what you meant to me, I didn't fight for you, and that's just as bad."

"Maddox …"

"Do you love me?" he asks, and I wish he didn't have to.

"So much it seems impossible."

"Do you want to marry me?"

"Even more than I love you."

His mouth slants into a grin, and I'd give anything for those lips to turn off the fears bombarding our moment. After everything we've been through in the last few weeks, they have no business creeping back in. As if reading my thoughts, he leans in and waits for me to meet him halfway. He lets me linger on his lips, giving more than he takes until I feel resettled and whole again. This man will forever have my heart for many reasons, but he always knows what I need without my having to ask.

"We found our way back to each other," he says, a hand framing my cheek, and I lean into it, loving the way he holds me steady, builds me up, and treasures me in ways no one else ever could. "And we'll spend the rest of our lives making up for lost time. That's all that matters."

With a nod, I blink back a gleam of tears—blissful ones this time. "Can you ask me that question now?"

"Which one?" He smirks, and I want to kiss it right off his face.

"You know."

Lowering, he holds up the ring. "Carmen Delilah Bennett, will you make me your forever groupie, lyric tester, lover, father to your children, and devoted husband?"

"You're so much more than that, Maddox. You're my everything. Yes, I will marry you … tonight if I could."

Smiling, he slides the ring onto my finger and rises to take me into his arms. As we sway, I hum our song, never feeling the words as much as I do now.

He soon draws back to press his lips to the ring on my finger.

"This is more than a symbol of my commitment," he says.

"Yeah?" I lean back and revel in the tender way he looks at me. He loves with his entire body, but his eyes most of all, and seeing that love pointed at me will never get old. "Tell me what it means to you, my love."

His lips press to my knuckles almost as if he's battling his emotions and can't find the words. I hold him tight, hoping it sends the message that he can turn it loose, and if he needs it, I'll support and steady him the same way he does for me.

"When I asked Nana how she loved after loss each time," he begins, "her answer reminded me of us"

"That she loved each husband unconditionally and so much that it felt like they loved a lifetime's worth."

The most breathtaking love shimmers in his eyes as he continues to shatter me and put me back together with his sweet words.

"We've already loved enough for a lifetime, and nothing's better than knowing we get to do it again. This ring was given to Nana by my grandfather, her first love, and I've wanted to see it on your finger since we were kids. You, Carmen Delilah Bennett, are *my* first love." He lowers to kiss my neck. "My only love." Another press of his lips to my cheek, and I'm crying with him on his way to my lips. "And my last."

Chapter 22

Maddox

I have one last surprise for you," I say, as we walk toward Frankie's restaurant. "You're going to love it."

"Does it happen to involve you taking me back to my apartment so we can celebrate right? Because I would *love* that."

"Hmm." Should have thought this plan through a little better and worked that in. "Unfortunately, that will have to wait until after this final stop."

She lets out an adorable moan in protest before conceding. "Alright, but I'm going to hold you to it."

"God, I hope so."

I sling open the door and follow her inside. The hostess doesn't bother with a greeting as we approach. She waves a hand and leads us to the back room.

"What have you done, fiancé?" Carmen teases, glancing at me

over her shoulder before entering.

Before I can marvel at my new title, the small room erupts. "Surprise!" Everyone we cherish rushes to us in waves.

Both moms get to us first and take turns hugging, congratulating, and checking out the ring. Our fathers do the same, and then my siblings.

"It's about time," Cooper says, tapping my shoulder on his way to hug Carmen.

"I'm so happy for you." With her eyes glistening, Kendall pecks my cheek and follows Cooper.

Aaron's next in the receiving line, but Nana, proudly wearing her pie baking champion medal, elbows him in the ribs and butts in front. "What the heck, Nana?"

"Hush, boy. You'll have your time in the spotlight when you wise up and listen to your grandmother." He slinks back, knowing he shouldn't dare test that statement, and allows her to take her moment with us.

"Go on," I encourage her. "I know you want to gloat."

"Nope. There's plenty of time for that later." She winks. "I'm so happy to see these beautiful smiles on your faces." She pats us both on the cheek, reveling in what she thinks is all her handiwork. Then, she waves a hand at Carmen. "Let me see it."

Reading her intention, Carmen removes her left hand from mine and shows off the ring.

Nana gasps, surprising Carmen as well as herself. She hasn't seen her first engagement ring since she gave it to me nine years ago. Sorrow coats her cheeks, stealing my breath, my thoughts, and my strength. She doesn't cry often, and these tears feel different than when she got emotional at my homecoming. It's lined with ache and a longing for something she'll never have again.

"It looks perfect on you," she finally says without taking her eyes off Carmen's hand resting in hers.

"I'll take very good care of it," she tells Nana, her own emotions sparkling on her face, and wraps her in a hug.

"I know you will, sweet girl. Phillip would be so honored to see you wearing it, as am I." She brings me into their embrace. "I'm proud of you. You did it."

"Thanks, Nana." Now, I'm crying. What the hell?

We give our family the time they deserve—without their support, we wouldn't be the people we are today—but not a second more.

"I'm ready to celebrate our way," I whisper to Carmen after Jamie delivers the last toast, inviting the handful of lingering guests to the bar for another round.

"Music to my ears."

"Your place or ours?" I ask.

"What do you mean *ours?*"

"I'd planned to show you tomorrow, but I don't want to wait." Leaning in, I kiss her until the questions dissolve on her tongue. A few hoots and catcalls echo through the room, but I don't care. She deserves my best, no matter who's watching. "Come on."

We wave to our friends and family on the way out, thank them for coming, and step outside. Holding my hand in the truck, she's quiet on the ride, and I hope it's the cold air and tonight's unexpected events stealing her voice and nothing else.

The last turn takes us into our childhood neighborhood, half a mile outside city limits. Still, she awaits silently, making my veins pulse with anxious jitters.

"Close your eyes," I say, and she doesn't protest. She leans her head back and closes her eyes while I park the truck and climb out. "Keep 'em closed." After helping her down, I position her on the sidewalk. "Okay."

While she takes in the view of the gray stone house a block from our parents' houses, tears roll without a sound down her rosy cheeks. "It's our dream house," she finally says.

"And now we own a real one."

When the world got too big as kids, we would walk around the neighborhood and talk about our future together. We'd envision ourselves making a home together—the type of house we'd buy, how we'd make a tradition of cooking and enjoying meals as a family, and the games we'd teach our children in the spacious backyard.

"It's another dream come true, Carmen. It may not be worldwide fame or having your songs on the country music charts, but it's a dream we can experience together."

She takes my hands and faces me, her eyes showing me what she's about to say is important. "Even if I still wanted those things, nothing could top this. You make all my dreams come true simply by loving me. I hope I can do the same for you."

Her head starts to fall with sorrow over lost time, but I redirect her eyes to me by framing her face. "I have everything I've ever wanted in my hands, and I'm never letting go. We will sing and kiss when we feel like it, give Sadie plenty of siblings to play with, and fill our lives with love and adventure for the rest of our days. And we're going to start here tonight."

I reach into the back cab of the truck and grab the overnight bag I packed for such an occasion. "Let's go celebrate our way."

"Love to," she says, taking my hand. "But can we find a place to hang this first?"

She waves a sprig of mistletoe in the air, making me laugh. "Where did you get that?"

"I might have had an accomplice steal it from the gazebo for me. A little souvenir from our big day."

"I'm glad it's plastic. We can display it and make Sadie uncomfortable with our PDA all year round."

"I can't wait. No more mistletoe misses for us."

"Amen to that." After unlocking the door, I scoop my arms under her and carry her over the threshold, signaling the start of a forever meant only for a love like ours.

Our Song

A Love Like Ours

It took a thousand miles
It took too many years
For reality to hit me
Every journey led me here

The place where it all started
And where our life begins
So much I thought I needed
But all I needed was this

To watch the sunrise
From our porch
You pull me close
My hand in yours
Never have I been so sure

You will be my sunshine in the morning
The flight that sets me soaring
The place that I call home
You will be the words written in my pages

The reason why I am staying
The one who makes me known

It's nice to know the best is yet to come
It's nice to know our lives have just begun
Isn't it

Now for a thousand miles
And for all of our years
We'll never have to question
We have all we need here

I wish I had seen it sooner
But glad I see it now
From this day 'til forever
We'll make every second count

We'll watch the sunset
From our porch
You pull me close
My hand in yours
A life ahead
We're looking toward

You will be the song I won't stop singing
The future I believe in
The best part of my day
You will be my comfort and my laughter
My happy ever after
My favorite choice I've made
It's nice to know the best is yet to come
It's nice to know our lives have just begun
Isn't it

Oh, I can see it all now
Those years of us growing up
In this little town

Oh, I can see it all now
Our years to come growing up
In this little town

This will be
Our greatest story written
Our only game worth winnin'
The joy we hoped to find
This will be the love that lasts forever
That just keeps getting better
The highlight of our lives
It's nice to know the best is yet to come
It's nice to know our lives have just begun
Isn't it

SCAN WITH YOUR PHONE CAMERA TO
LISTEN OR VISIT
https://youtu.be/VrkM7w5qpwA

Leave a Review

If you enjoyed Book 1 of the Ember Falls Series, *Mistletoe Misses*, please leave a review on any or all these platforms: Amazon, Goodreads, BookBub, Barnes & Noble, social media, and others. Reviews are vital to authors and help us reach more readers.

I hope you will continue the Ember Falls Siblings Series when available (book 2: Cooper's story, book 3: Aaron's story, and book 4: Kendall's story) and give my backlist a try.

Thank you for reading!

Alexandra Grace

Acknowledgments

It's impossible to thank everyone who supports me and makes this authoring gig amazing. There are so many of you, from family, friends, readers, graphic artists, PAs, editors, and so many others. Please know that if our paths have crossed, you've had an impact on me, and I'm grateful.

To my street and ARC teams, you rock! Thank you for loving my stories and sharing them with the world.

For this book, I put my amazing development editor, Marisa, to the test, and she welcomed it with open arms. Her advice took this story to another level, and I couldn't do it without her or my beta reader team. Ellison, Patty, Taylor, and J.H., your beta feedback is vital and incredibly helpful.

One day while writing, I got the crazy idea to add the song Carmen wrote for Maddox to the book. But I am no songwriter, and I needed help. The first person I thought to ask was the extremely talented Jen Woodrum, and she didn't hesitate. She's an indie author, artist, musician, singer, songwriter, reel-making expert, mom, wife, psychologist, and all-around beautiful person and friend. After a brief conversation, she wrote the most perfect song to represent Maddox and Carmen's second chance and everlasting love. I'm blown away! Listen to Carmen's song on YouTube. Jen, you are the best, and I can never thank you enough for all the time and effort you put into this project.

Thank you for reading *Mistletoe Misses*. I hope you enjoyed getting to know the Ember Falls crew as much as I did.

💜 Hugs, Alexandra

Printed in Great Britain
by Amazon

48594449R00155